Castle Creek

An Alex Snyder Novel

Eli Flicker

To Martha

- Eli Flicker

i

1

December 21
Aspen, Colorado

Alex Snyder was awake long before his alarm went off. He stared out the large windows into the backyard, watching snowflakes drift to the ground. The flakes were just a precursor to the coming blizzard. Schools and businesses were closed, but the town was far from quiet. Adding to the population of about 7,000 were hundreds of winter enthusiasts occupying the town. That number would only continue to grow as Christmas came and went. Snowmass, Aspen Mountain, and Buttermilk were already filled to capacity, and the other major resorts would soon be full as well. The heavy snow wouldn't hinder any visitors.

Winter was Alex's favorite time of the year. He enjoyed skiing and snowboarding, but hockey was his passion. In high school, his team had gone to the state tournament, losing by one goal in overtime. He had been a forward, scoring two goals, but not enough for the victory. That had been his sophomore year, and after that, the team never made it back.

Most of his time as a kid was spent outdoors, which was one reason he had moved to Aspen. It was a beautiful place, not only in winter but also in summer. Fall was magical, when the trees turned yellow and orange and the mountains came alive with color. Spring was the only season he had yet to experience here, and he couldn't imagine that it was terrible.

Footsteps sounded from down the hall. Jen stood behind him, her blond hair still wet from the shower. A soft blue bathrobe was wrapped around her. "You okay?"

They had been married just six months. Jen was from Aurora, near Denver, while Alex had grown up in the northwestern corner of Minnesota, in the small town of Crookston. Four and a half hours north of Minneapolis, an hour and a half south of the Canadian border. They met while he was vacationing in Vail two years ago. But not everything was laid out for them. He was an FBI agent, working in Washington D.C, while she worked for an energy corporation in Glenwood Springs. A series of events had caused him to leave the bureau and move out here, and he still didn't like to talk about it.

"Yeah, I'm good. Couldn't sleep. There's a lot of stuff going through my mind."

Jen knew he still had reservations about spending the rest of his life in Aspen. "Do you want to talk about it?"

He shook his head. "Not right now."

"I know how committed you were to your job. It's going to take some time getting used to the slower pace out here."

"It's boring, Jen. My work takes up a lot of my time, and I can't have it be so dull. I need action, excitement. Here, I just sit at a desk all day, going through paperwork. This isn't what I want to do with my life."

"It'll get better. Trust me."

He checked his phone. It was 7:00. He had a meeting with Sheriff Paul Brown at 7:30. "I've got to go. I'll see you later."

"Aren't you going to eat anything?"

"I'll pick something up." He grabbed his wallet and headed outside. The snow was light, nothing heavy enough to accumulate. Not yet, at least. Eight to twelve inches of snow were forecast to fall from today into tomorrow morning, with several feet expected in higher elevations of the Maroon Bells. This year had already been particularly snowy, making up for the snow drought of the past few years. So far, over half the annual snowfall had already come down. That had kept the flow of skiers and snowboarders steady, which was good for the town's heavy reliance on tourism.

2

Alex turned onto Highway 82 and drove through town. It was still early, but the streets were considerably busy. Restaurants were already full of hungry customers. He wasn't hungry, so he headed straight for the police station. Maybe he'd pick up something after the meeting.

He missed the FBI. Two years ago, he had thought that his path was set. He would be an agent until he retired. Maybe get married. He knew that marriage could be difficult, because the job took up so much time. Even when he met Jen, nothing had really changed. He thought she would be willing to move out to Virginia, and he would be able to stay with the bureau.

That was before his partner was killed in a shootout. They were investigating drug trafficking in Washington D.C. It was late fall, a little more than a year ago, though it seemed much longer. The two of them discovered that a gang was operating out of a ghetto in a poor suburb of Baltimore. They went in without backup; a decision Alex lived to regret. Jarred would not.

He took some personal time and never went back. He ended up proposing to Jen, and then moved out to Colorado. Guilt nagged him, and he thought a change of scenery might help get rid of it. He and Jen got married six months ago and bought the house shortly after. He took the job here five months ago, and since then, life had been boring and uneventful. There was still a part of him that hadn't let go of the possibility of returning to the FBI. They were in need of agents, and the director had told him if he ever wanted to come back, a job would be there for him.

The police department sat on the eastern side of Aspen, just north of Highway 82, away from the tourist areas. Only a few vehicles were parked out front; most officers had already taken time off for Christmas. The force was fairly small, too small for the large amount of real estate it covered. Operating out of Aspen, Sheriff Paul Brown was in charge of the whole of Pitkin County. That was over 950 square miles of rough terrain, nearly as large as the state of Rhode Island. Aspen was the only town in the county large enough to have a police force. The rest of the county was fairly desolate and uninhabited. Thankfully, crime hardly existed in these areas, so Aspen was the main area of focus.

Alex parked his truck and headed inside. He was ten minutes early, but he knew that sheriff was already there. The dull scent of pine hung in the air as he walked through the doors. Christmas music played quietly over the speakers. The lobby was warm and welcoming, and had the feel of a small town. Allyson Turner, an attractive blonde, sat behind the desk, talking on her cell phone. She gave Alex a nod as he took a seat.

He took out his phone, and a message popped up on the screen. It was from Stephen Olmsted, a friend from Glenwood Springs who had recently graduated with a double major in environmental engineering and criminal justice from the University of Denver. An unusual combination, Alex thought. Jen had shared several classes with Stephen in college, which was how the two had become friends. Stephen wanted Alex to meet him at the Snowmass Grille in forty five minutes. He figured the meeting with Sheriff Brown wouldn't take all that long, so he accepted the invitation. He just wanted to be back home before the roads got too slippery. He was used to driving in the snow, but that didn't mean he was comfortable with it.

"Alex." Sheriff Brown called from the hallway. He was tall, with thinning brown hair and a mustache that had already turned gray. Though Alex didn't know his age, he suspected that the sheriff was somewhere in his fifties. He looked older and more worn now than when Alex had been hired. He knew Brown's second term was up next November, and he suspected that the sheriff wouldn't run again.

"Thanks for coming in today. Let's go back to my office."

He left his jacket on the chair and followed Brown down the hall. Alex was off until after Christmas, but he didn't mind coming in. Nothing better to do in this weather, and Jen had to work anyway. Brown's office was the second door on the right, and had a window looking out into the main area of police business, where most of the officers had their small desks. Alex was a detective so he got his own office on the other side of the space. Brown closed the door and invited Alex to sit. Then he

4

grabbed a manila folder from his filing cabinet and tossed it on the desk.

"Here you go," he said, sitting down across from Alex. "It's your first real case."

Alex took the folder and opened it. There was a picture of a middle aged man paper clipped to a stack of papers. On the bottom of the picture was the name 'William Olmsted.'

He looked up at Brown. "Is this guy related to Stephen Olmsted?"

"You know Stephen?"

"Yeah. I'm actually meeting him for breakfast after this."

"William was Stephen's father. He died exactly eleven months ago. January 21. First homicide here in over five years. My guys have looked at every possible angle in this case and haven't found anything. Olmsted was one of our own. A good officer and role model for the younger guys. He was shot in his home while his wife was out shopping. No fingerprints, no evidence at all. It was virtually a perfect crime. There've been no related incidents since then."

Alex flipped through the papers. "So you want me to find something you missed? It's been eleven months."

"It's mainly because of Angela, his wife. She's practically begging me to reopen the case. I figured a pair of fresh eyes might be able to find something we missed."

"Is there another reason?"

Brown leaned forward. "I know you're bored. This isn't what you signed on for. This case will give you something to do. I'm just asking you to talk to the family and do a little digging, and get back to me next week. I know I gave you some time off, but I'd appreciate if you could get to work on it today."

"Sure." He stood up to go. "This all you wanted to talk to me about?"

"Yeah." He lowered his voice, though they were alone in a room with the door closed. "Be careful around Angela. She's manipulative and cunning. We went to high school together. Something's been off about her since her husband's death. Just thought I'd warn you."

"Thanks," he said, opening the door. "I'll be back here in a little while."

He grabbed his jacket and headed outside. Large flakes were coming down, blowing in the wind. He hadn't talked to Stephen since mid-October. He wondered if it was a coincidence that he wanted to meet today, right after Alex had learned about his father.

2

Stephen sat alone in a booth at the Snowmass Grille. Since the place was only a short walk from Snowmass Mountain, it was usually full. Today was no exception. Snowmass Grille was Stephen's favorite place to eat in the area. He was from Glenwood Springs, but he managed to get down here often enough. Not only was the food delicious, but the building was beautifully decorated. Chandeliers dangled from the lofted pine ceilings, and several scenic paintings hung on the walls, including a stunning panorama of Maroon Lake. When the weather was warm enough, dining was available on the back deck, offering a view of the mountains. In the mornings, the smell of maple syrup hung in the air, but in the afternoon and evening, that changed to the savory aroma of grilled meat.

He checked his phone. It was 8:03. He glanced toward the door, but there was still no sign of Alex.

Stephen knew relatively little about his friend, even though they'd met over six months ago. Most of his knowledge came from Jennifer, whom Stephen had met at the University of Denver. He'd grown up here, she was from Aurora. He knew that Alex had grown up in Minnesota, attended college out east and then been recruited by the FBI. Alex was slow to trust others, and Stephen hoped to be able to earn that trust.

"Hey Stephen." Alex's voice jolted Stephen from his thoughts. He slid into the booth across from Stephen.

"Hey, man, what's up?" Stephen asked. Physically, he and Alex were similar. Both tall and muscular, Stephen's hair a little shorter and lighter. He was a few years younger, at twenty three, but Alex's handsome, boyish face, made them appear the same age.

"Not much. What are you doing down here? I thought you'd be at home, with all this snow coming."

"My mom asked me to stay with her this weekend. I didn't want to, with this storm looming, but she insisted."

"Are you two close?"

"Not really. I was an only child. I guess we were closer when I was young, but then I got more independent.

Alex's gaze fixed on him. "The sheriff just told me about your father. Why didn't you ever tell me about it?"

Stephen shrugged. "It never came up."

"We're gonna have to talk about it now. Sheriff Brown asked me to take a look into the murder. I'll have to ask you some questions."

"I don't think I'll be able to help you very much. You're better off talking to my mom."

"I heard she's the main reason that I'm investigating. Why does she want this looked at again?"

"Her husband was killed, Alex. My dad. And the guy is still out there. She wants him locked away."

"If the cops didn't find anything then, why does she expect anything to be uncovered now?"

That was exactly what Stephen had thought when she told him. Until he discovered the real reason. She didn't want him to tell Alex, but he did anyway. "She wants to do some investigating herself."

"Why? I don't think she'll find anything. And if she's doing it herself, why does she want us looking into it as well?"

"She wants to see the case file, for one. And talking with you may allow her to see it." Stephen shrugged. "You should be asking her these questions, not me."

"The case file's pretty thin. There's not much there."

"I'm just telling you what she said."

"What can I get for you two?" A young blonde waitress approached their table.

"I'll have a stack of blueberry pancakes." It was what Stephen ordered every time he was here.

"I'll take a cup of coffee and a piece of toast," Alex said. He handed her his menu.

"You're not hungry?" Stephen asked.

Alex sighed. "Not really." He looked Stephen in the eye. "I'm not sure I belong out here. I don't like my job. I don't know many people. And I just got married. Maybe it wasn't a good idea to agree to move."

"You're still getting used to all the changes. It's going to take some time. Do you think Jen would have agreed to live out east?"

"I'm not sure." Alex took a sip of his coffee. "It's just so different here, you know? All my friends are back in Minnesota and D.C. I've always wanted to live in the mountains, especially Colorado, but maybe I'm wrong."

"You've only been here a few months, Alex. Things will come together."

"Thanks." Alex quickly changed the subject. "So what was your dad like?"

"I didn't see much of him before he died. I was in my last year of school in Denver. And when I did go home, for holidays and stuff, we didn't talk much. I don't know why. Nothing had changed with either of us. We just never had a tight bond, I guess. He didn't really know how to raise a son. Maybe that's why I'm an only child. The last time I saw him was at Christmas. Everything seemed normal."

"What did he like to do?"

"He worked a lot. That's how it was when I was growing up. I didn't see him often. He liked to hunt and fish, but that was about it. The rest of the time he was working. We didn't share any interests. I liked hiking, skiing, and basketball. He wasn't really into any of those things."

"And your mom?"

To be honest, Stephen didn't really know what his mom's interests were. "She likes to read. She also works a lot. Since dad died, she's worked even more, like she can't stand the thought of being alone. She wants people to think that she's moved on, but I know that she's still grieving. She lives in this big house all alone, so she has plenty of time by herself.

9

"So let me get this straight." Alex seemed confused. "Your mother asked the sheriff to have this case reopened so she can get a glimpse at the case file?"

Stephen knew there was more to it than that, but he didn't tell Alex. "Something like that."

"Why'd the sheriff agree to that?"

"He and my mom are old friends. They went to high school together. He wanted to do something for her, I guess. I know he wants to get the guy who did this just as much as she does."

Their food came, steaming hot, and the conversation ended for a few minutes as they both ate in silence. His pancakes were delicious, as always. The snow grew heavier, beginning to pile up in the parking lot. Stephen had plenty of experience driving in conditions like this, but he was still glad that he wasn't going back to Glenwood Springs today.

"So what happened on the day your dad died?" Alex asked, finishing his toast.

Stephen thought back to that fateful day. He had been at home, but he couldn't remember exactly what he was doing. "I was at my apartment in Denver. Mom called me after dinner. I didn't really understand what had happened, but I got down here as soon as I could. It was probably eight or nine by the time I arrived."

"I skimmed through the police report before I came. Your mom found him, right?"

"Yeah." Stephen poured some more maple syrup on the pancakes. "Look, I don't know much about what happened that day. Like I said, it would be better if you talked to my mom."

"I was planning on it. Is it okay if I do that this morning?"

"Sure. She isn't working today. I can take you to her house."

Stephen finished the rest of his breakfast in a hurry. The morning crowd was beginning to thin out. They split the bill and he left a tip on the table, grabbed his coat, and followed Alex outside. Snow swirled up in his face, blown around by the cold wind. An inch or so of white powder already covered most of the vehicles in the parking lot. Alex headed for his truck to grab the

10

case file while Stephen hurried to his Audi and brushed the snow off the windshield. The car was brand new, an S4, just in from Germany. His mother had covered the down payment, as a 'Way to Go' for getting through college, but he still had to pay a hefty monthly payment. So far, it was worth it. It was an awesome car.

Alex joined him a second later with a small folder in his hand. He wasn't kidding when he said the file was small. "That's it?"

"I told you there wasn't much."

"So you think you'll be able to find anything that the sheriff missed?"

Alex shrugged. "I'll do what I can. Don't count on anything."

They drove on in silence, Stephen paying close attention to the road. His mother lived about ten minutes west of Aspen, in a beautiful newly built two story house with a large backyard. It wasn't the same house he had grown up in, but not too far from it. She still worked as an accountant, but Stephen suspected that her retirement was drawing near.

He heard Alex rifling through the file, but didn't look over. He was curious to find out what information it held, but didn't ask just yet. If Alex was right, there wasn't much, but hopefully he would be willing to share whatever it did contain.

Stephen turned into her neighborhood and drove past a few expensive homes. He pulled into the driveway of his mother's home. The house looked dark and empty. Maybe she had gone somewhere after all.

"You're sure she's here?" Alex opened the door and stepped into the snow.

"She was when I left. And there's no tire tracks leaving the driveway. I think she's expecting us."

They hurried up the sidewalk and he opened the front door. They stepped into a massive foyer that opened up into the kitchen. A single light shone beyond the kitchen, in the dining room. The light hadn't been visible from the street.

Stephen slipped off his shoes and jacket and led Alex through the house. Angela sat at the head of the dining room table, and she smiled as they walked in. Stephen saw the look of

11

surprise on Alex's face that was quickly erased. This probably wasn't what Alex expected his mother to look like.

Angela looked like a happy, middle-aged lady, which was exactly what she wanted people to think of her. Her sandy blond hair hung past her shoulders, and makeup had been applied neatly to her eyelashes and lips. She was dressed as if she were going to a fancy restaurant, not just staying at home. Though she was fifty six years old, Stephen thought she looked about forty five.

"Sit down." She beckoned them with her hand. "We have a lot to talk about."

3

As of 11:00 A.M., over thirty crashes had been reported in central Colorado, most concentrated between Aspen, Brecken-ridge, and Vail. Highway 82 was closed east of Aspen during winter, which made the only way out of town to go west, toward Glenwood Springs. Paul Brown had the authority to close down the highway, but he had yet to do so. All he had done was recommend that people stay indoors and avoid travel.

Vincent Martinez and Stuart Rockford had responded to three accidents already, and were on their way to a fourth scene. Rockford drove, heading west out of Aspen into the blinding snow. This section of highway had already closed twice this season due to the weather. Vincent thought that this storm was already worse, and wondered why the road was still open. He expected a closure was imminent, but it was impossible to predict Sheriff Brown.

This was Vincent's first winter in Aspen. He had moved up from New Mexico, and so far, he liked the new job. Vincent was in his mid-twenties, with thick black hair and dark brown eyes. He spoke Spanish and English fluently, a result of his parents routinely speaking their native language around the house when he was a kid.

"So what happened here?" Rockford sounded annoyed. They had been out since seven, and were just passing the roundabout where Highway 82 intersected with County Road 13.

Vincent manned the radio, while Rockford focused on the road, staying under thirty miles per hour.

13

"Reports of a multi-car crash," he answered. "It's only about a mile further.

A couple minutes passed, and they rounded a bend in the road. Vincent saw a few cars stopped on the road. "Right up here," he warned. "Slow down." Rockford pressed down on the brake pedal, and the vehicle skidded a little before sliding to a stop. Two vehicles sat in the ditch, with another two in the road, both badly dented. A handful of people, maybe ten in all, stood in the road, barely visible through the thick cloud of white. Vincent fought against the strong winds to push open his door. Ice pellets stung his face as soon as he was out of the car. Generally, Vincent enjoyed snow, but this year had already been too much. He was used to it, coming from the mountains of northern New Mexico, but never had to drive in a storm like this and be outside in it.

As Vincent approached the group, he saw that his estimate of ten people was correct. An elderly couple stood together, a middle aged man next to them. A family of four stood in a circle, while three young women waited near a battered Toyota Corolla.

"You folks okay?" Rockford asked. He had to raise his voice to be heard above the howling wind.

"We're fine," the old man answered, pulling his wife closer. "Just a little shaken up."

"Tow trucks are on the way," Rockford informed them. "What happened?"

Everyone had gathered around them, and it was one of the young women who spoke up. "We were heading east when our car hit an icy patch. We hit the van, which was heading west, and the others vehicles skidded into the ditch trying to avoid us."

"Were you under the influence of alcohol or drugs?"

"No."

He addressed the others. "That account sound right to all you guys?"

They all nodded.

"You aren't to blame for this." He spoke to the young lady. "This road should not have been open in the first place. Have you exchanged contact and insurance information?"

They had.

14

Two tow trucks had arrived while they were talking, and a couple more were on the way. The vehicles blocking the road were moved away first. "I don't want to make you folks stay out here any longer than you have to," Rockford said as the first tow truck drove away. "I'm not going to write up a police report. You all have insurance which will cover this. Any other issues will have to be figured out among yourselves. Does anybody need a ride back in to Aspen?"

Each had somebody coming to pick them up, so he and Rockford hurried back to the vehicle.

"Shouldn't we wait here until the other tow trucks come and everyone's gone?" Vincent asked, once they were in the warmth and shelter of the squad car.

"You wanna be out there in this weather?" Rockford asked incredulously. "I asked if anyone needed a ride, and they all declined. They're on their own."

Vincent shrugged. He wanted the day to be over as much as Rockford. He also wanted to make sure they were following protocol. But he trusted the senior officer. So he didn't protest as they headed back toward Aspen.

"I'll finish up the police reports," Rockford said as they neared the police department. "Why don't you head home and enjoy the rest of your day."

"Sure." Vincent had nothing planned, but hanging at home was better than being out in this weather.

Rockford parked behind the building but left the car running. He turned to Vincent. "I know that some guys have been trying to spread the rumor that I'm not doing my job correctly. Police misconduct, or some crap. That's complete bullshit. We have more important stuff to worry about right now than some false allegations."

"What do you mean?

"Brown is losing it. He's got a sour relationship with the public and with most of the cops we've got. Nobody really likes him anymore. He used to be a real nice guy, before you came. That's what got him elected. Something's happened in the past few months. Something big. And I'm not sure what it is. He's got one more year left in office, but I'm not sure if I can deal with him for that much longer. Everyone knows that he should

15

have closed Highway 82 in anticipation of this storm. Maybe if he keeps making poor decisions like this, there's a way he could get fired before his term is up. Most of the guys know I'm planning on running for sheriff next fall. For some reason, I'm not getting very much support. Hence these rumors."

Vincent could see both sides of the issue. Rockford was ambitious, there was no doubt about it. He hadn't heard anything about misconduct, but wouldn't be stunned if it were true. Spreading rumors obviously wasn't the right way to prevent him from being elected. On the other hand, Vincent had noticed that there was something off about the sheriff. Maybe someone else *should* take charge of the force. He just didn't know if Rockford was the right person.

Vincent didn't know how to respond so he got out of the car and headed for the back door. "See you later," he said.

It was warm inside, and it felt good after being out in the cold for so long. He walked past the lockers toward his desk when he nearly ran into Paul Brown. The sheriff looked exhausted but he put on a smile.

" Martinez," he said, "I need to speak with you in my office."

Brown led Vincent to his office and invited him to take a seat. Everything was in order, and it looked as if Brown was ready to leave for the day.

"You know the name William Olmsted?" The sheriff asked.

Vincent shook his head. He'd never heard the name before.

"How would you like to do a little detective work for me?" Brown queried. "I've been watching you, and you have some skills that are being wasted. I could definitely use you as a detective."

Vincent was surprised. "You already have Alex. Why do you need me?"

"He's used to the fast pace and action of the FBI. Not a small town like this. I think it's only a matter of time before he realizes that this job isn't for him. If that time comes, I want you to become the new detective for this force."

Vincent didn't want to be a cop for his whole life. He wanted to move up. He just hadn't expected it to be so soon. There were obviously others more qualified than him. But he wasn't about to protest. "All right. Tell me about Olmsted."

Brown sat down so they were facing each other. "Olmsted was one of my best officers. He was murdered eleven months ago. Somebody shot him in his home. We have yet to find out who that person is. His widow has been nagging me to do something for the past few months," Brown said. "We went to high school together, and still talk occasionally. It's been bothering me as well. This is the only unsolved homicide we've had in this town in a long time. A lot of things about this crime are odd. Like how nothing was taken from the house. No motive. But clearly Olmsted was targeted. The killer knew that he was home alone. All I'm asking you to do is take a look at things and let me know what you find. Head home before the snow gets real bad, take a look at the file, and do some investigating." He stood up and ushered Vincent out of his office. "I'll see you next week, Vincent. Merry Christmas."

17

4

Despite what Stephen had told him, he was a little surprised by the appearance of Angela Olmsted. On the outside, she seemed like a normal, nice lady. Not the angry, deceptive woman Brown had cast her as. But he concealed his surprise, and shook her hand.

"Nice to meet you," he said, stepping back toward Stephen.

"The pleasure is mine." She stood up, smoothing her skirt. "I'll go get us some coffee. It'll just be a minute."

She left for the kitchen, leaving Alex and Stephen alone in the dining room. Alex sat down across from Angela's chair and put the folder on his lap. This whole thing felt off. He put some things together in his brain. Angela had asked the sheriff to reopen this investigation just so she could get some more information about the death of her husband? He shook his head. It didn't make a whole lot of sense. But he had agreed to look into it, and the only real thing he had to go off of was Angela Olmsted. And he was in her dining room right now.

Angela returned a minute later, balancing three mugs of steaming coffee. She set one in front of him, the other in front of Stephen and then sat down across from him.

"Thanks for coming out today, with the snow and all."

"No problem." He folded his hands on the table. "I know this is a very personal case, but why do you want it reopened? Your husband has been dead for almost a year now."

"His birthday was a few days ago." Her voice was soft and full of sorrow. "I've tried to move on, but I can't. I need to

18

know who did this to him, and I need that person-" She caught herself. "I need justice."

"I understand. But it might not be that easy. I'm looking at an eleven month old cold case. For all we know, the person who did this could be in a different state or even a different country by now."

"I need to know." Alex thought he detected a hint of malice in her words.

"Okay. I'll do what I can."

"Where do you want to start?" She pushed her coffee cup away and leaned forward.

"I'm going to ask you a few questions about the day your husband died. Try to answer them as best as you can."

She looked surprised. "I already did that with another officer. It's probably right there in your file."

"I know. I already read through it. But there's a few other questions I have that weren't asked. Maybe you'll remember something new. Just relax and close your eyes."

She looked at him dubiously, but did as he said.

"Good. Picture yourself in that afternoon. It's 4:00 P.M. on January 21. What are you doing?"

Angela didn't answer right away. "We're finishing up a movie. Something with Tom Cruise. I don't remember exactly what it is."

"Who's we?"

"Me and Will."

"What happened when the movie was done?"

"I was going to make dinner, but we needed a few things. So I ran to the store."

"And what was Will doing?"

"I don't know. I think he headed upstairs to take a shower."

"So you left the house. What was it like outside?"

He saw her shiver slightly. "It was cold. But sunny. It had snowed that morning, because the roads were icy, and I almost went off the road."

"So you left the house around what, 4:30?"

"Yeah." She opened her eyes. "I already ran through this with the other guy."

19

"I know. But I'd like to go through it again."

She sighed and closed her eyes. "Fine."

"Walk me through the day from 4:30 until the time you got back home. Don't leave anything out."

"I went to City Market to get a few things. Then I stopped at the bank to deposit a check."

"Slow down," Alex said. "How long does it usually take for you to get to City Market?"

"I don't know. Probably around eight minutes."

"We'll go with ten, since you said the roads were a little icy. And how long do you think you were there?"

"Probably fifteen minutes."

"And then you went to the bank. How long does it take to get there?"

"Five minutes. And I was there for fifteen minutes. It was really busy. I remember that."

"And did you come home after that?"

"Yeah."

"How long is it from the bank to here?"

"Since the roads were bad, probably around fifteen minutes."

Alex did some quick math in his head. "You were probably gone an hour, give or take ten minutes. That means you arrived home between 5:30 and 5:45." He looked at the report. "It says here that you didn't get home until 6:00."

"What's the difference? It's fifteen minutes."

"It could make a big difference. It gives the killer only about an hour window to get the job done. He might have been watching your house to see when you left. Do you remember seeing any suspicious vehicles in the week leading up to this?"

"I can't remember back that far."

"Okay." Alex did some backtracking. "Did you shut the garage door when you left?"

"Yes. I always shut it when I go anywhere."

"And when you came home, did you park back inside?"

"Yes."

"Okay, so now you're in the garage. You just stepped out of the car. Is anything out of place?"

She squeezed her eyes shut. "I don't know. It was a long time ago."

"This is important. Think hard."

Her eyes shot open. "The back door was open. We never leave it open."

"Was there any reason that Will would've been outside while you were gone?"

"Not that I can think of." She leaned back and took a sip of coffee. "He could've gone outside to shovel, I guess."

"There was snow on the driveway?"

"Yeah. We had a few inches, but neither of us felt like shoveling."

"Do you mind if we go out to the garage? I'd like to take a look around."

Stephen stood up. "I may have neglected to mention that my mother moved recently. This isn't the house where my father was killed.

It would have been nice to know that before he came here. "How long ago did you move?"

"I've been here since May."

Seven months. "Any particular reason you moved?"

"Memories."

He left it at that. "Who owns the house now?"

"Nobody. It's only been for sale for a few weeks."

"Nobody? You've been here for seven months but you just put the house up for sale?"

"It's really none of your business."

"Okay..." His confusion was growing. "So the house is empty at this point?"

"Correct."

He looked out the window, above Angela's head. The snow was coming down heavier. But he was intrigued. "How far is it from here?"

"About a mile," Stephen answered. "But are you sure you want to head over there right now?"

Alex turned back to Angela. "If it's all right with you, I'd like to take a look around today."

"If you want to stay home, Stephen, Alex and I can go ourselves."

He shook his head. "I'll come." He grabbed his keys. "Better go start my car."

The drive to Angela's old house took about five minutes, even though they were going only a mile. The roads were covered with snow, and Alex didn't see any other cars out on the streets. Maybe it was a sign that they should stay indoors as well. The wind began to pick up, blowing the snow in all directions. Alex was glad when they had safely made it to the log house. It was hard to see through the snow, but he could tell that it was a nice place that would definitely sell for a high price.

Angela hastily punched in a code for the garage. She walked over to the door leading into the house and shut the garage, to prevent any snow from getting in. The space was completely empty. A door led out back, and there was a small window on the wall to their left.

Alex rubbed his hands to keep them warm. The garage was freezing. He walked over to the service door. "This was open when you arrived home?"

She nodded. "I'm pretty sure."

"Which means the killer could have come in this way. Do you know if the door was ever tested for prints?"

"I don't think so. They thought he came in through the front door."

"Why's that?"

A sudden realization dawned on her. "Probably attributed to the fact that I shut and locked the back door when I got home." She cursed quietly. "Dammit. How'd that slip my mind?"

"It's not your fault. He probably wore gloves anyway, seeing that there were no prints anywhere inside." Alex traced the killer's steps. "So he came in here and walked to the door." He pushed it open and was inside a large mudroom. "He walks through here into the hallway." He turned to Angela, who stood behind him. "Can you show me where you found Will?"

She brushed past him and entered a large open space. The living room. "He was lying on the ground right here. He was dead when I found him." Her voice trailed off and she wiped her eyes.

Alex flipped through the folder, which he had brought inside. Will died from a single gunshot wound to the chest. The bullet was from a glock. The report went on to say that nothing had been taken from the house. The killer had come in, shot Will, and left. Wouldn't have taken him more than five minutes. There were no fingerprints or DNA in the house other than the Olmsted's. Alex was beginning to understand what Brown had told him. It certainly seemed like a clean crime. But no matter how sophisticated the killer was, Alex knew that every criminal made some mistake. He just had to find out what the mistake was.

"Let's go back outside," he suggested. "I want to check something out."

They went back through the garage to the back door. Alex pushed it open. Wind driven snow fell heavily, blown toward the house. The wind came from the north, drifting the snow. Had the day of Olmsted's murder been like this? Angela said it had snowed the night before, and now was windy and frigid. If he was correct, and the killer had come in through the back door, he would have left footprints somewhere. But in the report, an officer said that the snow was undisturbed. The trees were sparse back here. Snow could have definitely drifted and covered up any footprints.

"Did you say that your driveway was shoveled after that storm?" he asked.

"No. We hadn't done it yet because it was so cold."

"The killer couldn't have parked in the driveway, because he would have left tire tracks. That means he probably parked in the street."

"But you said he came in the back door," Angela argued. "If he walked through the snow to get around there, there would have been footprints. And one of the guys who was here swore there were no prints."

Interesting. "And we know he didn't come in the front door, because footprints would've shown there also."

"What if he didn't drive at all?" Stephen spoke up. "What if he came from the woods?"

23

Alex thought it over. It made sense. The wind could have covered the footprints, but then again, the cops probably hadn't checked the back for prints. They had no reason to. "What's back there?"

"Trees. They go back a long way," Stephen said. "There's a snowmobile trail that extends for a while."

It definitely was a possibility. "I'll have to check it out. Tomorrow, when the weather's better. Do you remember the name of the guy who checked outside and said there were no footprints."

She thought for a moment. "I his name was Kessel.

Dylan Kessel. And he *had* come in to work today. "Could you give me a ride back to Snowmass Grille?" He wanted to get back to Aspen before the weather got even worse. "Kessel might remember something.

5

Stephen and Alex headed back to the Snowmass Grille. Stephen had already dropped his mother off at home. It took another ten minutes just to get back into town. He counted five cars on the road in a span of about two miles. There had been worse storms than this one in the past few years, and Stephen didn't like driving in them, especially in a new car.

They didn't speak much on the way back. Alex was browsing through the file, writing a few things down. He turned the radio on quietly and focused on the road, but his mind eventually wandered to other things. Christmas, for one. It was only a few days away, and he was still pondering what to get his girlfriend, Mariah. She was a year younger than him, and lived east of Glenwood Springs on I-80 in the small town of Eagle, which was overshadowed by Vail. They'd been together for almost a year now, and it was their first Christmas together. He would be celebrating at her parent's house. He had only met them once, so he needed to make another good impression.

"What are you getting Jen for Christmas?" he asked. Maybe Alex could give him an idea.

Alex looked up. "I don't know. I haven't really thought about it yet."

"How haven't you thought about it? Christmas is only four days away."

"I know." He closed the file. "It just doesn't feel like Christmas. I've still got time. I'll figure it out. What are *you* getting Mariah?"

"I don't know. I was hoping you'd have some ideas. What did you get Jen for your first Christmas?"

Alex thought for a moment. "I don't remember."

That didn't help him much. "So am I supposed to get her something big?"

"It's up to you. Is she the one?"

A question he'd reflected on a lot. "I think so."

"Make sure she likes it." He shrugged. "I don't know, man. Sorry."

He sighed. "I'll figure it out, I guess."

He pulled into the parking lot of Snowmass Grille a couple minutes later. The electric sign in the front door now flashed 'Closed', and Alex's truck was the only vehicle remaining in the parking lot. Snow covered the windshield and was piled high on top of the truck and in its bed. Stephen pulled up behind it, left his car running, and got out to help Alex brush the snow off and scrape away some of the ice below.

"Thanks, man," Alex said, opening his door. "I'll be seeing you around, I'm sure."

"No problem. See you later."

He returned to his car and drove back the way he had come.

It was past one o'clock when he returned home. He opened his mother's garage door and parked his Audi inside next to her Jeep Grand Cherokee. He headed inside through the garage, glad to be out of the snow and cold for the rest of the day.

He found her in the kitchen, eating a salad. She was scrolling through something on her cellphone, but put it away when she saw him.

"Alex say anything more to you?" she asked.

"Not really."

She sighed. "He didn't really give us anything helpful."

"What if the killer did come from the woods? The cops never considered that possibility."

"There is that," she agreed. "Taking a look into it could be worthwhile."

"What do you mean?" He grabbed two pieces of bread from the cupboard and started making a sandwich. "Aren't you going to let Alex do his work?"

She chuckled quietly. "I've learned long ago that most cops are incompetent. Alex does seem like a nice guy who knows what he's doing, But I can't trust him to handle this correctly. I still need to do some investigating myself."

"Alex is responsible. What don't you trust about him?"

"I don't know." She locked her phone and put it on the table. "There's just something inside of me telling me that I need to do this myself. This is my mission."

"I suppose there's nothing I can do to convince you otherwise?"

She smiled. "You could try."

He grabbed a plate from the cupboard and brought his sandwich to the table. "We're not doing anything else today, right?"

"I don't know. We might."

"Have you looked outside? It's nearly impossible to get anywhere."

"I said might. Only if it's absolutely necessary. Let's go through what we know. Grab me a piece of paper, will you?"

He opened the desk drawer and handed her paper and a pen. She drew a line down the middle and a line across, dividing the sheet into four quadrants. In the upper left, she wrote the word 'Suspects.' "We have none so far, so I'll skip that box." In the box next to that one, she wrote 'Transportation.'

"What's that mean?" Stephen asked.

"How did he get here?" She divided that box into two smaller ones, and wrote 'Alex' in one, and 'Other Cops' in the other. "Alex's theory differed from the guys who investigated originally. I know he's from the FBI and all, but I still think the Kessel guy that I talked to got it right. How could they have missed something like that? They would have known if there were any footprints at all in the yard. Maybe my memory's messed up, and I just thought that the back door was open. His whole theory is based on the fact that whoever killed Will came in through the back door.

"I know, but you seemed so sure of it," he responded.

27

"My mind could be playing tricks on me. All I'm saying is that we need to examine every possibility." She brought her plate to the sink and started a pot of coffee. "Did you get a look at whatever was in that file he had?"

"No. But from what he said, there's not much in it."

"But there's got to be something helpful. Is there any way we can get a look at it?"

He shrugged. "I don't know."

"Fine." She returned to the table. "This is going to be harder than I thought."

"You could always just let Alex handle it." He repeated his advice.

"I already told you; I don't want Alex in charge of this. I want to do it my way."

"There's not much we can do right now, mom."

"Just let me think for a moment." She sat with her head on her hands her eyes closed. "Can you get newspaper articles online?" she asked after a minute.

"Yeah. Why?"

"Grab my laptop and bring it over here." She pointed to where it was sitting on the coffee table in the living room.

He did as she asked, and Angela unlocked the computer. "You're better at this technology stuff than I am. I bet the Pitkin Tribune has an online website. Pull it up."

He got on the webpage for the Pitkin Tribune. He clicked on a link for the online paper. Once that page loaded, a sidebar appeared that had newspapers for every month going back a year. Newspapers were published and distributed on Saturdays, so that made for fifty two newspapers a year. He clicked on January of the past year, and was given four papers to choose from. January 21, the day his father died, was a Saturday. He chose January 28, since his death would definitely be in the paper the following week. The story of Will's death was on the front page.

No Suspects in Cop Murder
Written by Carrie Prescott-Walters

The Aspen police department has no suspects in the murder of one of their own. William Olmsted, age 55, was shot in his home on January 21. His wife was in town at the time of the incident, and she returned to find her husband dead of a gunshot wound to the chest. Detectives estimate that Olmsted was shot sometime between 4:30 and 6:00 on Saturday afternoon. They have not found any DNA or fingerprints linking an individual to the crime. Neighbors and friends have been interviewed, but no information has been proven helpful.

"I have known Will for twelve years," a neighbor said. "I can't understand why anyone would do this."

"This is a tragic loss for our department," Sheriff Paul Brown said in a recent interview. "Will served with us for over fifteen years and was a trusted and respected cop. We are working actively to find the person or persons who committed this crime and hold them accountable."

The investigation is ongoing, but no leads have been unearthed. At this time, the department is treating this as a random incident but is still advising residents to be on the lookout for any suspicious activity. It is unknown if Olmsted had any enemies or altercations that would make him a target. William is survived by his wife Angela and son Stephen. The funeral will be held at St. Mary's Catholic Church in Aspen at 10:30 a.m. this Wednesday. Anyone with any information regarding this investigation should contact Aspen P.D.

Stephen vaguely remembered reading the article. Walters was a friend of his mother's, and had helped her get through the most difficult period following Will's death. Though the article didn't really provide anything new, maybe Walters had some additional information on the case that might prove useful.

He could still recall the day of the funeral. It was bitterly cold. A police escort took them from the church to the graveyard where his father was buried. The church had been packed with mourners, officers and friends alike. His father was well liked and active in the community. Nobody knew why this senseless tragedy had occurred. But as time went on and no new leads were uncovered, the murder fell out of the news, as all crimes eventually do. Soon his father was just a memory.

"I'll talk to Carrie." His mother broke the silence. Walters was reliable and honest, and maybe she knew more than she put in the article.

"So what do we do in the meantime?" Stephen asked.

His mother glanced outside. "There's nothing more we can do in this weather. We'll just have to wait for something to fall onto our plate."

6

Of course I remember," Dylan Kessel said, leaning back on the chair in Alex's office. Kessel was one of the few officers who had actually shown up despite the snow. He was older than Alex, but still young by comparison, in his early thirties. He stood just over five and a half feet, with wavy brown hair that came across his forehead. Alex liked him because he was friendly and easy-going with a no-nonsense attitude.

"This was the main topic of conversation around here for several months after he died. Is this the first you've heard about it?"

"Yeah. Nobody ever told me."

"Everyone was afraid for a while, but eventually we got over it. Brown really wanted to find whoever did it, but he had to give up and move on. We all had to."

"What was your part in the investigation?"

"I was one of the first people on the scene. I talked to the wife, tried to get her to calm down. Then Jesse and I went outside and tried to determine where the guy came from." He leaned forward, tapping his fingers on the desk. "I heard the sheriff's got you looking into it? Does he think we might have missed something?"

He didn't want to explain. "I'm not exactly sure what his reasons are. Could I just ask you a couple questions?"

"Shoot."

He flipped open the file to the police report. "It says that you and Rollins determined that the killer entered and exited through the front door. How did you figure that out?"

Kessel spun the folder around so it was facing him. "The guy had to have parked his car on the street. We went around the whole house and didn't find any footprints. The sidewalk was covered in them. We had no idea if those belonged to the Olmsted's or to the killer, but it seemed the front door was the only way he could've gotten in."

"Do you remember if it was windy?"

"Yeah. It was freezing. And the snow was fresh, so it kept blowing up in my face when we were outside."

"So the wind could've blown fresh snow over any footprints that the killer left?"

Kessel thought about that for a moment. "Yeah, I guess."

"I talked to Angela Olmsted today. She remembered that the back door was open when she arrived home from the store that evening."

"I'm pretty sure she said that everything was locked."

"I know. Sometimes the mind plays tricks. She was in shock when you talked to her that evening. She probably forgot to tell you a few things. You should've interviewed her the following day or a few days later."

"Footprints would've been left on the side of the garage if he came through the back door," Kessel said. "That area was completely sheltered from the wind."

"I know. I don't think he parked on the street. I think he came from the woods."

Kessel stared at him like he was crazy. "Alex. You don't understand. It was *freezing* that day. Not just cold. You'd go numb in five minutes. Someone would have to be insane to be out in that weather for an extended period of time."

"Maybe the person who did this is crazy."

"Aren't all murderers crazy?"

Alex smiled and shook his head. "No. Well, some of them are. From what I've heard, this guy planned out every move. He knew what exactly what he was doing, when Will would be left alone. He probably watched him for a long time."

Kessel shrugged. "Whatever. You're the expert. I suppose Jesse and I could've missed something. I just don't see how someone could be out in that cold that long."

Alex thought of Minnesota. The cold here was nothing compared to that. He could recall times when the temperature dropped to thirty below. "How cold are you talking about?"

"I don't know. With the wind chill, maybe ten below."

"In Minnesota, sometimes the wind chill drops to fifty below."

Kessel shook his head. "You *are* crazy."

Alex reached across the table and grabbed the folder. "I gotta go. Thanks for your help."

"Anytime. Let me know if you find anything."

He walked back to his truck, shielding his face against the blinding snow. This time he was going home. He didn't want to be out in this weather any more.

And then his cell phone rang.

"Alex." Brown's voice was quiet and serious. "I need you to get over here right now." He gave Alex an address, a mile or two southeast of town. "I've got bad news."

＊＊＊＊＊＊＊＊＊＊＊＊＊＊＊

It took Alex ten minutes to get to Brown's locale. There were no other vehicles on the road. Not even plows. The roads were completely snow covered, and he was glad that his truck had four wheel drive. He turned off Highway 82 into a small neighborhood. A couple of police cars sat on the road outside of the first house on the right, lights flashing. Yellow crime scene tape stretched from a large tree in the front yard to the garage and over to another tree.

That wasn't good.

He parked behind one of the patrol cars and turned off the engine. He made sure his pistol was snug in his belt before stepping out of the truck.

Brown appeared out of the cloud of white, walking down the driveway to meet him. The expression on his face told Alex that something was seriously wrong. He simply motioned for Alex to follow him to the house.

They ducked under the tape and approached the front door. The door was wide open, and an officer Alex didn't recognize stood inside, taking pictures. Jesse Rollins stood on

33

the front porch, talking urgently to somebody on his cell phone. Brown sidestepped Rollins, kicking the snow off of his shoes, and stepped inside.

The subject of the photographer was a big man lying face up on the hardwood floor. Alex knew immediately that it was Daniel Carver, a fellow cop for Aspen P.D. From the looks of it, he'd been shot point blank in the forehead. A dark pool of blood had formed underneath his head.

"What happened?" Alex asked quietly.

Brown pulled him aside and spoke softly so that the photographer couldn't hear. "His wife made the call, but she's gone. Said someone was in the house. He also has a daughter. We're working on locating them. The thing is," he continued, casting a glance over his shoulder, "this seems awfully similar to Olmsted's death."

The same thought had flashed through Alex's mind. A murder on the same day that he reopened the investigation? "It's gotta be just a coincidence."

He shrugged. "Could be. I hope it is. But the similarities are there. I just got here a couple minutes ago." The sheriff took a deep breath. "Daniel was... he was a good man. Why would somebody want to kill him?"

"I don't know. Is his wife a suspect?"

"I don't think so." Brown paused. "We can talk later. I've got a dead cop here and his wife and daughter are missing. And the top priority I have right now is finding them both."

He turned and headed out the door, leaving Alex alone with the photographer, who left a moment later. A box of latex gloves sat on the table in the kitchen. He grabbed a pair and knelt down next to Carver's body.

There wasn't a lot of blood on Carver's face. Most of it was in his hair, making it sticky and darker than usual. The viscosity meant that the murder was recent; maybe thirty minutes ago. He turned Carver's head slightly. There was no exit wound, which meant that the shell was somewhere in his brain. That would be sent to Denver for the lab to analyze. Alex checked the rest of the body. There were no marks or scratches on the body to indicate that Carver had been in a scuffle of some sort. He didn't see any gunshot residue on Carver's forehead, which meant that the gun probably hadn't been pressed against his head. The killer probably knocked on the door, and when Carver opened it, he was greeted with a bullet. From the position of the body, Alex could assume that he had fallen backward after opening the door. There was no sign that Carver had been dragged across the floor or moved at all.

He left the body and walked into the kitchen. He wasn't going to find anything by examining the body. That was for the coroner. Forensics would be here any minute to dust for fingerprints and DNA. He didn't think they'd find anything. It looked like the killer was thorough. He wouldn't leave anything behind to incriminate him. His job now was to find out why anyone may have wanted Daniel Carver dead.

He checked the kitchen first, looking for anything out of place. There were no dirty dishes in the sink, no food left out on the counters. A newspaper sat on the table, next to a cell phone. Alex turned it on. Alex recognized the picture that popped up as Erin Carver and her daughter. If Erin had called 9-1-1 from her cell phone, then how would it have ended up on the table? Unless the Carver's had a landline. They did. He saw a phone sitting in its cradle on the desk. He'd have to check with Brown to see what number the call came from.

He checked the rest of the main floor, but didn't notice anything out of the ordinary. When he returned to the kitchen, there were two men and a woman examining Carver's body. Forensics. Paul Brown stood next to them. One of the men saw him and handed him a black cell phone.

"This was in his back pocket," he explained.

Alex took the phone. It required a six digit passcode to get in. A million different possible combinations. He'd have to make a few calls and see if he could get access to Carver's phone records. Maybe he had contact with whoever did this.

"What phone number did the call come from?" he asked the sheriff.

"It was a local area code. Not a cellphone. Erin must have called from the landline."

The phone had been in its cradle in the kitchen. If she had used that phone, it was unlikely that she had replaced it. It was more likely that she had called from somewhere else in the house. Maybe upstairs. He wanted to find exactly where the call had come from.

He grabbed a new pair of gloves and headed upstairs. At the top, a hallway led to the right. A bathroom was the first door on the left. There was another room next to it, the door slightly open. He looked inside. The daughter's room. He pushed the door open and stepped in. Like the kitchen, everything looked in order. The bed was made and all clothes put away neatly. It sort of looked unused. An idea popped into his head. He went into the bathroom next door, which he guessed was used solely by the daughter. There wasn't a toothbrush, toothpaste, or a hairbrush anywhere to be found.

Carver's daughter hadn't been here at all today. The only explanation Alex could think of was that she had been somewhere overnight. Maybe a friend's house or grandparents. He guessed that Daniel and Erin had been here alone this morning.

He stored that information in the back of his mind and walked across the hall to the master bedroom. This room was a little messier. On a nightstand next to the bed, he saw what he was looking for. The phone wasn't in its cradle. Which likely meant that Erin had made the call from up here. Maybe she'd been in the bathroom, heard the shot, and called 9-1-1. But something didn't fit. There was no signs of a struggle. If Erin had been up here when she made the call, had the killer come upstairs to find her? She could've locked herself in the bedroom and waited for them to get here. Why go downstairs where there was an intruder?

He went back downstairs. The three techs from forensics were dusting the entryway for fingerprints. He motioned for Brown to join him in the kitchen.

"Find anything?"

"Yeah. I think Carver's daughter spent the night somewhere else. All her toiletries are gone, and her room is very neat. It was just him and Erin here this afternoon."

Brown thought that over. "Could be. I'll have one of my guys check it out."

"Also, when we get back to headquarters, I'd like to listen to the 9-1-1 call. Something about this just doesn't feel right."

"What do you mean?"

"Erin probably made the call from upstairs. But there was no sign of any altercation up there. Why would she come down if she knew someone was in the house?"

"Your guess is as good as mine. Maybe that call will tell us something."

They went out onto the front porch, back into the snow. Despite the weather, a sizeable crowd of people had gathered on the road. A couple officers were keeping them back. Alex watched a news van roll to a stop behind one of the squad cars. A reporter with a microphone hopped out.

"Shit," Brown whispered.

After seeing the crime scene, Alex was beginning to agree with Brown. The death of William Olmsted had to be related somehow to this.

He was doubting his earlier words. There was no way that this was a coincidence.

7

Vincent arrived at Carver's house shortly after Alex. By that time, it was nearing 3:00 P.M. He parked behind a grey Chevy Malibu on the street and got out of the car. A large crowd had gathered at the end of the driveway, braving the blizzard. He ducked under the yellow tape unseen and approached the sheriff, who was standing in the middle of the driveway.

Vincent could tell that Brown was upset. "How the hell did the press hear about this?"

Vincent shrugged. One of the neighbors might have reported something. But how had the news crew from Grand Junction gotten here so fast?

"Sheriff?" A young brunette spoke loudly, trying to attract his attention. "Is it true that Mr. Carver is dead?"

Brown had no choice but to draw closer to the crowd. "It is," he replied curtly.

"Is this murder related in any way to the death of William Olmsted?" Carrie Prescott Walters chimed in. Vincent recognized her as the main writer and editor for the Pitkin Tribune. Her short, dark hair was drawn back in a bun. A streak of pink ran through the right side, as if she was trying to make herself look young and hip.

"There is nothing at this point to make us believe the two are related." Vincent could hear the lie in Brown's voice, and suspected Walters could also.

"What about his wife and daughter? Are they all right?"

"We are working now to locate them."

"Are you treating this as an abduction?" The brunette spoke up again.

"Like I said, we are attempting to locate Mrs. Carver and her daughter as we speak." He started toward the house. "I have nothing more to say at this point, and I advise you all to leave before this storm gets any worse. If anyone has any pertinent information, please talk to me or one of my officers."

The sheriff brushed past Vincent, shaking his head and muttering something. The crowd slowly began to disperse, but several people remained behind, including Walters. Tomorrow was Saturday, and this was definitely going to make the front page in the newspaper. Vincent followed Brown into the house, joining the forensics team inside.

He'd never seen someone who'd been shot before, but the sight of the body on the floor didn't disturb him like it might other people. He hadn't known Carver well, but heard that the officer had a good reputation.

"Anything?" Brown's question was directed to a young man kneeling on the hardwood floor.

"Afraid not," he replied. "Whoever did this wore gloves. The victim didn't fight back at all. He was definitely surprised."

Brown closed his eyes and exhaled slowly. "Okay. Get out of here. You've done your job."

As the forensics people filed out, two more officers came in and put Carver in a body bag. A couple minutes later, he and the sheriff were alone in the house.

"Did you or Alex find anything?" Vincent finally asked.

"Maybe. Alex is headed back to the station. He's following up on a few things."

"Nothing major?"

"Nope." Brown sounded resigned.

"Do you think this is related to Olmsted's death?"

"Everybody's asking me that. I think it is, but I'm not going to admit that to anyone else. It would just spread fear. We need to make the public think that we're gonna find this person quickly and easily. This'll definitely be in the papers tomorrow, and I bet Walters is gonna try to link this to Olmsted's death. She was obsessed with it. And knowing her, she'll somehow find a way to cast the blame on me."

Apparently there was some animosity between Brown and the reporter. "So what are we gonna do?" Vincent asked.

"I don't know. I'll leave a couple guys here, and head back and see if Alex found anything. I don't wanna be out in this weather anymore."

Brown stepped back out onto the front porch. "Jesse, you and Seth stay here until everybody's cleared out. You can leave after that. Make sure nobody can get inside. I know I'm not following protocol, but I don't want to leave you guys out here with this snow." He turned to Maya Tanner, who was standing beside Rollins on the porch. She was a young officer who had been hired at the same time as him. "Maya, go talk to neighbors, see if they saw anything. Come back and report to me when you're done."

Then he turned to Vincent. "Follow me back to the station. "Be careful."

Vincent could barely see the tail lights of Brown's vehicle as he drove through the snow. He guessed that six inches had already fallen, which meant that the snow was coming down at about an inch an hour. He kept the heat on high and the windshield wipers going until he pulled into the parking lot behind the sheriff. Only Alex's truck was in the main lot. Everyone else had either parked behind the building or hadn't returned from Carver's house yet.

He shut off his lights and hurried inside. No doubt there would be a ton of snow on his car when he came back out. It wasn't supposed to quit snowing until at least midnight. He assumed that there would be another half foot or more by tomorrow morning.

It was warm inside. Allyson Turner sat at the front desk, where she'd been since 7:00 this morning. She served as a dispatcher today and did whatever Brown requested. He gave her a nod as he walked past the desk.

Alex sat at his desk, the door closed. It was on the far side of the large, open area where most of the other officers had their desks. Alex saw Vincent and came out.

"Anything?" he asked.

Vincent shook his head. "I was only there for ten minutes or so. Brown answered a few questions and then most people left."

"I saw the news van when I left. How'd they get there so fast?"

He shrugged. "I don't know. Maybe they were already reporting on something else here and happened to hear that there was a murder."

"Maybe Carrie has a police scanner. I wouldn't be surprised." Alex looked over his shoulder. "Where's the sheriff?"

"He's coming. You've got a few leads?"

"Not really. I have Carver's phone, but it's going to take a while to get access to it. I tried calling his phone company but I couldn't get through. I'm not even sure if his records will be useful."

"What might not be useful?" Brown joined them outside of Alex's office.

"His phone records. I couldn't get through to the phone company."

Brown nodded. "I have Kessel working on locating his daughter right now. He'll let me know once he finds anything."

"Did you tell him that she might have spent the night with a friend?"

"Yes, I told him that."

"What about Erin?" Alex asked.

"What do you think?"

"I think it's logical to assume that she's been abducted. She wouldn't leave the house after her husband's been murdered."

"That's what I think, too," Brown agreed. "I considered asking the police chief in Carbondale to put up a checkpoint on the highway, but it's probably too late now and we don't even know what type of vehicle we're looking for."

"What about the call Erin made? Can I listen to it?"

"Right." Brown turned around. "You guys head into my office. I'll have Allyson transfer it over to my computer."

41

They each took a chair and positioned it around the computer. Brown entered a moment later and pulled up his email. He found the recording and clicked play.

"9-1-1, what's your emergency?"

"Someone's in my house." Erin Carver's voice was quiet and frantic. "They've got a gun. Please help me."

"Slow down." Allyson sounded calm and reassuring. "What is your name and address?"

"Erin Carver. 3212 Marble Street. Please hurry."

"Officers have been sent to your home. Where are you in your house?"

There was a long pause, and then, "I'm upstairs in my closet."

"Stay there, Erin. Can you find something in the closet that you can use as a weapon if necessary?"

There was some rustling, and then a creaking sound. Erin didn't answer, but Vincent could hear heavy breathing.

"Mrs. Carver? Can you hear me?"

There was some more noise in the background, and then a click as the call ended.

Vincent was confused by Erin Carver's actions. He assumed her closet would have been a relatively safe place to hide. Why would she have left it?

"You were right that she made the call from upstairs," Brown said to Alex. "Do you have any idea why she may have left the closet?"

"Could you rewind to the point where she says she's in the closet?" Alex asked. "I thought I heard something in the background."

They listened to the second half of the recording once more. It sounded like a second voice in the background, but it was so jumbled that Vincent couldn't be sure. But he threw it out anyway. "I think someone was talking to her."

"That's what I was thinking," Alex agreed. "It sounds like a man's voice. But it couldn't have been Daniel because he was probably already dead."

"But why would she leave the closet if the killer was talking to her?" Brown queried. "If I was in her position, I'd have stayed right where I was."

"We don't know what he may have said to her," Vincent stated. "He could have threatened her."

"If we give this to Kessel, do you think he'd be able to isolate the noise in the background?" Alex asked.

"I could have him try. I'm not sure if our equipment is advanced enough to do that."

There was a knock on the door, and Kessel stepped inside, as if on cue. He had a post it note in his hand, and he stuck it to the sheriff's desk. "Emma Carver's at the home of Rich and Sandy Wilcox. They confirmed that she spent last night at their place. I didn't give them any details, but said that some-one would be over shortly to talk to her."

"Good work," Brown said. "I've got one more thing for you to do. We listened to the 9-1-1 call that Erin Carver made. Are you able to isolate some background noise?"

"I'll do my best. Where's the recording?"

"It's on my computer in here. I'll go grab a cup of coffee. Let me know when you're done."

Kessel took a seat at the computer, and Vincent followed Alex out of the office. Brown turned around and handed Alex the post it note with the Wilcox's address. "You two up for another drive?

8

It was just starting to get dark outside when Carrie Prescott Walters arrived. Her long black coat was covered in snow, and her face was flushed red from being out in the cold. She kicked off her boots in the entryway and joined Stephen and Angela in the dining room. A hot pot of coffee sat on the table.

After reading the article, Angela had called Walters. Upon hearing that Daniel Carver had been murdered, and that Walters was at the scene, she insisted that Carrie join them for dinner. After that phone call she had disappeared into her bedroom, and Stephen heard her talking to someone else. Who that was and what the conversation was about, Stephen didn't know. And it was clear that his mother didn't *want* him to know.

"Thanks for coming, Carrie," Angela said, standing up to give her a hug. "I hate to make you drive some more in this snow."

"It's no problem." Walters poured herself a mug of coffee and rubbed her hands together. "I've been driving in snow for thirty five years. I've seen worse than this."

For as long as Stephen could remember, the two of them had been friends. Walters had been writing for the Pitkin Tribune for at least twenty years. Based on her excellent reporting, Stephen was surprised that she hadn't moved on to higher places. She lived in a condo in Snowmass Village and was recently divorced with no children. And she wasn't shy about voicing her opinions, especially when it came to politics. Everyone in the county knew she wasn't a fan of the sheriff nor the mayor, and she didn't hesitate to publish harsh editorials against them.

"You said that Paul was reopening the investigation into Will's death," Walters continued. "What's that all about?"

"I asked him to."

"You did what? I thought you moved on, Angela. Don't make them dig into this again."

His mother leaned forward. "I *need* to do this, Carrie. Whoever killed Will needs to pay."

"What makes you think the cops will find anything? They clearly didn't the first time." Stephen caught the disdain in her voice.

"*They* aren't going to find anything. But Stephen and I might."

Walters was confused. "Could you run me through this, please?"

"You know Alex Snyder, right? He's looking into it, but he's not gonna find much, if anything. I talked to him earlier today, hoping to get a look at the case file. I saw it, but there's not much in there. I'm gonna let Alex do the work, and if he overturns anything, I'll check it out myself."

Walters shook her head. "Do you know Daniel Carver?"

"Not well. I've spoken with his wife, on occasion."

"Carver is dead, and his wife and daughter are missing. The sheriff is pretty tight-lipped. I asked about Erin and Emma, and all he said is that they're working to locate them. I also asked if he thought that this was related to Will's murder. He replied that there was no reason to believe that, but I could tell that the thought had gone through his mind."

Angela took a deep breath. "And what do you think?"

Walters arched her eyebrows. "I have little information, so it's hard to say. From what I did hear, there was very little evidence in the house. I won't know for sure until I talk to the cops, but I'd say the odds are good that this is related to Will's death in some way."

"Let's just assume that the killer is the same guy. Is it a coincidence that he killed someone on the same day that the investigation was reopened?"

"I don't believe in coincidences." Walters said. "But I agree that the timing is very odd. I haven't reported on too many murders in my time, but I have watched a lot of crime shows.

45

What kind of killer murders one person and then waits eleven months to do it again?"

"A psychopath." Angela stood up. "Dinner will be ready in five minutes."

Once she was in the kitchen, Walters leaned over to Stephen and spoke quietly. "What is she planning to do?"

"I don't know." To be honest, he had no idea what his mother's plan was. "All she told me is that justice should be served."

"It's not her place to do that, even with what happened. Let's just assume you do find this guy. Do you think she has it in her to kill someone in revenge?"

Unfortunately, he didn't have to think about it. "I hate to say it, but yes."

"You've got to do something," Walters said seriously. "Revenge or not, that's still murder. She would end up in prison."

"Why can't you talk to her? You guys are much closer than we are. And how likely is it that she actually finds the person who did this?"

"Not very likely. But you can't take that chance."

He sighed. Angela was as stubborn as a mule. "I'll talk to her. But it may not do any good."

"Thank you." Walters seemed content with his answer.

They were sitting like that, waiting for dinner, when Angela's cell phone rang. It was sitting on the table next to Stephen, so he grabbed it. The display read 'Stuart Rockford.' The name meant nothing to him, but he answered any way.

"I've got a name and address for you," a deep male voice said quickly. "Emma Carver is-" He stopped abruptly. "Who is this?"

Angela rushed into the dining room and swiped the phone out of his hand. "What the hell are you doing?"

"Your phone rang, so I answered it," Stephen said. "What's the problem?"

She ended the call and shoved the phone in her pocket. "I don't need you answering calls for me."

Walters stood up and approached his mother. She must have heard what Rockford said. "I think you need to tell us what's going on here, Angela."

"It's none of your business, Carrie."

"I think it is. If Stephen or I are going to have any part in helping you, we need to know the full story. We don't keep secrets from each other, Angela."

It looked like they were going to get into a heated argument, but Angela finally relented. "Fine. Let me go grab the food first."

"Stuart is a cop," she began, once the food was on the table. "We met a year ago at a dinner."

"Stuart Rockford?" Walters interrupted. Stephen could tell by her tone that she didn't particularly like Rockford.

"Yes," she replied, with a twinge of annoyance. "As I was saying, we met about a year ago. It was right after Will died. He was very kind to me, and we got to talking. He expressed some disapproval toward Brown, and I found myself agreeing with him. We ran into each other several times afterward, but didn't really talk until he called me out of the blue a week ago. He said that he would help me find whoever killed Will. And of course, I accepted. He's called a couple times yesterday, and already three times today."

Something was off about this whole thing. "Why would he want to help you?"

Angela sounded offended. "I don't know, maybe he's a good person? And feels sorry for me?"

"Good person? No." Walters was shaking her head. "I think I know what this is all about." She pushed her plate aside. "I've covered news in this city for almost thirty years. I've gotten to know nearly all the cops on this force. Stuart Rockford joined about six years ago. I'm not sure where he came from, but there was something about him that I just didn't like. He acted like he was in charge, and he was disrespectful toward authority. Paul has been sheriff ever since Stuart came here. I've talked to him numerous times, and I get the strong impression that he does not like Paul. This is just a theory, but hear me out. Stuart could be using this as a way to put himself into the spotlight." She held up her hand to keep Angela from interrupting. "He wants to be sheriff next year. I know that much. What better way to gain notoriety than to solve these murders? If he gets credit for this, it'll make him look good and Paul not so good. He's using you to help solve this. It's not about your feelings. He just wants to find out who did this in any way possible, and this just happens to involve you."

Walters' theory made sense, Stephen thought. He didn't know who Stuart Rockford was, but it was clear that Carrie didn't like him.

"I will admit that your explanation seems reasonable," Angela finally said. "But to be honest with you, I don't give a damn why Stuart is helping me. If he's just using me to further his career, so be it. All I'm concerned about right now is finding out who killed my husband."

Walters sighed. "I know I can't do anything to change your mind, Angela. I just hope you know that you're getting into a tricky situation." She stood up and pushed in her chair. "Thanks for dinner. I'd better get going."

"Are you sure you want to drive home in this?"

Walters put on her coat and gloves. "I'll be fine. Think about what I said. I'll talk to you later."

A draft of cold air entered the house as Walters left. Stephen helped his mother clear the table, then headed into the living room.

"Do you agree with Carrie?" Angela asked, joining him on the sofa.

"Kind of. I wish you'd let Alex do what he can instead of working against him."

"I'm not working against him," she defended herself. "It's just a different angle."

"Same thing. I know you have your mind set, so I'll help you and get this over quicker."

"Thank you." She pulled out her cell phone. "Now that you know about Stuart, I suppose it's all right if you hear what he has to say."

She dialed a number and put it on speaker. Rockford picked up in two rings. "I found out where Emma Carver is. She was at a friend's house last night. I texted you the address a minute ago."

"Yes, I know. I saw it. I don't want to try getting out there tonight. It's getting dark."

"It wouldn't do any good. Alex and Vincent are on their way there now."

"Where are you right now?"

"I just got home. I'll head back in tomorrow, see what happened. I'll let you know whatever I find out."

"Thanks." Angela hesitated for a moment before her next question. "Why are you doing this?"

Rockford didn't answer right away. "What do you mean?"

"Why are you helping me? Going behind Paul's back?"

"I don't like the way he's doing things. And I don't think his methods are going to help us find the killer."

"So why don't you work on your own? Why involve me?"

"This whole thing revolves around your husband, Angela. Don't you want to know who killed him?"

"Of course I do. I'm just saying that it's a little odd how you're just feeding me information."

"I can hang up right now and never talk to you again, if that's what you want."

"No, please don't. I just want to know the whole reason behind this."

Stephen heard a loud sigh. "Fine. A lot of people in the county agree that the sheriff is making some poor decisions. We have factions forming within our own department. If I can solve this case, with your help of course, it will give me a real shot at becoming sheriff in November, and it will make him look even more incompetent."

"I used to like Paul," Angela agreed, "but my feelings have changed. You do whatever you have to do. I have one goal and you know what that is."

"Okay. I'll call you if I learn anything."

She let the phone slide out of her hand, and they sat in silence for a few minutes before Stephen finally spoke. "I know Carrie doesn't believe in coincidences, but do you? You have to admit that it's odd how all these things are happening at the same time."

49

She walked away without answering. "I'm heading upstairs. We'll decide what to do tomorrow."

He was beginning to regret getting involved in this.

9

Alex and Vincent pulled up in front of the Wilcox home at about 7:30. Several lights shone from inside. At least somebody was home. They hurried from the car up to the front door, which opened even before Alex knocked. In the doorway stood a middle aged woman with shoulder length hair that was blonde to the point of nearly being white. She was short and petite and had a worried look on her face.

"Is it true?" she asked quietly, stepping out onto the front porch. "Is Daniel dead?"

Alex simply nodded. "I understand Emma spent last night here?"

She nodded. "I'm Sandy. Emma got here around five o'clock last night and has been here ever since. She found out a few hours ago and locked herself in my daughter's bedroom." She squeezed her eyes shut and rubbed the bridge of her nose. "I can't imagine what's going through her mind right now."

"Do you mind if we come in?" he asked. "It's a little windy out here."

"Of course. I'm sorry." Sandy stepped aside. "This is my husband, Rick."

Rick stood behind Sandy, and was probably two heads taller than her with a mass of graying hair. Alex had never seen either of them before and placed the couple in their mid to late forties.

Alex stepped forward and shook his hand. "I'm Alex Snyder, and this is Vincent Martinez. Does Emma have any relatives nearby?"

"Her grandparents live in Glenwood Springs," Sandy responded. "They're on their way here right now."

"God, I can't believe this," Rick said. "Daniel's dead, and what about Erin?"

"It appears that whoever killed Daniel took her. Do you think I could try and speak with Emma?" He just wanted to get this over with.

"She hasn't said a word." Sandy sighed. "I doubt you could get her to say anything."

"How much does she know?" Vincent asked.

"It's all over the news. She knows the basic details."

"I understand. But it's my job to at least try and talk to her."

Sandy stepped aside. "Good luck."

Luck wasn't on his side. Emma didn't say a single word to him. The snow was still coming down when he arrived home. Twelve hours after he'd left home, there was a dead cop, a missing woman, a devastated daughter, and a vengeful widow. And instead of one murder to look into, he now had two.

He hung up his coat in the mudroom and headed into the kitchen. He had texted Jen earlier to let her know that he wouldn't be home until around eight. She replied that dinner would be waiting. And it was.

She sat with her back to him, her blonde hair falling around her shoulders. He came up behind her and kissed her, and then sat down across from her.

"You've had a busy day," she said, pouring him a glass of wine.

He sighed. "I guess everybody knows by now what's happened."

"Yeah. I watched the news tonight. It's the top story on every local channel, and even made the national news. There's a lot of pressure on you guys."

"I know." He tapped his fingers on the table. "I honestly have no idea what to do."

"Run me through your day. Maybe I can give you some help."

Jen was smart, logical, and good under pressure. He always thought she would have been a good agent, or even a politician. "I met with the sheriff at seven, and he told me about William Olmsted. Why wasn't I aware of that?"

She shrugged. "I don't know. People don't like to talk about it. I figured Stephen would eventually tell you. I mean, didn't you ever ask him about his parents?"

"Yeah. I guess he never actually told me about his dad."

"So what did you do after the meeting?"

"I went to breakfast with Stephen, and then we went to his mother's house. You ever met her?"

"I don't think so."

"She's... interesting. She's set on finding whoever killed William and getting revenge on that person. I asked her a few questions, but it happened so long ago that I don't know if she really knew what she was talking about. I'm gonna head over to her old house tomorrow and check a few things out.

"Then I heard about Daniel Carver and headed over to his house. He must have been shot right when he opened the door. And his wife's missing."

Jen shook her head. "That's awful. Do you think it's the same person who killed Stephen's dad?"

Alex sighed. "It's kind of early to tell, but I'd guess that it is. The sheriff's already convinced."

"So what do you think?" Jen asked. "What would be a motive for this?"

"I honestly don't know. These could be random victims. Let's just assume that they *are* connected. The fact that these murders are eleven months apart suggests that the killer is patient. And the neatness shows that he is smart and organized." He finished the wine and put the glass down a little too hard. "I'm sorry. I'm not really hungry. I just need to do some thinking."

"I understand." Jen started clearing off the table. "Let me know if you need anything."

Alex grabbed the Olmsted file and headed into his office with a full glass of water. He closed the door and opened his laptop. The internet might have some additional information on Will's death that wasn't in the file.

He had one new email, and he clicked on it. The name 'Sara Wright' appeared, and he sat back in his chair, surprised. Wright was one of Alex's partners from the FBI. His preferred partner. They had developed a close relationship, both in their twenties and having similar interests. Since Alex had left the bureau, however, the two had not stayed in contact. She hadn't even come to his wedding, the only member of his team not present. Which was why the email caught him off guard.

He opened it and read.

Alex,

I hope you are growing accustomed to your new life. It is so much different here without you. We have a new member from Baltimore, and he is nice, but nothing can replace you. I am so sorry that I was not at your wedding. There are several things I would like to talk to you about. I am in Denver for a week celebrating Christmas with my family. Could we meet for dinner some night? I'd love to see you.

Sara

He felt a pang of sadness in his chest. Just thinking about Sara brought back a lot of memories. Ones he wished were still being created. Sara had once had feelings for him. He and Jen had started dating around the same time, so nothing had happened between them. He always wondered if she had missed his wedding because she resented that he had chosen Jen instead of her. Here was a chance to set things straight, catch up, and maybe even get some help on the current case he was working Denver was a long drive, especially in winter, but he felt that this meeting was important.

His response was short, stating that he would like to meet with her. Pushing Sara to the back of his mind, he opened a new tab and typed in 'William Olmsted.' Thousands of results came up, and he scrolled through them. Many were newspaper articles, and he read several of them, but none gave him any information that he didn't already know. Several articles were similar in that they criticized Paul Brown for his failure to find the person responsible. There weren't even any named suspects. He read several articles by Carrie Prescott Walters, who was especially harsh on the sheriff. It seemed like she definitely had something against him. Based on comments below the article, she wasn't the only one who felt that way. He had the feeling that the citizens of Pitkin County had a negative attitude toward the sheriff, and he couldn't really blame them.

Mayor Janet Danielson was also up for re-election in November, and Alex thought she would likely get elected for a fourth term. There had been little growth in the city, and tax rates had gone up, but Danielson had a large base of followers. Alex had never met her, but had heard rumors that there were tensions between her and the sheriff.

He read a few more things, but found nothing helpful. Tomorrow morning, he planned to head back to Angela's previous home and check out the landscape. If the killer had actually come from the woods, he wanted to know how.

The snow was finally winding down as he headed up to bed.

10

It was dark and cold when Alex woke up the next morning. He threw on a sweatshirt and a pair of jeans and left the bedroom quietly. He started a pot of coffee before heading outside. Wherever he looked, he saw white. The first rays of light were just beginning to appear in the east, already warming the air. He didn't want to take the time to get out the snow blower, so he shoveled a path down the driveway, doing just enough so that he would be able to back his truck out. The street was still snow-covered, but Alex expected that the plows would be out in full force and arrive in the neighborhood soon.

He hurried back into the garage, grabbed his cross country skis from off the wall, and tossed them into the back of the truck. The fresh foot of snow meant that skiing would be difficult, but hopefully it was the heavy kind so he wouldn't sink in too deep.

He kicked off his boots in the mudroom and poured himself a cup of coffee. He had a text from the sheriff, which read, 'Meet me in the conference room at ten.' That gave him about two and a half hours to check out Angela's land, which should be more than enough time.

He ate a bowl of cereal and drank two cups of coffee before heading out. Jen was still sleeping when he left at seven fifteen, but he'd told her last night where he would be in the morning.

He didn't see any other cars out on the road. Most streets were plowed by now and there was no wind, so the roads weren't too slippery. This was his favorite time of day, when most of the world was still sleeping and there were no distractions. Several questions drifted through his mind. Were the two murders related? Where was Erin Carver? What was Angela planning? Unfortunately, he could only guess the answers to these. Maybe Sheriff Brown had some news. But he wasn't optimistic.

He parked on the street in front of the house, but another question popped into his mind. Why hadn't Angela sold this house yet? She had moved several months ago, so why hold on to this additional property?

Snow lay in drifts in front of the house. Alex couldn't even make out where the driveway started under all the snow. He wasn't looking forward to this, but had decided that it was easier and quicker than getting his snowmobile loaded up.

He walked around to the back of the house, his boots sinking into the snow. A chilly breeze had picked up, blowing from the north, but once he was behind the house, the wind was blocked by the trees. Thick pines stretched around most of the house like a barrier, their branches sagging under the heavy snow.

He bent down and attached his skis. Once that was done, he grabbed his poles and skied to the point where the open land met the trees. A wide trail cut into the forest, twisting out of his view. For some reason, he felt fairly certain that the killer had come this way. And if that was the case, this trail had probably been used. So he decided to see where it led.

It was considerably darker beneath the thick canopy of the trees. He followed the trail as it wound its way through the pines. After about ten minutes of skiing, the trees began to thin out. Alex broke free from the forest and skidded to a stop. He was in a large open area, what he assumed to be a meadow in the summer. An icy pond sat off to his left, the surface blown free of snow by the wind. Drifts lay everywhere, some more than ten feet high. He was staring straight at a side view of the Maroon Bells, and it seemed as if they were close enough to touch. Three sides of the meadow were surrounded by trees, while the fourth side was barren and gently sloped upward.

He skied over to the frozen pond, which was less than a hundred yards across. It was odd for such a small body of water to be found in a place like this. It had been a wet autumn followed by an early, cold November, so maybe the water had ponded and froze before getting a chance to evaporate.

He turned and scanned the woods, wondering if this was the end of the trail. The trees were definitely more sparse, but there was no obvious path. Then he noticed something on the far side of the meadow, directly across from him. There was a break in the trees. A large one.

As he skied over to check it out, he realized that it wasn't a trail, but an old logging road. It was slightly wider than the trail he had been on, but only a little more than the width of an SUV or pickup, at least at this point. There were countless roads like this in Colorado, many of them crisscrossing the Mosquito and Gore ranges and the San Juans near Telluride and Ouray. Not many of them were used any more, but they were there. The road headed north, back into more trees. Alex had followed the trail west from the Olmsted's, for about two miles. Unfortunately, he had to be back in town in less than an hour. Skiing back to the truck would take another twenty minutes. He didn't have time to follow the logging road. He knew of another way to figure out where it went. It would just have to wait until after the meeting.

He pulled into the parking lot next to an old red Monte Carlo an hour later. By the time he entered the conference room, there was only one seat left, next to the sheriff. The rest of the chairs were occupied by a couple of deputies and several other officers.

The sheriff was passing out folders to everyone. He handed one to Alex and turned on the TV that was mounted on the wall behind him. "Let's get started right away. I've notified you all about what happened yesterday. It saddens me to say that Daniel Carver was pronounced dead at his home."

A photo of Carver appeared on the screen. He was a tall, big man, with short reddish hair and a similar colored beard. Alex estimated him at 6'5, maybe three hundred pounds.

"He was with us for over fifteen years," Brown continued. "The search is still underway for his wife, Erin.

Unfortunately, we have not had any new developments since last night."

The screen switched to a photo of William Olmsted. "This is Will Olmsted, as you all know. He too was murdered in the same fashion eleven months ago."

"Do you think the same person is responsible?" Deputy Charlie Porter asked.

"It seems... likely." Brown searched for the right word to use. "Both men were shot in their homes. And both crime scenes were incredibly neat, with practically no evidence left behind. The one major difference is that Erin Carver is missing. Angela Olmsted, Will's wife, was not home at the time of Will's death."

"Maybe he didn't realize that Erin was home," Porter suggested.

"That's unlikely," Alex said. "A person with this level of organization and neatness wouldn't miss that fact. He probably went in knowing that he'd have to either abduct Erin Carver or kill her."

"Did you ever deal with anything like this while you were in the FBI?" Brown asked.

All eyes turned to him. "No. There are a lot of unusual things about this case. His level of neatness shows that he's very sophisticated. But he'll eventually make a mistake, and we need to be there to catch him at that point."

"What if the killer's a she?" Maya Tanner spoke up. She was young, bright, and eager, just out of college. Tanner was short and pretty, her blond hair tied at the back of her head in ponytail.

"Men are responsible for over ninety percent of murders," Alex replied. "This could be the work of a woman, but it's not likely."

"Tanner and Young, I'd like you to work on getting phone records for Carver and his wife. Let me know what you find."

Brown spoke again once the two officers were gone. "Whatever is said here is not to be shared anywhere else," Brown said once the door was closed again. "I don't want the whole town in a state of panic."

"I'm pretty sure it's too late for that," Rockford muttered under his breath.

Dylan Kessel stood up and joined Brown in front of the TV. "Last night I listened to the 9-1-1 call Erin Carver made and attempted to isolate some of the background noise in the recording. I wasn't able to get all of it, but I did get the words 'Come down here.' And it was definitely a man's voice."

"We thought Erin was probably upstairs when she made the call," Alex said. "That verifies it."

"But how did he get her downstairs?" Rollins asked. "I mean, there's a guy with a gun. Why would she go down?"

"Maybe he threatened Daniel," Kessel said. "She might not have known he was dead."

"That makes sense," Brown said. "Let's assume he was in and out in three minutes. We got there eight minutes after Erin's call. That means he'd already been gone for five or six minutes when we got there." The sheriff turned to Vincent. "Martinez, pull footage from every traffic camera in the area around the time Carver was shot. There were probably very few cars on the road. A neighbor said they saw a red vehicle. Start with that."

"Tanner said one of the neighbors saw a black Cadillac on Saturday evening at Carver's house," Brown continued. "The neighbor was walking her dog, and she heard Carver and a man arguing."

"Did she say who it was?" Rockford asked.

"She thought it was Jerry Voyen, and I confirmed that he does drive a Cadillac."

"Has anyone talked to him?"

"I sent Wyatt out to bring him in."

"What were they arguing about?"

"I don't know. I guess we'll find out when he comes in."

It was quiet for a minute, then Rockford said, "So what do we do now?"

"What do you mean?"

"I'm talking about a search," Rockford continued. "What if Erin is out there, waiting for us to come find her? Are we just going to sit here and do nothing?"

"What do you want me to do?" Brown replied. "For all we know, she could be out of the county by now. I don't have the men or resources to waste on a search."

"Then how are we supposed to find her?" Rockford asked.

"We find who killed her husband and we'll find her," Brown said.

Alex didn't want to share any information he'd discovered about Olmsted's murder quite yet. "Did Olmsted or Carver have any enemies that you know of?"

Brown shrugged. "I guess when you're a cop for that long, you might have some."

"I think it's interesting that neither Carver nor Olmsted were killed in uniform," Alex said.

"Does that really matter?"

"I don't know, I'm just throwing stuff out there. This guy could have a thing against cops, or it could be something completely different. We need to find out if there's any other connection between these two."

"On it." Kessel headed for the door.

"I'm still working the Olmsted angle," Alex continued. "But your top priority right now should be finding Erin Carver."

Brown nodded. "You've got something going on right now?"

"Just following a hunch," Alex replied. "I'll be in my office. Let me know if you find anything."

"You do the same."

The sheriff seemed hesitant to give him orders. In the first few months, that hadn't been the case. Alex didn't like taking orders, unless they were from a superior. And even though Brown was the sheriff, Alex felt that he had more knowledge and common sense. He did things his own way and didn't like it when others told him what to do.

He closed the door to his office, brought up Google Earth on his computer and typed in 'Aspen, Colorado.' He didn't know Angela's address, but he located his own home and was able to find his way to her house from there. The thick cover of the trees prohibited him from finding the trail he had been on. He moved west, searching for the meadow. It appeared a minute later, a tiny square on the map. He zoomed in as far as he could and pinpointed the start of the logging road. The trees here were thinner, and he was able to follow the road's faint outline as it twisted north. About two miles further, the road emerged to intersect with a county road connecting Aspen and Snowmass Village. Anyone who traveled the road could have noticed the logging road. It's entrance wasn't overgrown with shrubs or way off the beaten path. But how did the killer know about the meadow and know that a trail led to the Olmsted's? It definitely had to be someone local. He zoomed out for a wider view and noticed a house, a little farther west of the meadow. The meadow could very well be part of that person's property.

Alex knew what he had to do now. Find out who owned that house.

11

Vincent sat at his computer, pulling traffic camera footage. Aspen didn't have a lot of cameras and some of those that were up didn't even work. Unfortunately, the area near Daniel Carver's home had no cameras at all. Carver's house was located south and east of town. The nearest camera was located on a street post in the actual city of Aspen on Highway 82, over a mile away.

Vincent found video from 12:40 P.M., the time that Erin Carver's call had come in. It was almost impossible to see anything because the snow was falling so heavily. For the first three minutes, Vincent didn't see any vehicles. At 12:44, two black pickup trucks drove by, both headed west. At 12:50, he spotted a pair of tail lights. At this point, he couldn't see anything except for two tiny red lights. The camera was wet and blurry from the snow. He stopped the camera and zoomed in as far as he could. The vehicle was headed west, and he could see well enough to tell that it was a small sedan. Unfortunately, he couldn't tell what type of vehicle it was or pull a license plate number. But the time frame fit.

He jumped ahead on Highway 82 to the next camera and saw the vehicle going straight through the intersection. The next camera, at North Mill Street, wasn't working, so he had to move on to the second stoplight in town. But he didn't see the vehicle anywhere. That meant he must've turned onto Mill Street. Vincent guessed he would've gone north, because heading south led right into the business and tourist areas. There were a few more cameras he could look at, but footage from those would be difficult to access, requiring permission from local businesses.

The door to the conference room was still shut so Vincent decided to take a peek at Carver's phone records and credit card transactions. They had finally gained access to them late last night. He didn't have high enough security clearance to be doing this, but he knew the password and used that to log in. Carver's last call had been made the night before his death, to a local number. No calls had been placed on Friday. He didn't have access to the Carver's landline, but he suspected there would be little activity on that as well. He had used a credit card Thursday evening at Plato's Restaurant, one of the pricier places to eat in the city. Maybe with their daughter gone for the evening, the Carver's had decided to go out for a nice dinner. They just didn't know that it would be the last dinner they ever had together.

The records told him next to nothing. Carver probably didn't even know who killed him. It wasn't likely that he had any contact with his attacker. The forensics team hadn't found any fingerprint, hair, or DNA samples. All they had was one footprint in the snow, a size eleven boot. Unless they got a major break from the public, there wasn't a lot to go on.

The door to the conference room swung open and the sheriff stepped out.

"Did you find anything?" he called to Vincent.

"I caught a small sedan heading west on Highway 82 at the first stop sign in town. He's on one more camera before disappearing."

Brown approached his computer and Vincent showed him the grainy image of the small sedan.

"Damn it," Brown cursed. "If it wasn't snowing so hard we could have the model and color of that car and its license plate. Send that shot over to Kessel and see if he can enhance it with any of his stuff."

Vincent emailed the shot to him and stood up. It was half past eleven and he was hungry. "Is it okay if I take my lunch?"

"Go ahead." Brown stared off at something behind him, and his voice was distracted. "Check in with me when you get back."

He drove across town to Subway, ordered a sandwich and then went back to his car to eat it. Vincent went through things in his mind. Was Erin Carver still alive? And if so, where was she? Maybe she was being kept alive for a reason. If so, he had no idea why. There hadn't been a ransom demand and Vincent didn't think this crime was about money.

What about William Olmsted? How was his death related to this? Everyone seemed to think it was the same person, but he wasn't sure. As Alex had pointed out earlier, there was an eleven month separation between the two murders. He was no crime expert, but he thought that was very unusual.

He finished the spicy Italian sub and balled up the wrapper. He was frustrated. Even though he wasn't in charge, Vincent felt that he should have a bigger part in this investigation. He knew he was young and inexperienced, but he also felt that Brown was close minded and incompetent, like Rockford had said.

He drove back through Aspen, leaving the radio off. Traffic was fairly light, considering that it was nearly Christmas. All local businesses and restaurants were open for business on the last major shopping day before Christmas. He arrived back at the station several minutes after noon. He knew his words couldn't influence the sheriff, but maybe Alex could.

Vincent spotted Alex leaving the conference room. He caught him before the door to his office closed. "Can I talk to you for a second?"

"Sure." Alex invited him in. "What's up?"

"Do you approve of the way Brown's handling all this?"

"I'm mostly working separately from him. I guess I don't really have any criticisms."

"Could I ask you a couple questions, then? He's pretty busy and he doesn't really care about my opinion."

"Shoot."

"If the same person killed Will and Daniel, why would they take an eleven month break?" Vincent asked.

"The main reason I can think of is maybe he was in jail for a while. Maybe a minor crime that only got him locked up for a few months. But it's a little different with this guy because he's so *neat*. He wouldn't get caught for a felony or misdemeanor.

Another reason is if he were out of the state or out of the country, which is a little more difficult to check out. I think the guy we're looking for is incredibly patient, so it is possible he was able to wait eleven months, for whatever reason. A third thing we haven't discussed is the possibility that he hasn't stopped killing at all. There could be murders we don't even know about. Could be he's just now returned here."

"Is there any way you can check that out? Don't you have access to a lot of things since you used to be with the FBI?"

Alex sighed. "Unfortunately, I lost most of those privileges when I left. I'll see what I can do and keep you informed. Until then, just comply with whatever Brown says. He knows what he's doing." But Alex said it as if he didn't believe his own words.

Stuart Rockford intercepted Vincent as he was headed back to his desk. He was in a hurry.

"There's been another murder."

****

Rockford peeled out of the parking lot and turned west onto Highway 82, lights blazing. He took another turn on to Mill Street, following another squad car that was driven by Jesse Rollins.

"So what's the deal?" Vincent asked, nearly slamming his head on the window as Rockford took a turn way too hard. "You wanna slow down a little?"

Rockford didn't answer his second question. "Allyson said the call came from a boy. He told her that his father is dead."

A tingle ran down his spine. He hesitated before asking the next question. "Do we know who it is?"

"Sam Preston."

Vincent closed his eyes and took a deep breath. Another seasoned veteran; and unlike Daniel Carver, Vincent didn't know a single person who didn't like Preston.

Rockford turned on to Red Mountain Road, and Vincent took it that he wasn't in the mood to talk anymore. It was five more minutes before they reached Preston's house. The roads were still iced over, with mountains of snow on either side. Rockford squealed to a stop behind Rollins and hopped out of the car. Vincent followed. His pistol was loaded and ready, but he doubted that he would need it. The killer was surely long gone by now.

A Toyota minivan sat in front of the house. The driveway was completely cleared of snow. The house was sprawling and surrounded on every side, except the front, by a thick ring of trees.

The passenger door of the first vehicle opened up and the sheriff stepped out. The look on his face showed nothing short of defeat. A third vehicle rolled to the stop behind him, driven by Charlie Porter. He and Alex hopped out and joined them.

"Shooter's gone," Brown said quietly. "According to the kid, at least. He said Sam's dead, but I've got an ambulance coming up here anyway. Let's go in."

Brown led up the long, steep driveway, his gun drawn. Vincent noticed that the sheriff and Porter were the only ones in uniform; odd, considering that they were responding to a crime. Nobody else was officially on duty. As they approached the van, the front door of the house swung open. Rockford raised his pistol, but Brown grabbed his arm and shook his head. A young boy stepped outside, decked out in winter clothing. Vincent guessed that he was maybe ten or eleven years old. He didn't say anything, but it was evident by his red eyes and wet cheeks that he had been crying.

Porter stepped forward and bent down on one knee. "Come here, Kevin."

The little boy ran into Porter's arms and buried his face in the deputy's shoulder. He turned and mouthed 'Go inside,' and the others filed past, up the sidewalk, and into the house.

They found the other three children in the dining room. Two girls and an older boy sat on the ground, their backs to him. Vincent soon saw why. Sam Preston lay on the ground in front of them, the floor bloody beneath him. He had been shot in the chest. There was no doubt in his mind that he was dead. Alex checked for a pulse but found none, confirming what he already knew. Vincent felt a sick feeling in his stomach and turned away, not wanting to look at the body any longer.

Brown was the only one of them who had any children, and he was eventually able to coax them out of the kitchen. The four of them stood there for a few moments until Rockford broke the silence.

"Dammit," he cursed. "Why Sam? Why is this happening?" He turned to Alex. "Isn't this *your* thing? Why haven't you caught this guy yet?"

"How the hell am I supposed to know who did this?"

"You're from the FBI." Rockford raised his voice. "Paul said you're an expert. I think he's giving you too much credit."

"Shut up, Stuart," Rollins said, coming to Alex's defense. "What's your problem?"

"My problem? You're a deputy." Rockford lashed out at Rollins. "You have at least some influence over Brown and I don't see you using it. You just sit on your ass all day doing nothing."

Rollins laughed. "You ever wonder why you're not a deputy, Stuart?"

"No, but I wonder why the hell you are."

Rollins moved toward Rockford but Alex stepped in between them. "Get out of here, Stuart. Go find Brown and see what he wants you to do."

Rockford was about to protest, but changed his mind and stormed away from them. Rollins exhaled slowly and lowered his hands. "We gotta do something about him. I don't trust Stuart for a second."

"I didn't mention this to anybody," Vincent said, "but he neglected to write up a police report for at least two of the accidents we responded to yesterday."

"Why didn't you do it?" Rollins asked.

"He said he was going to handle it."

"That's definitely not the first time," Rollins stated. "I've worked with him for six years. It's just been getting worse lately."

"I agree that this is a real issue," Alex said. "But we need to push this aside for the time being. We're standing right next to a dead body and it doesn't seem to be bothering either of you."

"Sorry," Rollins apologized, and Vincent immediately felt ashamed. "What do you want me to do?"

"Take a look around," Alex said. Preston's body lay to the right of a table. An overturned chair was beside it. Broken glass was scattered across the floor, shards of it stuck to Preston's shirt. This was not nearly as neat as Carver's murder.

"Careful where you step," Alex warned. He had found some plastic gloves and tossed a pair to Rollins and Vincent.

"So what do you think happened?" Rollins asked, going down on one knee next to the body. "What's with all this broken glass?"

"I don't know," Alex said. "It looks like it's from a drinking glass, or maybe a wine glass. Maybe we can have some fingerprints pulled from it."

"Give me a theoretical situation, at least."

"Okay. Let's say the killer knows Preston. He comes over here, they have a drink, Preston gets shot. Or maybe Sam and his wife were having lunch. It's possible that the glass just fell off the table, but based on how far it's scattered, I'd say it's more plausible that it was thrown down with a lot of force. That would be my first guess. Preston was sitting at the table when he was shot." Alex positioned himself so that he was directly across from the overturned chair. "Let's say I'm the shooter. There's no way I could've broken in, because Sam would confront me or run, not just sit here. So let's say I'm sitting here at the table, talking to him. For whatever reason, I decide to shoot him. I realize I left my prints on this glass, so I gotta smash that. Then... what, I take his wife and get out of here?"

"He could have forced Sam into the chair by threatening his wife or kids," Rollins suggested.

"Maybe," Alex said. "Something's not right here."

"What about the kids?" Vincent asked. "One of them must have seen this guy."

"Let's hope so. You go talk to them. But if they didn't see anything..."

Alex didn't finish his thoughts.

69

12

Stephen felt very uncomfortable with what he and his mother were about to do. Before they left her home, he had been on the internet. Posing as a police officer was illegal and could elicit a fine of up to $1000. He had tried to talk her out of it, but Angela was convinced that her idea was just about the only way to move forward in her investigation.

Stephen and Angela pulled up in front of the Limelight Hotel at 1:00. Apparently, Emma's grandparents had no lack of money. He wore a suit and tie, which made him look "very handsome and fashionable." His mother wore a sky blue jacket, black pants, and a pair of knee high black boots. They were supposed to look like detectives. He thought he would definitely be able to pass, but Angela looked like she was dressed for dinner at an expensive restaurant.

"Just follow my lead," she ordered, applying the last bit of makeup to her eyes. "Emma's in Room 212. Stuart told me that they'll be expecting us. You'll flip your wallet open, but quickly enough so that they can't quite get a look. I'll take it from there."

"Whatever you say." He stuffed the keys into his pocket and stepped outside. It was cloudy, but the air was still relatively mild. He followed Angela around the side of the building and in through the main doors. She approached the large front desk, where a young receptionist sat, talking on a phone. A nametag on her shirt said 'Kelsey.' She held up a finger and mouthed 'One minute please.' It was more like three or four minutes before the conversation was finally finished.

"What can I help you with today?" she queried.

"We're here to see the Asher's," Angela said. "They should be expecting us."

Kelsey flipped through a stack of papers and removed one from the middle. "Yes, I was told that they would be expecting you. They are in Room 212. You'll just go up the stairs and take a right."

Angela thanked her and rounded the corner, heading for the stairs. Her boots clicked on the wood floors, echoing throughout the otherwise quiet main level. A spacious lounge, empty but for a few people, sat off to their right. This was Stephen's first time in the Limelight, one of Aspen's finest hotels.

They took a right at the top of the staircase and headed down the hall, stopping in front of Room 212. Angela turned to him, brushing a strand of hair out of her face. "You know what to do, right?"

He nodded. "Nothing to worry about."

She knocked hard on the door three times. Stephen had his wallet in his hand, ready to flip it open. He stood to her left, so he would be the first one into the room.

The door opened slowly, and an elderly man appeared in front of them. He had short gray hair and wore a pair of black glasses. Stephen put his age at around seventy.

"We're with Aspen P.D.," Stephen said, flipping his wallet open, but not long enough for the man to see actual credentials. "We'd like to talk with Emma."

He pushed the door open wide. "Come on in."

Stephen and Angela followed him through a short hall, where his wife stood waiting. She stepped forward and extended her hand.

"Lisa Asher," she said, her tone brusque. "We've kind of been left in the dark here, so I'd appreciate if you could let us know what's going on."

"There's not much to say, unfortunately," Angela replied. "The sheriff's leaving us out of the loop on this one. There's been no success yet locating Erin. We believe whoever killed Daniel abducted her."

"Why would someone do this?" Lisa asked, her voice beginning to tremble. "And what are you doing to find my daughter?"

"We don't know why this happened, but we are doing everything we can to locate Erin." Angela said sympathetically. "Hopefully, talking to your granddaughter will give us a lead of some sort."

Lisa stepped aside. "She's in the bedroom. You can talk to her, but I'm not sure what you'll get out of her. She's hardly said a word since we picked her up."

Emma sat on the bed, her back to the door. The Asher's closed the door behind them, leaving Stephen and Angela alone with Emma. She didn't even turn when she heard the door close.

"Emma," Angela spoke, stepping closer to the bed. "My name's Angela, and I'm here to ask you a few questions."

Emma turned toward them. "Who would do this?" she asked, her voice barely more than a whisper.

"That's what we're trying to figure out," she replied. "We need your help. It's very possible that your mother is still alive. You could help us find her."

Emma didn't answer immediately. "How did my dad die?"

"He was shot."

"And my mom? Did he hurt her also?"

"I don't know. Nobody's heard from her since yesterday morning. I'm going to ask you a few questions, Emma. Is that all right?"

She nodded, wiping her eyes. Stephen couldn't imagine what Emma was going through. She was only thirteen. Losing both parents would be devastating.

"When was the last time you were at home?"

"Thursday afternoon. I went to Evelyn's house before dinner."

"Did your parents have anything planned for Friday?"

She shrugged. "I don't know."

"Did you talk to your parents at all after you went to Evelyn's?"

She shook her head.

72

"Did your dad have any conflicts or arguments with anyone recently?"

"I don't know." Her voice faltered. "He doesn't like to talk about work around me."

"Did you notice anything odd over the past week?"

She shook her head.

"Anything on Thursday? Try to think."

"Well...there was a red car sitting on the street." Emma paused. "I'd never seen it before."

"Do you know what make or model it was?" his mother queried.

She didn't answer. Stephen saw a tear roll down her cheek. "Promise me that you'll find my mom."

Angela gave her a hug. "I will do everything in my power to find her, Emma."

The Asher's were waiting outside the door. "Did she say anything?" Lisa asked anxiously.

"She was able to answer a few of my questions," Angela said. "I just hope she's able to recover from this. I can't imagine what she's going through."

Lisa nodded sadly. "Will you please keep us updated?"

"Of course. Please call us if Emma remembers anything else."

"Definitely. Do you have a card?"

Angela felt her pocket. "Looks like I forgot it in the car. Do you have a piece of paper?"

She scribbled down her number, and they left the room quietly. They didn't speak until they had passed an older couple coming down the hall.

"A red car. That's all we've got. Do you know how many red vehicles there are in Pitkin County?" Angela was unhappy.

"You didn't expect her to be a much of help, did you? She wasn't even around yesterday. And she's probably in a bit of shock right now."

"I know." She thanked the receptionist and they walked through the sliding glass doors and into the cold. "You have any theories?"

"I don't think he was killed because of an argument or dispute. This is something deeper than that. It could be something from Carver's past."

Angela was about to respond when her cell phone rang. She fished it out of her pocket and answered.

"Carrie?"

Stephen couldn't hear the conversation but saw his mother's eyes grow wide.

"Thanks. We'll be right there."

"Carrie said there's been another murder. A guy named Samuel Preston." She slammed the door shut. "Let's go."

Stephen pulled up behind a gray Ford Explorer on Red Mountain Road ten minutes later. They got out and hurried down the road toward Preston's house. A small crowd, maybe ten people, were bunched together at the end of the driveway. A heavy, metal roadblock had been set up at the end of the driveway, and two officers stood near it, keeping everyone back. He and Angela joined Carrie Prescott Walters, who stood at the front of the crowd, a notepad and pen in her right hand.

"Carrie," Angela said, keeping her voice low, "what's going on?"

"I don't have many details," she responded. "I just got an anonymous tip that there'd been a shooting up here. It sounds like Samuel Preston is dead."

Stephen had never heard the name before. Then again, he'd lived in Glenwood Springs for the last year and didn't spend much time in Aspen. Walters said the name like she knew Preston personally.

"How long have you been here?" Stephen asked.

"I don't know, fifteen minutes. These two guys-" she pointed to the officers standing near the block- "got here right after me. Everyone else is inside."

Stephen looked up the driveway. It was fairly steep and long, so that the house was barely visible. There was no way to tell what was going on inside. The two cops had radios to stay in touch with whoever was inside.

"Sir," Walters called out, her words directed toward the cops, "Can you tell us what's going on?"

"Sorry, ma'am." The taller cop responded. "I have orders not to say anything."

"Can you confirm that Samuel Preston is dead?"

"I can neither confirm nor deny that."

"Is the rest of the Preston family all right?"

"Ma'am, I already told you that I am not authorized to say anything." He glared at her.

Carrie folded her arms, but didn't press the officer any further. Ten minutes passed, with no activity from the house or the officers. Stephen turned to Angela. "How long are we staying here?"

Her mouth was set. "Until we get some answers."

13

"You got anything?" Alex asked. He was talking to the forensic tech, who was working alongside him in the kitchen.

"There's not a lot here. I'll send some of this glass back to the lab and see what they can do. Unfortunately, it might take a while to get some results."

"Any hair or DNA?"

"We got a couple strands of brown hair. I'll have them tested also, but I don't know if it'll be enough to get any results."

"All right." Alex thanked him. "Let me know if you find anything else."

Rollins joined him in the kitchen a few seconds later. "Anything?"

"Maybe." Alex wasn't feeling optimistic. "There's so many pieces of glass and they're all so small that fingerprints, if there are any, will be hard to match up."

"Why do you think he broke the glass instead of just taking it with him?" Rollins wondered. "He had plenty of time, right?"

"Seems like he did," Alex agreed. "Maybe something startled him, or he did this on purpose for some reason. Either way, he's getting sloppy. Carver's murder was much neater than this. And much less... risky. With four kids, I'm surprised he still went after Preston. It makes me think that he isn't a random victim."

The body was out of the house and now en route to the coroner. There an autopsy would be done as well as a toxicology

76

report. Those procedures would take a little more time, maybe as long as a few days. That was a lot of time to wait with potentially no results.

"What now?" Rollins asked Alex.

"I don't know. I'm about done here. Why don't we go find Vincent and see if the kids told him anything?"

"Doubt it," Rollins said, following Alex toward the back of the house. "They're probably in a state of shock."

Vincent was standing outside on the sidewalk. Preston's children were nowhere to be seen, nor was the sheriff.

"Did you talk to them?" Alex asked.

He shrugged. "Sort of. We were able to get a general idea of what happened."

"Do you want to run us through it?"

"All four kids were gone this morning. The girls were at a birthday party, and the boys were at a movie. All four arrived home at approximately the same time. This is what they found."

"Who dropped them off?" Rollins asked.

"The boys said it was someone named Mandy. We have someone back at the station trying to figure out who that is. Neither of the girls said anything. I'm not even sure if they're old enough to understand what happened."

"Where are the kids now?"

"Dana and Maya came a couple minutes ago and took them back to the station. They'll try to contact some family. How long ago do you think this happened?"

"At least an hour," Alex said. "I'm not skilled enough to pinpoint an exact time."

Rollins looked at his phone. "It's 1:45 right now. The call came in at what, 12:50?"

"Right. The coroner should be able to narrow it down to within fifteen minutes. I'm guessing that he was killed sometime between 12:00 and 12:45. Did the kids say how long they were gone?" he addressed Vincent.

"No. Probably at least two or three hours."

"So our guy had a pretty large window. He must have been watching from somewhere, to make sure the kids were gone. This was planned out pretty carefully."

"Will forensics come up with anything?" Vincent asked.

"Maybe. The glass is all over in there." He turned and looked over his shoulder. Why weren't there more officers here? "Where's Brown?"

"He's inside somewhere."

"This is Julie's minivan?"

Vincent nodded.

"Alright." Since he had no idea where the sheriff was, Alex decided to take charge. "You two head to the coroner's office and see what he can tell you about cause and time of death. I'll stay here, talk to Brown, and then head back to the station. Meet me there when you're done."

Vincent and Jesse headed down the driveway. Alex hoped they wouldn't have any trouble getting past the crowds and cameras. He wondered how news of Preston's murder had spread so quickly.

When he turned around, Paul Brown was standing in front of him. He didn't look happy. "Where are they going?"

"I didn't know where you were, so I sent them to the coroner's. That's fine, right?"

"I guess so." The sheriff rubbed his chin.

"What were you doing in there?"

"Just finishing up with Rockford and Porter. They'll stay here and take another look around. You and I are going to head back into town. I've got Kessel working on a lot of stuff right now. He could use some help."

The sheriff bent down and took a deep breath. Alex kept forgetting that the sheriff was thirty years older than him. But was this taking that much of a toll on his body? "I can't believe this is happening," he said. "Daniel and Sam. Two good men."

"We're gonna find them, Paul. Trust me on that."

Brown composed himself and the two of them took the long walk down the driveway. Brown saw the large crowd that had gathered and stopped in his tracks.

"Shit," he cursed. "Not this again. Is there another way we can get out of here?"

"I don't think so," Alex said. "The car's parked right at the end of the driveway."

Brown sighed. "You have any experience dealing with the media?"

"Some. I've done press conferences before."

"You want to handle this?"

"Is that an order or a question?"

"It's a question."

"Yeah, I can take care of it."

"Thanks." Brown started walking again. "Just don't say too much."

Questions started up as soon as they neared the crowd. Brown skirted the edge of the driveway, leaving Alex to be bombarded with inquiries.

"Is the same person who killed Daniel Carver also responsible for Samuel Preston's death?" Carrie Prescott Walters asked.

Of course Walters was here, he thought. She could smell a crime a mile away.

"At this point, we believe so."

"Have you made any progress in locating the person responsible?" another voice called out.

"We are following several leads at this time," Alex answered. "A press conference is planned for later this afternoon. Questions will be taken and answered at that time. Please call the tip line that has been set up with any pertinent information."

A few more questions drifted toward him, but most people began to scatter as he joined Brown in the patrol car. He'd seen Angela and Stephen standing behind Walters, and made contact with Angela. Something had flashed in her eyes before she quickly turned away.

Alex and the sheriff drove back toward Aspen in silence.

Dylan Kessel was waiting in the conference room when Alex and Brown got back to Aspen. It was nearly three o'clock, and the sky was dark and threatening more snow. Like it had been the last few days, the building was fairly empty, with only a few officers working at their desks. If it had been up to him, he'd have brought in every available officer, Christmas or not, but it wasn't his call.

Brown shut the door and turned to Kessel. "Tell me you've got something."

"Possibly," Kessel said. "I started with Mandy. She dropped the boys off after the movie and is on her way in here right now. I figured you'd want to talk to her."

Brown nodded. "What else?"

"I've started going through Sam's phone records. It was surprisingly easy to gain access to them. The one thing that stuck out was that he made a phone call at 12:09 to a number in California. The call lasted fifteen minutes."

"Any idea who that call was made to?"

"I'm still working on it. I can only do so much on my own."

"Alex can help you once we're through here."

"Dispatch says the call came in at 12:50, right?" Alex said. "If the call Sam made ended at 12:24, that only leaves thirty minutes until the 9-1-1 call. And there were at least a few minutes between the time he was killed and the time the call was made. And we thought that Sam may have had a drink with whoever killed him, which means he probably knows the killer. That's a pretty narrow window for our guy to shoot him, grab his wife, and get away from the house before the kids arrived home."

"But it could happen," Brown stated. "They could've only talked for five minutes or so, and then he's out of there with Julie by 12:35."

"Or maybe he had a drink with his wife," Kessel said.. "Doesn't that seem a little more likely?"

"Maybe." Brown wasn't convinced. "But I don't think Julie drinks."

"How do we know she wasn't drinking water?"

"Forensics took a liquid sample, and we'll get it back soon. We'll know for sure then."

Brown continued, "If either of you see this Mandy before I do, send her to my office. I'll be waiting. Kessel, keep doing what you're doing."

Porter came up behind the sheriff. "Jerry Voyen is here to talk to you."

"He took his sweet time getting here," the sheriff muttered.

Alex followed Brown down the hall and joined him in the interrogation room. Porter and a couple other officers watched from outside.

Voyen looked calm and collected, Alex thought. He was a prominent lawyer in Aspen and had recently defended several high profile clients. Voyen had thick gray hair and was in his early sixties, and though Alex hadn't dealt with him personally, he knew Voyen wasn't someone to cross. For some reason, Bob Seger's song *Fire Down Below* popped into his head.

Here comes the banker and the lawyer and the cop
One thing for certain it ain't never gonna stop.

Besides not having a banker present, Alex thought the lyrics rang true.

"I hope you brought me in here for a good reason," Voyen said, tapping his fingers on the table impatiently. "I don't appreciate being interrupted on my afternoon off."

"I can assure you that this is important, Mr. Voyen," the sheriff said. "Does the name Daniel Carver ring a bell?"

"Of course." His tone turned sympathetic. "I heard what happened yesterday. It's terrible."

"When was the last time you saw Daniel?"

"Thursday night. I had a few questions for him about a case, and his car was having repairs done, so I gave him a lift home."

"What questions did you have?"

"Is that really important?"

"A neighbor heard you two arguing when she was walking her dog. What was the argument about?"

"We were discussing politics and happened to be on different sides of an issue."

"Where were you on Friday around noon?"

"I was at home."

"Can anyone confirm that?"

"My wife." He fixed the sheriff with a hard stare. "I had nothing to do with this. I would not kill someone over a

81

meaningless argument. Daniel and I got along well, and I'm sorry that he's dead. So if that's all, I think I'll be going."

The sheriff stepped aside. "We're sorry to have bothered you."

"I don't think he did it," Alex said once Voyen was gone.

Brown nodded, but Kessel stepped into the room before the sheriff had a chance to speak.

"Sam was on the phone with a guy named Erik Lawson right before his murder," Kessel said. "He's from San Francisco. Does that name sound familiar to either of you?"

"Should it?"

"There's a guy who lives here in Aspen with that same name. My gut tells me that's no coincidence. They gotta be related."

"Did you call the Erik Lawson from California?"

"Yeah. There was no answer, so I left a message. Now I need to find the Erik Lawson from Aspen and give him a call." He paused. "Did Voyen give you anything?"

Brown shook his head. "We don't think he did it."

"Mandy Cordova is here," Porter called from outside. "She's waiting in your office."

Mandy Cordova was a small Hispanic woman in her thirties. She had shoulder length brown hair and wore a large ring on her index finger. She sat across from Brown's computer, her fingers tapping nervously on the desk. Alex grabbed a chair and pulled it up next to Mandy.

"What's this all about?" she asked.

"You took Jack and Isaiah to a movie this morning, correct?"

"Yes." Her gaze alternated between him and the sheriff. "They went with my son."

Brown leaned forward. "When the boys arrived home, they found their father dead in the kitchen. Someone shot and killed him."

Mandy's eyes went wide and she covered her mouth. "Oh my God," she whispered. "Who would do that?"

"That's what we're trying to figure out. We'd like to ask you a few questions."

"I'm afraid I won't be of much help. I didn't even go inside when I dropped the boys off."

"That's all right," Brown said. "You may have seen something that could help us."

"Okay. What do you want to know?"

"What time did you drop the boys off?"

"I don't know. I think it was probably around 12:45."

"And you came from town, driving up Red Mountain Road, correct?"

"Yeah."

"Did you notice anything odd on the drive there? Did anything stand out to you?"

"There was this one car that I passed. We were almost to the house when he flew past me. He was going way over the speed limit and nearly hit me when I went around one of the curves."

"You say he. Did you see the person driving?"

"Yeah. It was definitely a man. I couldn't tell any physical features, if that's what you're wondering."

"What kind of vehicle was this guy driving?" Alex asked.

"It was a red sedan of some sort. Pretty small. I'm not sure what make or model."

"I don't assume you noticed the license plate number?" Brown queried.

"No. I didn't think much of it at the time."

The sheriff stood up. "Thank you for your time." He handed her his business card. "Please call if you remember anything else."

"I will." As she opened the door to leave the office, Mandy Cordova turned around.

"Julie and I aren't very close, but her sons and my boy are best friends." She had tears in her eyes. "Please find her."

14

Vincent and Jesse pulled up in front of the office of Mitch Warren, the county coroner. Warren did autopsies, toxicology reports, and pretty much anything else related to dead bodies in Pitkin County. Vincent guessed that he wasn't used to dealing with two bodies in such a short time.

Vincent followed Rollins through the door, a bell jingling as they entered. Warren appeared from the back room, where Vincent assumed Preston's body was. Warren was a short man, standing about five and a half feet tall with short, balding hair. He was the epitome of what a coroner would look like, Vincent thought.

"I've got the body in back," Warren said, gesturing with his right hand. "Do you guys want to come take a look?"

"I wouldn't say that we want to," Rollins replied, grimacing. "More that we have to."

They followed Warren toward the back of the building. A blue sheet covered all of Preston's body except the face. There was no more blood on his face, just a big hole in his forehead from the gunshot. Without that hole, it may have looked as if Preston was just sleeping instead of dead.

"The shell matches the one that killed Daniel Carver," Warren explained, pointing to a small bag that sat on the table. "It's the same guy. Shot's almost in the same place, too. These kills are practically the same."

"Can you give us an approximate time of death?" Rollins asked.

Warren exhaled loudly. "It's been at least two hours. I'd say the time of death was somewhere between 12:30 and 12:45. I can't get any more exact than that."

That was almost exactly the same time that Daniel Carver had been shot. Vincent made a mental note of it.

"Anything else you can tell us?" Rollins said.

Warren shrugged. " He had something to eat and drink right before he was shot; lunch, I would assume. I didn't find any ligature marks or defensive wounds. I'll call the sheriff later and tell him what I find. My tests on Daniel Carver are nearly complete. I should have those results by this evening."

"All right. Thanks for your time."

"I've worked here for twelve years and I've had about a total of five homicide victims that whole time. And now I have two back to back. What the hell is going on here?"

"Your guess is as good as mine," Rollins answered. "We'll do our best not to give you any more."

"Good luck," Warren replied. "I'll be here all afternoon if you have more questions."

"That was pointless," Rollins said as they stepped back outside. "We already knew the time of death was around 12:45."

"We know for sure it's the same guy now," Vincent pointed out.

"We figured that anyway," Rollins said, pulling out of the parking spot and heading back east. "I feel like we could be doing a lot more than we are."

Vincent didn't respond. Rollins was critical of the sheriff, but he wasn't willing to step up and take charge. Vincent didn't understand that, and he wanted to point that out, but managed to restrain himself.

He tried to put things in order inside his head. There were a lot of things he had to process, but not a lot of evidence. Traffic cams, cell phone records, and witnesses could provide information, but was that really evidence? What they needed was something concrete, something from the scene of the murder. In Daniel Carver's case, there had been absolutely nothing. Today, he hadn't had a chance to really look for anything. He wasn't sure if Alex had found anything useful. It seemed like they were at another dead end.

"Conference room," Brown ordered as soon as he saw them. "We may have something."

Vincent followed Rollins into the conference room, joining several other officers who were already seated.

"We've got a lot to talk about and a lot to do," Brown said, closing the door and taking a seat at the head of the table. "Forensics was able to pull two prints from the glass on the floor. Adams is running them through national databases as we speak. If this guy has a criminal record at all we should at least get a partial hit on the prints. The house is still being dusted for additional prints, but it's unlikely they'll come up with anymore. A few brown hairs were found on the table, and I suspect they belong to the killer, but we're not going to be able to get anything from them."

"Sam made one call this morning," Brown continued. "It went to a number in California. The area code indicates that it went to someone living in or near San Francisco. Kessel figured out that the number called belongs to a man named Erik Lawson. That name should sound familiar to some of you, because there's a guy here in Aspen by the same name. He's in his seventies, and lives on some property southwest of town. I don't know if this other Erik Lawson from California is related to him, but we'll find out soon enough. We've made calls to both Lawson's and will continue to do so until both of them answer."

"Alex and I also talked to Mandy Cordova a short while ago. She was the woman who dropped off Preston's sons at home. She says she dropped them off at 12:45, which fits in with our timeline. She also saw a red sedan driving recklessly down the mountain toward town. One of Daniel's neighbors also reported seeing a red sedan in the neighborhood yesterday. So I'll have one of you pull vehicle registrations for all red sedans in Pitkin and the neighboring counties."

"We talked to Mitch Warren," Rollins added. "He said the time of death was between 12:30 and 12:45, but couldn't narrow it down any more than that."

"Sounds right," Brown agreed. "Now I'm going to turn things over to Alex."

Alex moved to the front of the room. "On January 21, William Olmsted was murdered," Alex said. "I think it's safe to say that his death is related to these murders in some way. For whatever reason, our guy took an eleven month break. I mentioned to Vincent earlier that he could've been in prison. If he was in prison, his fingerprints are in the system, and we should get a hit. But we should have someone double check it just to be sure.

"I thought you said this guy was neat and knows what to do to avoid getting caught," Rockford pointed out.

"It's unlikely that he has a record, but there is a chance, and we need to turn over every stone. The kind of precision and neatness he's operating with suggests that he's... seasoned. I'd say late thirties or early to mid-forties. He could have been a whole different person fifteen or twenty years ago."

"We have three victims so far. The fact that he went after Sam Preston, who was married with four kids, makes me think that these kills are not random. He could've chosen a much easier target with fewer potential witnesses. Sheriff, do you know of anything Olmsted, Carver, and Preston were working on together that could be the cause of all this?"

"We rarely have anything of importance happen here, Alex. Maybe they uncovered a scandal regarding some celebrity. I honestly have no idea. What could they know or be involved in that's worth killing for?"

"I don't think it's something they know," Alex replied. Nothing was stolen from any of the homes, and there were no signs that the killer was looking for anything. It could be something they were all involved in, maybe years ago. I'll do some digging and see if I can find anything in common between the three of them, besides the fact that they all were cops."

"So what am I supposed to tell the press?" Brown asked impatiently. "I've got a conference coming up in an hour. Everything you've said is speculation. I can't just go out there and say we have no idea who is behind this, and that we have no leads. That'll spread even more fear."

"What do you want us to be doing?" Rollins questioned. "This guy is good, and we're doing all we can. We just gotta follow up on these things and hopefully we'll get somewhere."

"Tomorrow, we need as many of our officers working as we can get," Alex advised. "Both kills have happened just

87

before one o'clock. If the pattern follows, there'll be another one tomorrow. You should have some officers out starting around noon, and if a call comes in, one of them may be able to intercept our guy. Make sure everyone off duty is cautious and alert, especially those at home."

Alex spread a map of the city out on the table. "Carver's house is down here." He drew a circle around the southeastern part of town. "Preston's is up here." Another circle, north of town this time. "We know that after leaving Carver's house, our guy ended up on North Mill Street. If he continued down Red Mountain Road toward town from Preston's house, he would end up on North Mill Street as well." He draw a large circle just north of town. "Patrols tomorrow should be focused in this area. With any luck, we'll be able to catch him somewhere in this area."

"We also need to look for anyone who had a recent conflict with Carver, Preston, and even Olmsted. It's likely that our killer feels he has been wronged and is seeking revenge."

"All right." Brown stood up and pushed the map aside. "I know we've lost two of our own and we're all a little angry right now. But we need to stay focused. Everyone just needs to stay extra cautious, and if we turn over every stone, we will find this guy. So let's get back to work. Martinez and Rollins, work on contacting the Lawsons. Porter and Rockford, see if you can get anything else from traffic cameras. Tanner, take a deeper look into Jerry Voyen, see if his alibi checks out. Kessel, keep checking cell phone and credit card records. Alex, find me another connection between our three victims. Any findings come directly to me."

There was a knock on the door, and Allyson Turner stuck her head in.

"Sheriff, someone just called and said they discovered a body."

15

The shock absorbers on Angela's Jeep Grand Cherokee were definitely taking a beating. Stephen knew that they were on an old logging road, but he had no idea where they were going.

"If you don't slow down," he cautioned, "we're going to slide off the road."

"I know what I'm doing."

"Where are we going?" he tried for the third time.

"You'll see."

A moment later, the trees thinned out, and a large clearing appeared before them. Angela pushed on the brakes, the jeep's wheels sliding several feet on the snow and ice before the vehicle came to rest.

He opened his door and stepped outside. The sun had disappeared, clouds taking its place. A cool breeze blew through the trees, sending snow raining down in the forest.

"This is a place your dad and I discovered a few years ago. You should see it in the summer. It's quite spectacular. I was thinking about what Alex said, how the killer could have come through the woods. I didn't tell Alex, but that trail leads to this meadow. Your father knew about all the old logging roads, and he figured out that this one lead to the meadow we discovered."

"Why didn't I know about this place?"

"You were in college when we found it. I didn't see any real reason that you needed to know about it."

Stephen looked around him. One side of the meadow opened up to the mountains. The view wasn't spectacular now, but he guessed when the flowers bloomed and the mountains lost their snow it might be a pretty place.

"So why are we here?" Stephen asked. "It's nice and all, but what's the point?"

"I just want to get a layout of the area," Angela replied. "I haven't been back here in a while." She stepped into the snow, her feet sinking down into the powder. By the time they reached the middle of the meadow, his boots were full of snow, the melting water soaking through his socks to his feet.

"Our old house is that way," she said, pointing more or less to the east. The logging road had led south from Owl Creek Road and though it had been winding, you could draw a pretty straight line directly south from the start to end. Following her finger, he could just make out an opening in the trees. That must be the trail that led back to the house.

"West of here is Snowmass Village," she continued. "North is back to Highway 82. South of here, though," she turned so her back was to the jeep, "that could be worth looking into. The Maroon Bells are down there, but that's still a good five or ten miles from here. In between, there's a sizeable chunk of land. What we need to do is figure out if that's owned by the state or owned privately. The government owns so much of this state that there's a good chance this land is accessible to everybody. Hell, I doubt if this meadow actually even belongs to us."

Stephen stared at the drifts of snow surrounding him. "Is that what you want to do now? Figure out who this land belongs to?"

"That was the idea."

"Even if it's privately owned, anyone could have access to this place. It's not like it's monitored or anything."

"I know. But who would know that this logging road leads to this meadow, and that there's a trail beginning here that leads back to our house?"

"What if it's somebody we know?" Stephen said. "Who else would know about that trail?"

Angela didn't seem surprised. "I hate to say it, but I was thinking the same thing."

They stood in silence for a minute, letting that sink in. Stephen tried to think of any enemies his parents had. Had someone been angry with his father because of an arrest? Stephen knew that cops commonly made enemies. He couldn't think of any enemies his mother might have, but based on her behavior the last few days, he wouldn't be surprised if she had some.

Stephen was about to ask another question when he heard the sound of a motor in the distance. It slowly grew louder, until it was evident that the noise was coming their way.

"What the hell?" Angela said. She hurried through the snow, to the edge of the meadow where the trees gave them shelter. Stephen followed her. From there, they still had a view of Angela's vehicle, but whoever was coming would not be able to see them.

An old gray truck pulled up next to the jeep a few seconds later. Stephen thought it was a Chevy, but he couldn't say for sure. The truck looked ancient. It was partially rusted over and looked like it had never been washed.

"Who the hell is that?" his mother asked. She was farther back in the woods, several yards behind him.

"I don't know," he whispered. He was too far away to see the driver.

There was a soft click from behind him. He turned to see Angela loading a small, black pistol. She stepped forward and handed it to him. "Just a precaution."

He pulled off his gloves and accepted the gun. It felt slightly reassuring in his hand. He was no sharpshooter, but he could hit anything he aimed at. Needless to say, he had never actually had to use a weapon when his life was in danger. He left the safety on and waited.

A tall man stepped out of the truck a moment later. He wore a hat, sunglasses, and a blue jacket. Stephen wished he were closer so he could get a better view of the guy.

"What's going on?" Angela voice startled him. She was right behind him now, nearly knee deep in snow. He had found a patch of hard ice and stood a foot taller than her now.

Stephen pointed to the truck and the man with the blue jacket. He was headed toward the center of the meadow, scanning the trees as he went. Stephen gripped the pistol tighter and eased the safety off. He wasn't going to use it unless his or Angela's lives depended on it. Was it possible that this guy wasn't looking for them? He couldn't think of any other reason why the man might be out here.

Angela had moved from her spot and was heading into the woods. He could tell by her path that she was headed back toward the jeep. He followed, moving as quietly as possible in the deep snow. In a few seconds Stephen was deep enough into the trees so he knew he couldn't be seen.

His mother was waiting a few yards ahead. The snow here only reached up to his shins. The trees surrounded him were weighed down by snow, occasionally losing some as the wind gusted higher. It was truly isolated out here.

"Do you have any idea who that is?" Stephen asked, keeping his voice quiet even though he knew he wouldn't be heard.

She had caught her breath by now and continued in the direction of the jeep. "Well, he's got a gun. I caught a glimpse of it as he was walking. I'm assuming that means he's coming after us."

"How are we gonna get out of here?"

"If you'd just shot him that wouldn't be a problem."

Sometimes his mother had no sense of right or wrong. "He hasn't done anything yet. I can't just shoot him."

"Fine. Here's what we're gonna do. There's no cell service out here, so we can't call for help. We're gonna freeze to death if we try wandering through these woods. We need the car. I'm gonna have to back up to the wider section of the road where I can turn around. We'll get as close to the jeep as possible without him seeing us. I parked close to the trees, so it should just be a few yards from the woods to the vehicle. I'll use remote start, and we'll get into the jeep as fast as possible and get the hell out of there. If he starts shooting, you're gonna have to use that pistol."

They approached the edge of the woods, where the Jeep was waiting. Stephen caught a glimpse of the man in the meadow. He was on the far side, away from them, which was good. He did, however, keep glancing around him in every direction, which only gave them about ten seconds to get into the jeep unnoticed.

"Ready?" Angela asked. She had the keys in her hand, her finger on the button that would start the vehicle.

He checked the pistol once more. Convinced that it was loaded, he nodded.

"On three, we go." She inched closer to the car. "One, two, three."

The Jeep roared to life, and they sprinted to the car, snow flying up behind them. Stephen threw open the back door and jumped inside. Before he could even sit up, the car was in reverse, bouncing backward along the icy path. He heard a gunshot and a loud crack. Angela screamed. He scrambled to the other side of the backseat and opened the window. His first shot went well left of the man, who was now running toward them. He heard the second bullet ping off metal. He had no idea where the third shot went.

And by that time, they were around the curve and out of sight.

16

Paul Brown took his time getting back to his office. He had the mayor of Aspen and an FBI agent waiting there. This was a conversation he was not looking forward to.

The press conference had gone fairly well. He was able to answer most of the questions directed toward him. A few he answered cryptically, and when pressed further, he just moved on to the next inquiry. Of course, Carrie Prescott Walters was in the front row, throwing difficult questions at him. He hadn't seen the local paper yet today, but he was certain that Carver's murder would be on the front page. He guessed papers statewide and even nationally would be focused on his city tomorrow.

Afterward, an older man had approached him, along with Mayor Danielson. He could tell by the man's attire and attitude that he was government. He had introduced himself as Agent Baxter, and he would appreciate some more insight into the case so he could determine if the FBI should be called in to take over the investigation. Brown hoped that wouldn't happen for two reasons. First, it made him and his people look incompetent. Second, he wouldn't be the one calling the shots, and he hated taking orders from others. This was his case. He was going to be the one to solve it.

Danielson, of course, wanted the crime to be solved as quickly as possible. Brown didn't like the mayor, and she didn't like him. She was a short, stout woman in her forties. This was her third term as mayor, and, like him, she was up for re-election next fall. She seemed to want to stay as mayor of Aspen until she died. All Danielson cared about was maintaining the town's positive image. He couldn't argue with that, but she acted as if she were responsible for everything good about Aspen.

He'd sent Jesse Rollins, Vincent Martinez, and Charlie Porter to a wooded location west of town where a body had supposedly been discovered. He had wanted to go and check it out himself, but the press conference could not be pushed back. Porter and Rollins knew what they were doing, and he was sure Vincent wouldn't mess anything up. If there was actually a body, and it was one of the women, it could tell them a whole lot. It could also make for another uncomfortable conversation with Emma Carver or Preston's children.

The door to his office was open about halfway. Baxter and Danielson sat next to each other, abruptly ending a discussion they were having. He shut the door and walked around their chairs to his desk.

"So," Agent Baxter leaned forward, "I was given very little information on this case on my plane ride here. Would you please fill me and Mayor Danielson in on your recent activities?"

This guy was already rubbing him the wrong way. "I assume you at least know of the William Olmsted murder. He was killed in his home on January 21 of this year. Carver's murder was pretty much the same MO as that one. For that reason, we have to assume that all these deaths are related. The only difference is that Olmsted's wife was... left alone, while Daniel Carver and Sam Preston's wives have both disappeared."

"And you think they were abducted," Baxter said.

"Yes. There's no reason they would leave their children. I didn't mention at the press conference, but somebody supposedly discovered a body. I sent a few of my officers to check it out."

"One of the women?"

"There haven't been any missing persons reported. So unless it's a hoax or something, yes, I believe it is one of the women."

"Mrs. Danielson tells me you have been sheriff of Pitkin County for seven years now. Do you have any experience dealing with homicides?"

"Pitkin County has the one of the lowest crime rates in the state," Danielson interjected. "Homicides rarely happen here."

"Thank you, mayor," Baxter said, dipping his head, "but I'd like to hear the sheriff's answer."

"Like the mayor said, we don't see many homicides here. So no, I don't have much experience," Brown admitted. "That's not to say that I haven't dealt with any murders as a police officer. I've just never dealt with anything this severe."

"I must say that this is a unique situation," Baxter stated. "And the fact that all the victims are cops is one of the reasons it caught our eye back in Denver. I even received a call from the Director of the FBI in Quantico. He's quite concerned. Have you informed all your officers that one of them may be the next target?"

"I have."

"I'd like to see the file for the Olmsted case, if you have it available."

"My detective has it at the moment. I can make a copy of the file for you."

Baxter nodded. "That would be great. I take it there was a lack of evidence with that crime, which is why the case went cold?"

"Correct."

"Did you have any suspects then, and do you have any now?"

"No. Olmsted was a well-liked guy. There were no fingerprints or DNA at his house. My guys found a couple fingerprints at Preston's house, and we're running that right now."

"Are your people getting anywhere?" Mayor Danielson asked. "This is one of the busiest times of year, and I don't want a serial killer running loose through town."

"I understand that," the sheriff replied, trying to remain calm. Each time he spoke with her, the mayor seemed to get more irritating. "My officers are pursuing multiple leads. It's not like I'm going to sit back and let this guy continue to kill."

"From what I've heard, you're not making a lot of progress," Baxter said, taking control of the conversation. "It seems you could use a little help. Since you have lost two of your own, it may make your department more." He held up his hand as Brown was about to protest. "I know. You don't want the FBI come in and make your department look incompetent. But if there is truly a serial killer on the loose, we can't just sit back and let you handle this. I'll send in a few agents tomorrow morning. You will work alongside them. I know you won't admit it, but if you need any help before then, let me know." He pulled out a business card and put it on the desk. "I'm flying back to Denver this evening, but don't hesitate to contact me."

He left Danielson and Brown facing each other. The mayor leaned forward, her gaze dark.

"Don't screw this up, Paul. I don't want people afraid to come here. If you don't close this thing, you'll have some major trouble on your hands. More trouble than you have right now."

"Are you threatening me?"

"Just warning you. I've turned this city in the right direction. Don't you dare ruin this for me."

"Please get out of my office." He stood, reaching for the phone on his desk as if to call for an escort.

Danielson turned and strode out of the office. She hit her foot on the door as she was leaving, which gave him a little satisfaction. He closed the door once more and called Alex into his office.

"So," Alex said, taking the empty seat across from him, "how'd it go?"

"Not great." He gave Alex a quick rundown of the meeting. "We're going to have agents in here tomorrow morning. Please tell me we've got some substantial leads."

"I'm still working on my end. You'll have to check with the others."

The FBI was giving him less than twenty four hours to catch a killer that had eluded him for eleven months. Success didn't seem very likely.

17

Alex returned to his office, enjoying the brief break from staring at his computer screen. He was technically off in about a half hour, but he knew he would be here much later than that. But every hour that passed, he knew that the likelihood of finding Erin Carver and Julie Preston alive decreased.

Alex focused his attention back on the screen. He was searching for any connection between Sam Preston, Daniel Carver, and Will Olmsted. Obviously they were all police officers, but he felt that this went deeper. It was possible that their guy was killing cops at random, not that he had any particular target in mind. But there was also the possibility that each officer was selected for a reason. Sam Preston knew the killer, or so it seemed. That suggested that he was not a random victim.

This guy was different in another way. Olmsted, Carver, and Preston had all been killed while off duty. That suggested that the killer had a grievance against the three of them. He wasn't striking out at the uniform or department as a whole, but rather these individuals. This reaffirmed the notion Alex had that the victims were not random.

He had been digging for almost an hour, and he had next to nothing. It was hard because he didn't know exactly what he was looking for. Each of them had grown up in different locations. Olmsted was from Glenwood Springs, Carver from Phoenix, and Preston from Aspen. He couldn't find any overlap from their early lives, which made him belief that this was related to something that had happened here in Aspen.

Olmsted went to the University of Colorado-Boulder and returned to Glenwood Springs. He was an officer there for six years and then spent the next twenty two in Aspen.

Carver joined the Army out of high school. He served one tour in Iraq and then attended a community college in Flagstaff. Alex didn't exactly know how he ended up in Aspen, but he had been a cop here for sixteen years.

Preston went to college somewhere in New York. He moved around Virginia, Pennsylvania, and New York, working for several departments before coming to Aspen suddenly in 2000. Like Carver and Olmsted, he had served the people of Pitkin County for over fifteen years.

Obviously, Alex didn't have access to every single detail about their personal lives. He knew more about Olmsted than the others, just from his meeting with Angela. They didn't have time to talk to every friend and relative of Carver and Preston. The connection between the three men, if one existed, was something from the past, something he couldn't find on paper.

He found some information on all three wives as well. Julie Preston and Erin Carver were both from the Denver area, while Angela Olmsted was from Aspen. Julie Preston was a stay at home mom. Erin Carver worked as a teacher for Aspen Public Schools. Angela Olmsted had an accounting degree and worked with a firm located near Glenwood Springs. The women varied in age, Angela the oldest at fifty five and Erin the youngest at forty.

An email flashed across the top of his screen. It was from Sara Wright. Her email from earlier had been forgotten in the business of the day. She wrote,

I know it's short notice, but tonight would work best to meet with you. Text me back and let me know if that works.

It was already almost six. Sara was in Denver, over three hours away, and he still had a mountain of work to do. He sent her a text, asking if they could meet tomorrow morning for breakfast. Vail was about halfway between Aspen and Denver, so he suggested meeting there. Sara texted back right away, agreeing to meet at Big Bear Bistro at 8:30. He'd have to leave home no later than 6:30 to get there on time. Alex knew the meeting would take up at least half of his day, but he felt that Sara might be able to give them some insight on this case.

He'd checked on inmates recently released from prison who had served less than a year and lived near Aspen. The list was very short, and he was quickly able to rule all the names out. It was very likely that the killer had not served any time in prison, at least not recently.

Alex needed a break. He left the door to his office open and walked over to Kessel's desk. Kessel was hunched over his computer and didn't even notice Alex until he tapped him on the shoulder.

"Find anything?" Alex asked.

Kessel shook his head. "Brown assigned me to phone and credit card records. I don't think that's going to turn up anything. If one of these guys was looking into something, and that's why they got killed, then it might be worth looking at cell phone records. But they weren't killed because of something they knew. This was revenge." He looked up at Alex. "I mean, that's my theory."

"No, I totally agree with you," Alex said. "It's beginning to look more and more like revenge."

Kessel sighed. "So am I supposed to keep going through these?"

"I'll talk with Brown and see if there's anything else he needs you to do."

"I want to help catch this guy," Kessel said. "I'm willing to do whatever you need me to do.

Alex nodded. "I'll pass that along. Keep looking and I'll be back in a few minutes."

Alex checked on Stuart Rockford next. Rockford had been combing through traffic cameras with Charlie Porter, but Porter had gone to investigate the reported discovery of a body. He didn't really want to talk to Rockford because of their earlier encounter, but he needed to know if the officer had found anything.

"There's hundreds of vehicles on these cameras," Rockford complained as Alex approached. "I narrowed the time frame down to between 12:45 and 1:00. Cameras mounted on the stoplights on Highway 82 photographed three red sedans. But I can rule each of them out because two contain children and the other was driven by an elderly woman."

"Damn," Alex said. "So if he didn't cross 82 at any point, that means he's somewhere north of town."

"Probably," Rockford agreed. "Of course, there's a few roads west of town that meet with the highway. He could have taken back roads to get there, thus avoiding the cameras."

"True," Alex said. "Still, I think it's safe to assume that he's somewhere north of downtown, or possibly west. Have you looked at every camera in town?"

Rockford nodded. "There's not a lot, you know. There's some businesses with security cameras that capture vehicles on the quieter streets, but we'd need permission to access those."

"Is there any way you could get permission?"

"It's Saturday. Most of them are closed right now."

Alex nodded. Monday was a long way away, but there wasn't much he could do. "So all we know is that we're looking for a red sedan?"

"I went back through the cameras from yesterday," Rockford said. "I zoomed in on the vehicle Vincent saw and I'm pretty sure it's a red Chevy. I'm not a hundred percent sure, but based on the shape of the vehicle, it's a good bet."

There were a lot of Chevys in Pitkin County. Then he remembered something Mandy Cordova said. "The woman who dropped off Preston's kids at home said she saw a red sedan coming down Red Mountain Road. It definitely could've been a Chevy."

"Chevy's are pretty popular in this area," Rockford said.

"Okay," Alex said. "Get me a list of everyone who owns a red Chevy sedan in Pitkin, Garfield, and Gunnison counties. Put it on my desk when you're done."

"Got it," Rockford said. He turned and got back to work.

Alex nearly ran into Ethan Adams as he went to get a cup of coffee. Adams had been tasked with running the fingerprints and trace evidence through national databases. Alex figured he was about finished by now.

"Ethan," he called after the senior officer. "Any hits on that fingerprint?"

Adams shook his head. "It's not in any databases. If we had the whole hand, we might be able to get somewhere, but I've got nothing with just that print."

"All right," Alex said. "Thanks."

He wasn't feeling very thankful as he walked back toward his office with a fresh cup of coffee. The coffee was bad. The weather was bad. He wasn't getting anywhere. At least he was doing real work, he thought. This was serious, but also a welcome relief from the endless days of paperwork. He now had to catch this guy before any more lives were lost.

He glanced around the space before heading back into his office and realized how overwhelmed they all were. After this was over, he needed to talk with Brown about hiring more officers.

He pulled out his phone and went back to his office. Brown had given him numbers for both Erik Lawson's. He tried the number for the Erik Lawson from San Francisco first. There was no answer, and he didn't leave a voicemail since he knew several had already been left. He dialed the number for the other Lawson, and on the third ring, a gravelly voice answered.

"Is this Erik Lawson?"

"Yeah. Who are you?"

"My name's Alex Snyder and I'm with Aspen P.D. Do you have a minute to talk?"

There was an audible sigh on the other end of the line. "What'd I do?"

An odd question. "Nothing, sir, I just have a few questions regarding an investigation we're conducting."

"Come on out. I'm here all night."

Alex hung up, surprised that Lawson hadn't asked more questions. He looked up the address for Erik Lawson of Aspen.

Lawson's property was adjacent to Angela Olmsted's land..

18

Vincent Martinez followed Jesse Rollins and Charlie Porter through the knee deep snow farther into the woods. Teddy Ryan led the way. He was the cross country skier who discovered the body. Ryan looked like a snowboarder. He was in his twenties with long blond hair and dark sunglasses. Apparently, he had just happened to come across the body way out here in the middle of nowhere. Vincent wanted to ask what the hell Ryan was doing out here, but he instead deferred to Rollins and Porter, the senior officers.

They trudged through the woods, coming to Castle Creek a minute later. The creek was frozen solid from the string of temperatures below freezing. The creek ran north to south, but they crossed over it and kept going.

"How much further is it?" Porter asked.

"Not far," Ryan said, keeping his gaze ahead. "It's at the edge of the tree line up here."

The first sign of the body was a dark blob in the snow. They fanned out around the body, making a circle around it. There was no doubt that it was, in fact, a body. Black clothing stuck out from the snow, but it looked like the body itself was buried in the snow.

"This is what it was like when I saw it," Ryan said. "I didn't touch anything."

"And you were just skiing past here?" Porter asked, the doubt evident in his voice.

"Yeah, there's a trail right through here." He pointed to the north. "I've watched the news, man. I thought it might be one of those women."

"Sure," Porter said. "We'll need to get a statement from you when we're finished here."

Ryan agreed. "I had nothing to do with this, if that's what you're thinking. I just came across it."

Porter nodded, but didn't say anything. Vincent believed Ryan but didn't voice his thoughts.

"Body recovery's on the way," Porter said to Rollins. "Should we find out who this is?"

Vincent and the two other officers knelt down near the body and started to dig the snow away, while Teddy Ryan watched from a distance. There was only a light coating of snow over the body, which had fallen heavily until about eight or nine p.m. on Friday night. Of course, the snow could have drifted, but Vincent thought that the body probably hadn't been here more than twenty four hours. Mitch Warren would be getting yet another body, and he could determine the C.O.D.

They had scraped away enough snow from the body by now. The dead woman lay face down, her brown hair frozen in clumps. She was clothed only in a long sleeve shirt and jeans. No gloves, hat, nothing. Vincent didn't know which of the women it was because he didn't know what either looked like. But Porter and Rollins exchanged a look, and on the count of three, they rolled the body over.

Her skin was white, ghost like. Strands of hair were frozen to her cheeks and forehead. It looked as if she had been dead a while; but then again, that was just Vincent's opinion. Maybe that's what the cold did to you.

"Erin," he heard Porter whisper. So this was Erin Carver. She was a petite woman, but probably attractive, if not encased in ice and snow.

"Who is that?" Ryan said, his gaze fixed on the body.

Nobody answered.

A couple officers came with a body bag a few minutes later. Porter attempted to call the sheriff, but there was no signal. They stood in silence as Erin Carver was carried out of the forest. Even Ryan was quiet for a moment.

They stuck some yellow tape up between the trees, outlining the scene. Nobody would be out here with the cold, but it was procedure. Each of them went into the woods on each side a little further, but found nothing. Vincent didn't know what he was looking for; a scrap of clothing or a footprint? He came back empty handed and joined Rollins and Porter by the yellow tape.

"We need you to come in tomorrow morning and give your statement," Rollins told Ryan.

"Sure," Ryan said. He skied off to the north and disappeared from view a few seconds later.

"It wasn't him," Porter said a moment later. "He's not smart enough."

Rollins nodded. "I agree."

"But don't you think it's kind of odd that he's out here in the middle of nowhere?" Vincent asked, taking a few large strides to catch up.

"Something about his story doesn't add up," Rollins agreed. "I just don't think he killed her. If that was the case, why would he lead us to the body?"

Porter shrugged. "I'm just so confused by all of this. I just wanted a quiet Christmas for once."

The car came into view a second later. The red sun was setting behind the trees, the sky growing dim as light began to fade. The wind had lessened, now just a gentle breeze that rustled through the trees. They were past the shortest day of the year, Vincent realized. Days would start getting longer, but winter had a solid grip for the next three months.

It was so calm that for a minute Vincent forgot about everything that was happening.

19

Several hours had passed, but Stephen hadn't completely calmed down. The Jeep had sustained minimal damage, just a large dent in the passenger door. Angela had retreated upstairs, only coming down to grab a bite to eat. Very few words had been exchanged between the two of them. He sat on the bed in the guest room, wondering what to do. He wanted to leave, but knew that was no longer an option. Now that he was involved in this case, there was no way he could walk away. He'd tried multiple times to convince Angela to let the police investigate, but she had her mind made up. Nothing could change it. That was the way it had always been, as long as he could remember. His mother made a decision and stuck to it, even if it was foolish. She did things her own way, and there was nobody who could change her mind. In a way, her stubbornness was good, because she stuck to her values, but in situations like this, it was an Achilles heel.

That really only left him with two choices. Option one was to keep doing what he was doing; helping her out as much as he could. There was a second option, one that he had just thought of a few minutes ago. His cell phone lay on the bed next to him. He could pick it up, dial Alex's number, and tell him what was going on. Alex obviously knew to some extent what they were doing. Stephen didn't think he knew what Rockford was up to. If Alex knew what was going on, he would make sure that Angela couldn't do any other stupid things.

He was torn. He didn't want to betray his mother, but if he just stood by, something bad could happen. The day had already been bad. One of them could have easily been killed. He didn't like the feeling of not knowing what was going to happen. And the direction that Angela was taking relied a lot on luck.

As he was reaching for his phone, there was a knock on the door. Angela stepped in, and took a seat at the small desk that sat against the wall. She had taken a shower and was now wearing black leggings and a black sweatshirt.

"How's it going?" she asked casually.

"Fine, I guess. What's with all the black?"

She glanced down. "I don't know. I just wanted something comfortable."

He knew that wasn't it. "Come on. What's going on?"

"I've been doing a lot of thinking and a little research. What we should have done is called the sheriff and told him about the guy in the meadow. They could've intercepted him before he got back on the county road, and this might've been all over."

"That probably would have been the smart thing to do. You think that's the guy who killed dad?"

She nodded. "Who else would be out in that meadow at the same time we were?"

"I don't think we had any cell service, even when we got back onto the county road. He would have been gone by then."

She shrugged. "Maybe. But I still think we should have tried. Anyway, I talked to an old friend who works for the city. I think our next step is to find out who owns the property surrounding that meadow. The only way we're going to be able to do that is by going to city hall. It's obviously closed for the night and doesn't open until eight on Monday morning. We don't have time to wait, so I gave her a call. She owes me a favor, so she said she could get me in there tonight."

Angela had so many contacts that he had never even heard of. "Who's this friend?"

"Nobody you'd know." She brushed off the question. "Anyway, we're meeting her there at 8:30, which is an hour from now. She'll let us in, and then we're on our own. She could get in real trouble for doing this."

"Then why is she?"

"Like I said, she owes me one. I've been waiting for a while for her to pay up. I'm not forcing you to come."

"I'm coming." He stood up. "I'll grab something to eat before we go. Anything else you want to tell me?"

"Nope. I'll join you in a minute."

****

Angela waited until he was gone and then walked across the hall to her bedroom. She had a call to make. Five rings later, Rockford picked up.

"Yeah?"

"I may have something." She hadn't spoken to him since the previous night. "Where are you?"

"At my desk."

"Can anyone hear you."

"Nope." Yet she heard him lower his voice. "What is it?"

"Someone took a few shots at Stephen and me earlier today. We think it's our guy."

"Why didn't you call earlier?"

"That's not important. We're fine. If I give you a vehicle description, can you get me a list of people who have one registered to them?"

"Sure. What's this guy look like?"

"Look, I don't have time to go into detail with you right now. Can you meet me tomorrow morning?"

"Yeah, that should work. I just don't want anybody to see me with you."

"Fine. I'll text you the location. The vehicle was a gray pickup truck. Really old."

"Did you get a license plate or model?" She could hear Rockford's fingers working on the keyboard.

"No. We were in a hurry to get out of there."

"How old are we talking?"

"I don't know. At least twenty years, probably more."

"This is going to be tough," he answered a few seconds later. "Especially since I don't have the make or model. We only have online vehicle records for cars made in this century. I'd have to see if I could dig out the paper copies."

"Where are those kept?"

"I don't know. I'll figure it out, okay? Don't call me again tonight. I'll be here late. Just send me the time and place and I'll meet you tomorrow."

Rockford annoyed the hell out of her. But they both needed each other; she needed closure, and he wanted this to bolster his career. Rockford was used to getting his way and expected people to do whatever he said. Maybe that was why he was having problems with the sheriff. But he got results and that's all she cared about at this point.

She pocketed the phone and fixed her hair in the mirror. Kelly had only agreed to unlock a back door for them; she hadn't said how exactly to find property records. It was understandable, since Kelly could get in real trouble if anybody found out what she'd done. Of course, Angela wouldn't sell her out. She didn't plan on attracting any attention, and even if they did get into any trouble, she felt confident that she could deal with the sheriff.

If Rockford could give her a list of names, Angela knew she could narrow it down. She just needed a list of some sort, because as of right now, she had absolutely no suspects.

She shut the door to her bedroom and joined Stephen in the kitchen.

Aspen was abuzz with activity. Not surprisingly, this was one of the busiest times of the year. It was the final Saturday before Christmas, and all the local shops were open late to accommodate last minute shoppers, as well as the higher number of tourists that arrived over the holidays. Angela drove, turning the Jeep onto a side street, the location of City Hall and several other government offices. She hoped that nobody noticed the large dent in her vehicle.

There was only one vehicle in the parking lot at City Hall. It was parked in the back corner of the lot, a new-looking dark colored sedan. Angela pulled up next to it, recognizing it as Kelly Christensen's vehicle. The two women had first met at church over twenty years ago, and had formed a close bond. She and Kelly had remained tight, until Kelly moved away for a few years. Now Kelly was back, and she and Angela were still rebuilding their relationship.

"I'll be right back," she told Stephen, turning off the car. Angela stepped outside, the breeze chilly on her skin. Kelly leaned against her car, visible only in the light cast by the streetlamp. With her black jacket and dark hair, Angela may not have even noticed her had there not been light.

"Here you go," Kelly said, pressing a key into her palm. "Bring this back to my house the moment you are finished here."

"Don't worry," Angela replied, shoving the key into the pocket of her sweatshirt.

"When you get inside, you'll be in a long hallway," Kelly said. "You'll want to enter the last door on the right. It'll be the only one that's unlocked. Don't turn on any lights. Security comes by sometimes, and if they see something, they might stop and check it out."

"Got it," she said. "Thanks so much for doing this."

"I guess I owe it to you," Kelly answered. Angela could still hear the anxiety in her voice. Kelly had always stuck to the rules, something that annoyed Angela. People had to live life, not be afraid of going outside some verbal boundaries.

"I still appreciate it. I'll be seeing you in a little bit." She turned and walked around the Jeep to the driver's side. "Let's go," she said, opening the door. She grabbed her cellphone and hard drive. Once she plugged it into the computer, everything on memory would be copied onto the drive. That meant they could go through some of the files at home instead of staying longer at city hall.

Stephen stepped out of the car, nodding to Kelly as he walked past her. They were in a less crowded section of town, away from the tourists and restaurants. Hopefully nobody would notice their car in the lot and consider it suspicious.

They rounded the side of the building, staying close to the siding. The door was about fifty feet from the corner of the building. Angela grabbed the key from her pocket and inserted into the lock. It felt a little jammed, but after wiggling the key a few times, she felt something click. Stephen shoved open the door and they stepped inside.

The door slammed shut behind her, leaving them in complete darkness. A light came on ahead of her, and she realized that Stephen was using the flashlight on his phone. It illuminated a wide corridor, like Kelly had said. It felt a little more like an abandoned warehouse than a government building. The walls and ceiling were white, and their footsteps echoed down the hallway.

"What are we looking for?" Stephen whispered. They were nearing the end of the hallway and has passed several locked doors.

"Right up here." She pointed forward and to the right. There was one more office before the intersection. The placard read 'Kathleen Orso.'

Stephen shone his light around the room. It was fairly spacious, and much nicer than Angela would have thought, given the rest of the building. The name Kathleen Orso sounded vaguely familiar. She had heard it around town somewhere, but nowhere did it say what Orso's job was. Based on the office, Angela guessed she was fairly high up, maybe close to the mayor.

"Don't touch anything," she warned, approaching the desk. She wore gloves; Stephen didn't. She hoped that he listened to her and didn't touch anything accidentally

Stephen shone the flashlight at the desk as Angela booted up the computer. While the computer woke up, she checked out the rest of the room. Orso was neat; besides her computer, all that was on her desk were a few family photographs. Angela recognized Orso from these photos; she was an older woman, probably in her sixties, with short gray hair and striking blue eyes. She looked like the kind of person you didn't want to mess with. Which was why Angela needed to make sure they left no trace of their presence.

There were several posters on the walls, none especially unique. The drawers of her desk were filled with folders; probably hundreds of them. They were filed alphabetically, 'A' in the first drawer on the left and 'Z' in the bottom left. She flipped through of few of them quickly, each file having one or two words written across the front. They made no sense to Angela.

The screen lit up, and she returned to the desk. It asked for a password. Kelly had never told her that.

"Shit," she whispered. "I don't know the password."

"Here." Stephen dropped a slip of paper on the desk. "She gave it to me when you got back in the car."

The password was a long assortment of letters and numbers. One that would be hard to remember, but also extremely difficult to crack. Angela wondered how Kelly knew it.

She typed it in, then shoved the slip of paper into her pocket along with the key. They might need it for later. The monitor flashed to the home screen, a scenic ocean picture. Several icons popped up on the left side of the screen. She clicked on the one that said 'Property.'

"How long is this gonna take?" Stephen asked, standing over her shoulder.

"I don't know." The PDF was taking a while to download, and she didn't want to spend all night in this office. She pulled the flash drive out and handed it to Stephen. "Find the spot to plug this in. Once everything's on there, we'll get out of here."

"Found it," Stephen said a minute later. The application still hadn't loaded, and she was getting impatient. A second later, the words 'Copying files' popped up on the screen, followed by 'Download Complete.'

"Pull it out," she ordered. "We've got all we need."

20

Alex drove west out of Aspen, following the directions on his GPS. He took the curves slowly, the road still icy from the storm. Lawson's house was about halfway between Snowmass and Aspen, but without the city lights and activity, it felt miles away.

Alex took a left onto a gravel driveway. The trees closed in around him, the only light coming from the beams of his truck. He passed a large pole barn before pulling up in front of the house. He parked behind a battered pickup truck that sat in front of the garage. A sole light shone in the front window of the house; no garage or porch lights. Alex got the impression that Lawson wasn't going to be very forthcoming. He hadn't been very friendly on the phone; then again, it was 9:00 P.M. on a Saturday night.

He locked his truck and walked up the front steps. Though it was tough to tell in the dark, the structure looked like a modern farmhouse. In this area, people tended to have more land, and it definitely seemed like Lawson did. He'd love to live out here and have some acreage.

Alex knocked three times on the door. He reached into his pocket and started the recording on his phone. That way he could listen to the whole conversation again if he needed to. He just got the feeling that Lawson knew something. The man hadn't even seemed surprised that Alex wanted to talk to him.

A white haired man opened the door, pulling Alex from his thoughts. He was slightly shorter than Alex and probably almost fifty years older. The expression on his face was something between curiosity and irritation.

Alex extended his hand. "I'm Alex Snyder. Thanks for allowing me to come out."

Lawson took it, rather grudgingly. "Erik Lawson. But I'm sure you already know all about me."

Alex stepped inside. "I don't want to take up too much of your time. I'm sure you've heard about the recent murders. We're up against the clock here, and you may be able to help. Do you mind if I ask you a couple questions?"

Lawson chuckled. "I'm not a suspect, am I? I don't exactly recall killing anyone."

"No, but you may be able to help us out a little bit." Lawson's demeanor was a bit confusing. Alex didn't want to share too much information regarding the case. So far, he and Brown had both been careful with what they had said to the media, not wanting to let word out that they had no suspects.

"Your son has the same name as you, correct?" Alex asked.

"Yeah. Erik. He's my only son."

"And he lives in the San Francisco area right now?"

"Yeah. What does he have to do with this?"

"I'll get to that," Alex said. "Is the name Samuel Preston familiar to you?"

"He was the cop who was killed earlier today, right?"

Alex nodded. "Had you heard of his name before today?"

"He and my son were good friends in high school. I knew him pretty well, but hadn't spoken with him in, well, I guess five years or more. It's a shame he's dead. He was such a nice kid."

"Did Erik and Sam keep in touch after high school?" Alex queried.

"Not that I know of. I think they both went their separate ways. Maybe once in a while they talked. I mean, they're a thousand miles apart." Lawson paused. "Why are you asking me this? You need to talk to my son."

"We've tried multiple times to reach him, but he's not answering his phone. When was the last time you heard from him?

"He texted me a couple days ago," Lawson replied. "He's on vacation in South America. He's not in any kind of danger, is he?"

Maybe that's why Lawson wasn't answering his phone. "We don't think so. The real reason I'm here is because Sam Preston made a call to your son right before he was killed. They talked for over twenty minutes. If what you say is correct, that the two of them didn't talk very much, then that call was out of the ordinary. That's why we'd like to talk to your son, but like I said, we can't reach him, so we turned to our next best option, which was you."

Lawson shrugged. "Sorry I couldn't be of much help. If I hear anything from him, I'll let you know."

"Did your son grow up in this house?" Alex asked.

"Yeah. I've lived here for fifty one years.

Alex handed Lawson his card. "One more question before I go. Do you recognize the name Daniel Carver?"

Lawson shook his head. "Never heard of him."

"How about William or Angela Olmsted?"

Lawson shook his head. "Nope."

Alex parked next to Jen's Toyota in front of Dean's Bar and Grill. Neither had eaten in hours, so they agreed to meet for a late dinner. Dean's was located in Snowmass Village, another haven for tourists. Most of the tables were open at this late hour. He found Jen sitting at a table in the corner, sipping from a glass of water. She wore a purple sweater, her blonde hair curled.

"Hey." Alex slid down in the chair across from her. "How was your day?"

"Fine." She set the glass down gingerly. "The aspirin's finally working. How about you? I heard there was another murder."

He exhaled slowly. "Yeah. Samuel Preston. Did you know him at all?"

"I recognized his photo. I don't think I ever talked to him. He has four kids, right?"

"Yeah. They're with relatives right now. Somebody's going to have to talk to them, but I think all four of them are in shock right now. His wife, Julie, is also missing. That's taking a toll on them."

"That's so terrible," Jen said quietly. "And you found Erin Carver?"

He nodded. Brown had called before he had arrived at Lawson's and told him the news. "How'd you hear about that already?"

"It's online. There's been three articles posted just today. All by Carrie Prescott."

"How does she get the news so fast? Erin Carver wasn't found more than two hours ago. I don't understand how she already got an article up."

Jen shrugged. "She's a pro, I guess." She paused as the waitress came to take their order. "So I take it you had a busy day?"

"Yeah." It was hard to believe that the morning had started with him skiing behind the Olmsted's house. "You'd think I'd finish the day with a lot more information than I started with. But we didn't make that much progress."

"You have any suspects yet?"

"Nope."

"So what have you been doing all day?"

"A lot of office work. Looking for ties between William Olmsted, Daniel Carver, and Samuel Preston. I looked around Preston's house. Nothing too exciting or productive."

Jen folded her hands on the table. "So what do you have planned for tomorrow?"

Here's where he had to tell her about Sara. "Do you remember Sara Wright? She was one of my colleagues in the FBI."

Jen nodded. "Yeah, I remember her. Didn't she have a thing for you?"

Alex smiled. "Yeah, I guess. You know nothing happened."

"So why'd you bring her up?" Jen asked.

"She's in Denver this week, and she's wondering if I want to meet tomorrow morning for breakfast."

Jen's smile disappeared. "What does she want?"

"I don't know. We haven't talked since I left. I think she just wants to catch up. Plus, she could be a major help on this case."

"Does she still have feelings for you?"

He reached across and squeezed her hand. "It's been a long time. And she knows I'm married. You don't need to worry about it."

Jen sighed. "I know. I just thought we were going to do something together tomorrow."

"With this case there's no way I can take any time off. We're doing our best to catch this guy. Once this is all over, I promise that I'll take a week off and do whatever you want."

A smile tugged at the corners of her mouth. "Okay."

Their food came, and they ate in silence for a few minutes. Diners left, no new ones entering. Alex thought about this case and mentally compared it to the other ones he had worked on in the FBI. Many of the cases he had worked involved revenge, like this one. Unfortunately, he didn't have a team of experts to work with to solve this one. No one to bounce theories off of. Of course, some things he could figure out on his own. They were dealing with a single killer bent on revenge. Of that he was ninety nine percent sure. He was targeting cops and their wives. That greatly narrowed down the victim pool. All potential targets had been warned and were on alert. He realized that he was a possible victim. But Alex wasn't too concerned. He had only been in Aspen six months. Whatever the reason for these murders, it went back to something that had happened a while ago. At least that's what he thought.

"So where are you meeting her tomorrow?" Jen asked, pushing her plate aside. "Denver's a long way from here."

"We're meeting in Vail." The ski resort town was two hours from Aspen and two hours from Denver. "I'll have to leave here around six thirty."

Jen whistled. "That's a long way for a meeting. Don't you have a lot of work to do tomorrow?"

"Yeah. But a fresh set of eyes can't hurt."

117

"Okay. So you'll get back at what, 12:00? And then you'll be working on this case the rest of the day?"

"You got it."

Jen sighed. "So what am I gonna do all day?"

"I don't know." He thought for a moment. "I've got a ton of work to do. You want to help me?"

"Doing what?"

"I can get you into my database and have you run a few things for me."

"Am I even allowed to do that? I mean, since I'm not a cop."

"It's not a problem if nobody knows about it. It would really help me out, and give you something to do."

A man stumbled past their table and put his hand on Jen's shoulder. The one thing that immediately caught Alex's eye was the snake tattoo that ran up his arm. "I'm sorry, miss." He stopped and ran his hand along her arm. "Wow. You *are* pretty. Can I buy you a drink?"

Alex immediately stood up. "Get your hands off my wife."

The man put his hands up and backed away from the table. "Just a misunderstanding." His eyes locked with Alex's before he turned and headed for the restroom.

21

It was past eleven when Angela and Stephen returned home. They had dropped the key off at Kelly's house before circling around town to Angela's. They hadn't spoken much on the way home; both were wondering what might be on the flash drive, and if it would help their investigation in any way.

Stephen was hungry. While Angela went upstairs to grab her laptop, he ate some of the chicken from the previous night. He debated calling his girlfriend, Mariah, to let her know exactly what he was doing, but he figured it was a little bit late and could wait until tomorrow.

He was just finishing when his mother came down the stairs. She opened her laptop and set it on the table, then disappeared into the basement. A couple minutes later, she returned with a bottle of champagne. He poured a glass, even though he didn't particularly like champagne.

"If we find anything here," Angela said, "don't tell anybody. This could give us a real advantage over the cops."

She plugged the flash drive into the side of the laptop. It was amazing that a device that small could hold so much information. Technology had advanced so far, Stephen thought, in just a few years. When he had graduated from high school six years ago, technology wasn't a major part of the curriculum. Now, almost everything revolved around smart phones, computers and other devices.

A box popped up on the screen, asking for a password, Angela pulled the little slip of paper out of her pocket and typed in the combination.

Immediately the screen shifted to the home screen of Kathleen Orso's desktop. They now had unrestricted access to everything on her computer. On the left side of the screen was a folder that said 'Property Records.' Angela clicked on it, and a new tab popped up. The next screen asked which area of Pitkin County they wanted to search. Angela chose Aspen. Then she clicked on southwest Aspen, and a long list of names popped up on the screen.

"I'm guessing these are all the people or businesses that own property southeast of town," she said, scrolling through the list. "More than I thought."

"What exactly are we looking for?" Stephen asked. He didn't see how all the names of residents of Aspen could help them.

"We need to find out who owns the land surrounding the meadow," she said, continuing to scroll down. "I don't know how anyone could know that a trail led to our house unless they lived or live in the area and explored it."

"I know I said this earlier, but I'm going to say it again; is it possible that it's someone we know?"

She turned and looked him in the eyes. "That's thought has been in my mind the whole afternoon. I don't recall taking a walk back there with anyone besides your father. What if it's one of your friends?"

"I never knew about the meadow until today," Stephen replied. "Sure, my friends knew about that trail, but none of them knew about the meadow." He looked past her at the screen. "Is that link for a property map?"

"Looks like it." She clicked on it, and a PDF began to download. Stephen had already emptied his glass and didn't want another, so he got up and grabbed a beer from the fridge instead. When he came back, Angela was looking at the map.

"Here's our old house." She pointed to a dot on the screen. "Our property is outlined by this black line. I'm guessing the meadow is about here." She made a circle with her finger on the screen, which looked to be just west of their property line. "I don't think it's technically our land. Which means it's national forest land." There was a large chunk of outlined land that was part of White River National Forest. "But as you can see," she

120

continued, "it's really thin right where the meadow is. Just to the north and west is a slice of land belonging to a guy named Erik Lawson."

"Do you know him?"

"Nope. Our property is close, but it looks like he lives off of a different street. We're not exactly neighbors."

They scanned the rest of the map, but all the rest of the land near the meadow was either part of White River National Forest or the Maroon Bells Wilderness. Nothing else private. They looked through the rest of the folders on Orso's computer, but none really stood out. Just words.

It was approaching midnight, and Stephen was tired. The day had been long and busy. Now all he wanted to do was sleep.

"I'm going to head up to bed," he told her.

"Sure," she responded, not looking up from the screen. "Sleep well."

"What's the plan for tomorrow?"

She shrugged. "I guess I'll look through the rest of these files and see if there's anything interesting. Find out some more about this Lawson fellow. I'll figure out a plan for tomorrow."

****

Angela finished sifting through Orso's documents, but there were none relevant to her husband's murder. Apparently, Orso dealt with all things property related in Pitkin County. She ejected the flash drive and stuck it in her purse. She'd probably end up going through it again tomorrow, and maybe something would stick out then.

She looked up a phone number for Erik Lawson and wrote it down. It was too late to call him, but she'd do it first thing in the morning.

Angela stuck the bottle of champagne in the cupboard, turned off the lights and moved to her recliner in the living room. The day had been largely unproductive. She wondered if the sheriff and Alex had managed to find more than she and Stephen had.

That brought thoughts of Stephen to her mind. She wondered how they had drifted so far apart. He hardly felt like a

121

son to her anymore. That was the consequence of going a full year with little contact. She was proud of him, of course. In a few years he was going to be very successful. She just wondered what had happened in the past year. It largely had to do with Will's death. From experience, she knew a tragedy like that had the power to either draw people together or push them apart. In this case, the latter had occurred. She had grieved, and was still grieving. Stephen hadn't really been there to support her. Instead, he'd moved on with his life, leaving her mostly alone. The only one she had to confide in was her sister in Lakewood and her friend Carrie. And even those two didn't really understand what she was going through. What she'd needed was an immediate family member to help her through it, and there was nobody but Stephen who could even partially understand.

She and Stephen lived only forty five minutes apart, yet had only seen each other once since January. She wanted to be a part of Stephen's life, because if they drifted even farther apart, she would grow old alone. She'd hoped that this... mission... would bring them together and help her life to start moving again.

She sipped from the glass and grabbed her cell phone. She needed to talk to someone. And the only person she knew would be up at this hour was Carrie.

"Angela." Carrie always answered by addressing who was calling her, which annoyed her.

"Hey, Carrie. I just need someone to talk to."

"You doing all right?"

"Yeah, I guess. I'm just disappointed that today wasn't more productive."

"Well, I've got some news for you. I don't know if you've heard or not, but they found the body of Erin Carver."

Angela hadn't heard. "When did this happen?"

"I don't know, I guess it was around six o'clock. It was south of town near Castle Creek. Some cross country skier discovered the body in the woods.

"Were you out there?"

"Yeah. Three cops were just leaving when I arrived. I'm trying to figure out who discovered her so I can talk to that person."

"Two dead cops, a frozen woman and another missing woman," Angela said. "What do you make of it?"

"I've never covered anything like this," Carrie answered. "It's like something out of a crime show. But in shows, the bad guy always gets caught. I don't know if that's going to happen here."

"He will get caught," she said, with more force than she meant.

"Do I want to know what you and Stephen were up to today?" Carrie asked.

She smiled. "Probably not. I can tell you that we may have a couple of leads."

"That's good, I guess."

"Yeah. Hey, I've got a question for you. Do you know a guy named Erik Lawson?"

"I wouldn't say I know him, but our paths have crossed a few times. His wife died a few years ago, I think. He's pretty reclusive. Why do you ask?"

Angela explained the property map she had seen. "He's the only one I can think of who would know about the meadow."

"What meadow?" Carrie sounded confused.

Then Angela remembered that she hadn't told Carrie about Alex's theory. "Alex Snyder thinks that whoever killed Will came from the woods behind our house. It's kind of a long story."

"I see," Carrie said. "Look, Angela, I've got some stuff to finish up tonight. Give me a call sometime tomorrow. Please don't do anything stupid, okay?"

"I won't." Carrie sounded like her mother. "We'll talk tomorrow."

Before heading up to bed, Angela sent a text to Stuart Rockford. They were going to meet at Poppycock's tomorrow morning for coffee. She walked over to the window and stared out into the darkness, wondering how her life had changed so quickly.

22

Alex arrived at Big Bear Bistro at 8:25. Somehow he had managed to get here early, even though he left ten minutes later than he should have. It was just two days before Christmas now, so it wasn't surprising that the small cafe was nearly full. He headed inside and got a table near the door so Sara could see him when she entered. Alex was still tired, but he could feel the coffee kicking in. It had been a late night and an early morning. He had run through every piece of the case in his mind and tried to put some things together that didn't seem to make sense. There were so many questions and so few answers. He had the feeling that there was more to this case than met the eye. Much more.

Once again, his mind drifted back to his family in Minnesota. He had been looking forward to seeing them next week when he and Jen flew out to Fargo. They still lived up in northern Minnesota, on Cass Lake near the town of Walker. Both of his older sisters were married and lived in the suburbs of Minneapolis. His younger sister was at the University of St. Thomas and was finishing her last year in college. His family had been tight growing up, and he wished he lived closer to them.

"Alex." Sara's voice startled him. She pulled out the chair across from him and sat down. "It's good to see you again."

Sara Wright was older than him, but only by a couple years. She had dark brown hair and darker skin because of her Native American heritage. She was about five and a half feet tall, slim and very attractive. He always thought she looked more like a nurse than an agent, but he would never tell her that.

Alex felt a little awkward. After all, they hadn't even spoken since he left the bureau, and at that time, she still had feelings for him.

"I'm doing all right. Glad we could get a chance to talk."

"So am I." Sara slid out of her jacket and draped it over her chair. "Look, before you say anything, I just want to clear something up. You obviously know that I had feelings for you. At that time, you and Jennifer were already dating, and I'm sorry that those got in the way of our friendship. I've moved on since then, and I hope we can remain friends."

"No need to explain," Alex said. He was surprised that Sara remembered his wife's name. Jen and Sara had never even met.

Sara held up her hand. "I missed your wedding, and for that I'm truly sorry. I know everyone else from the team was there, and I wasn't. My grandmother had just passed away, and I was worn out and a little depressed. I know that doesn't make it all right, but I was going through a bit of a hard time."

"Sara, it's fine." Their wedding had been a large event, but he had always wondered why Sara hadn't been there. After all, she had been one of his best friends. "It's all in the past. I accept your apology."

Sara exhaled quietly, but Alex noticed it. She had been nervous. "Thank you. So how's life in Aspen?"

He shrugged. "Fine, I guess. I've got a nice house, a beautiful wife, and a good job. What more can I ask for?"

The waitress delivered two mugs of coffee, and Sara took a long sip before answering. "Nothing, it would seem. So why don't you sound happy?"

He sighed. "I miss the action. Most of the time I just sit at my desk filling out paperwork. It's not like being out in the field, facing danger at every turn."

"You chose this," Sara reminded him.

"I didn't know it would be this boring. I mean, I thought I would be solving crimes as a detective and doing something important. But I'm not. Aspen's a great place, but there's very little crime. Which is good, obviously, but it makes my job boring."

"You can always come back, you know," Sara said hopefully. "There's always going to be a place for you if you change your mind."

Alex nodded. "I made the decision to leave after Jarred died. Jen loves this state. I don't know if there's any way she'd leave."

"Have you told her how you feel?"

"She says I just need to give it some more time. Everybody says that."

Sara shrugged. "I don't know what to tell you, Alex. I can't say 'Things are going to get better,' because they might not, you know? I believe you've got to follow your passion in life. You need to figure out what that is and talk to Jen. You're what, twenty six? You've still got practically your whole life ahead of you."

The waitress came by to take their orders, creating a break in the conversation. Alex wanted to talk about something else, something not centered on his life.

"How about you?" he asked. "How's Washington?"

"Good, I guess. It's not the same without you. We got a new guy, Cade. He transferred from the Kansas City field office. He's cocky and always wants to be the hero, but I don't really like him. Everyone else is still around, and like always, we've got our share of cases."

"Do you have a boyfriend?" Alex asked.

She smiled. "As a matter of fact, I do. We met several months ago at a party."

"Really?" Even though Sara was extremely pretty, she had never had a boyfriend for more than a few months.

"He's a pilot. Friend of a friend."

"I guess you guys don't see each other much."

"Not a lot. He does a lot of international flights. But that's fine. Our work is really important to both of us."

Alex understood. Agents worked long, odd hours, which was the reason many never married or started families. "They give you some time off for Christmas?"

"Yeah. Just a week, but it's really nice. I'm working like sixty, sixty five hours a week. I don't mind it as much as some people might, but it's nice to be out here. This is only my second time in Colorado, if you can believe it. The mountains here are so different than the Appalachians, you know? So much prettier, isolated. I love it."

"You should see the Maroon Bells," Alex said. "They're incredible."

"So I've heard," Sara answered, digging into her pancakes. "Is Aspen overrun by rich people and tourists, like they say?"

He shrugged. "Yes and no. A lot of them just have summer places out here. It's pretty nice in the fall, because there are fewer tourists, and it feels a little more like a normal mountain town."

They ate in silence for a few minutes. Which was weird, because they usually always had something to talk about. Alex figured that after a year there'd be a ton to say to her, but maybe he was wrong.

"So has *anything* exciting happened at all?" Sara asked. "You must have had at least a few cases to work on."

"One of the reasons I wanted to meet with you sooner rather than later is because there's a case I'm working on right now," he replied. "You've probably heard about two cops who have been murdered?"

That got her attention. "No. Wifi's very limited where I'm at this week. I'm taking a break from everything. What's going on?"

"Two cops dead in two days. One of their wives was found frozen to death yesterday afternoon, the other is still missing. We think it's related to a similar case from last January where another cop was murdered."

Sara pushed her plate aside and leaned forward. "Sounds like a case we might see. Is the FBI involved at all?"

Alex shook his head. "Not yet. You know how it is. Small town law enforcement hates being bossed around by any larger agency. Especially since we lost two of our own. We dealt with it all the time. Our sheriff had a meeting with some guy they sent from Denver, and he made it clear that Aspen's going

127

to be flooded with agents pretty soon. I can see both sides of this, but the sheriff's not happy about it."

"So give me the specifics. You guys must have some leads."

"We're following up on a few things, but I'm not even sure if we can call them leads. This guy is meticulous, Sara. All we have between the two crime scenes is a partial fingerprint and a few strands of hair. Our first victim, Daniel Carver, was shot in his home on Friday morning. His wife went missing and her body was discovered in the middle of a forest yesterday. Carver's was part of our force for fifteen years. The crime scene is about as neat as you can get, no trace evidence, footprints, anything. His daughter was at a friend's house, and neighbors saw a suspicious red sedan in the area around the time of the murder.

"Yesterday, another cop by the name of Samuel Preston was murdered in his home, and his wife went missing. All four of his children were gone at the time. We think the victim and shooter knew each other because there was a broken glass on the floor in the kitchen and a chair was tipped over. I'm guessed that they had a drink before he was shot. We tried pulling fingerprints off some shards of glass, but so far we've got nothing. A witness claims to have seen a red sedan driving recklessly down the road when she was bringing the kids back home. So all we've got right now is a guy in a red sedan driving around shooting cops and taking their wives."

"Any sign of sexual assault on the wife?"

"Don't know yet. We have one coroner in the county, and this is already more bodies than he deals with in six months."

"What about the earlier case you were talking about? The one you thought this might be linked to?"

The restaurant was now completely full, and Alex didn't like talking so openly about this in public. But he also didn't have any time to waste. Asking Sara to move their conversation to somewhere more private would take time he just didn't have. So he lowered his voice and continued.

"Another cop, by the name of William Olmsted. I'm friends with his son. January 21, he was shot and killed in his home, just like Carver. No evidence. You should see the case file." He spread his fingers. "About this thick. But I can't understand why the killer would take an eleven month break. And to make matters worse, Olmsted's wife wants revenge. So far, she's stayed out of our way, but that's bound to change."

Sara took a long drink of coffee. She was thinking about what he had just told her.

"Seems like a lot to handle. I can tell you what I'd do, but I know you've already done it. Is there any link between these men, besides the fact that they're all cops?"

"Not that I could find, just that they all served in Aspen for over fifteen years, which I found kind of interesting."

"What about the wives?"

"Nothing. Different backgrounds, different occupations, all from different cities."

Sara set the mug down with a thunk. "They were all cops in Aspen for over fifteen years. Look into that. I'm obviously not getting the full picture, but I know you've probably got to get back to Aspen as soon as possible. But that's what I would do."

"Thanks," Alex said. "I'll look into it."

He paid the bill and left a tip on the table. Sara pushed open the big wooden door, and he followed her outside. It was already considerably warmer out than it had been when he'd left home. Vail had seen some snow from the recent storm, but not as much as Aspen. It sat in piles on street corners, but today those piles would be melting.

"So," Sara said, stopping next to a white Chevy Malibu. "It was good to see you."

"You too," Alex said.

"I'm glad we could get things cleared up. You know if things don't work out here there's always a place for you back in Washington."

"I know."

She reached for the door. "You better get going. Let me know what happens, will you?"

"Sure. See you later, Sara."

He headed toward his truck, his thoughts wandering. They had both moved on with their lives, and clearly she no longer had feelings for him. He just hoped that they could remain friends, even though they lived so far apart.

His cell phone buzzed as soon as he turned the key in the ignition. Paul Brown was calling.

"What's up?" he asked in greeting.

"Where the hell are you?" The sheriff sounded angry and irritated. Not a good sign.

"I'm in Vail."

"What are you doing up there? We're working on a case, you know."

"I was with meeting someone regarding the case. I worked with her in the FBI."

"Fine. Just get back here as soon as you can. There are some new developments we need to talk about."

23

Vincent Martinez waited in the large conference room with Paul Brown and Dylan Kessel. It was almost noon, and they were all waiting for Alex Snyder. There had been several new developments already this morning, and the sheriff didn't want to proceed until Alex knew about them.

The results from Daniel Carver's autopsy had come back. The bullet that killed him was different than the one that killed William Olmsted, who had been shot with a Glock. Both were popular handguns, and in a state where a large portion of the population owned firearms, it would be difficult to make a list of potential suspects. Though the weapons were different, Vincent was still fairly certain that it was the same killer. He could just be trying to throw them off by using a different handgun.

Warren had almost determined that Preston had drunk a beer before he died. Nothing had been done yet with his body, because Warren had decided to run some tests on Erin Carver first. His findings were interesting. There was a large amount of alcohol in Erin's system, definitely more than the legal limit. Warren also found small amounts of morphine, as well as a few other drugs that Vincent couldn't even pronounce. The coroner concluded that Erin had died sometime on Friday evening; most likely between 8 and 10 P.M. She couldn't have survived for more than an hour or two out in the cold, so that meant that she was with her killer for at least a few hours in the afternoon and late evening. There were also ligature marks on her wrists, which suggested that she had been bound for an extended period of time. Had he gotten her drunk and then sent her out into the storm, knowing she wouldn't find her way off the mountain? It was odd, Vincent thought, to kidnap a woman, get her drunk, and send her out into the snow. Warren had found no evidence of sexual assault. He had several more tests to run before moving on to Preston's body.

They had a couple lists to go through as well. One was a list of red Chevy owners in Pitkin and the surrounding counties, which numbered near a hundred. The others lists included contacts of Carver and Preston, and determining if any of those people may have had something to do with the murders.

The door swung open, and Alex walked in. He threw his jacket over the chair and set his phone on the table.

"So did your colleague give you any suggestions?" Brown asked.

"Let's just say I have a lot to do," Alex replied. "What's going on?"

Brown told him about the autopsies. When he was finished, he asked, "What do you make of it?"

"I still think it's the same person, if that's what you're asking. He probably just changed weapons to throw us off."

"That's what I thought, too."

Alex nodded. "He probably messed up Erin's system so she wouldn't be able to find her way out of the woods. I don't think it mattered, because the cold would've killed her anyway."

Brown sighed. "We're running into a lot of dead ends here. Amanda's trying to talk with the kids, but they aren't saying much of anything. We have a list of red Chevys, but apparently there's a lot of them in this area. And both of these families were well-liked and have a ton of friends."

"Let Jen talk to the kids. I bet she could get something out of them."

"What do you think Jen will be able to do that Amanda can't?"

"Amanda's not very friendly. And her kids are out of high school. Please," he insisted. "She'll be able to help."

"Fine." Brown relented. "Tell her to get here ASAP."

"One more thing," Alex said. "If you had a friend over, you'd probably offer them a beer, right?"

"What?"

"You don't drink a beer with an acquaintance. You drink it with a friend. Sam had a beer right before he died. I'm almost certain whoever killed him was a friend. Where'd you get this list of his and Carver's contacts?"

"We compiled it from the list of contacts on their cell phones," the sheriff replied.

"I don't care about Carver's contacts right now. I don't think he knew the person who shot him. Get me a list of Sam's. Not just those on his cell phone, but anyone he talked to regularly over the past year. I'm gonna go call Jen."

"Kessel, get that list for Alex and put it on his desk. Martinez, I want you to go to Precision Small Arms and get a list of anyone who has purchased a Springfield XD-S in the past two years. It's a relatively new model, so our guy must have purchased it pretty recently. Get that list as quick as you can and report back to me."

Vincent drove across town to Precision Small Arms. There were several firearms sales places in town, but Precision was the most popular place for handguns. It was Sunday morning, but luckily the sign in the front window flashed 'Open.' There were only two other vehicles in the parking lot; a Ford F150 and a Toyota Tacoma. He parked next to the Toyota and headed inside.

"Can I help you?" A large, bearded man sat behind the counter. He had a nametag clipped to his shirt that said 'Edward.' The other customers were nowhere to be seen. Vincent wasn't in uniform, so he flashed his police badge. "I'm with Aspen P.D. I'd like to ask you a few questions."

"Yeah?" Edward stood up and leaned across the counter. "Like what?"

"Do you sell a Springfield XD-S here?" Vincent asked.

"Sure I do."

"Is it a popular model?"

"They're selling," he replied simply. "What are you doing here? I don't like having cops around my store."

Vincent felt a flash of irritation. "I'd like a list of everyone who's purchased a Springfield XD-S over the past few years."

133

"I'm afraid I can't be of much help."

"Why not?"

"I respect my client's privacy."

"I don't see how this infringes on that."

"It's the fourth amendment, Mr. Martinez. Maybe you should take a look at our Constitution before coming to this country."

Vincent tried to control his anger, but it was difficult. "You can either get me a list of names right now or I'll be back in an hour with a warrant.

Edward scowled at Vincent. "Wait here."

He pushed through a door behind the counter and disappeared. Vincent took a quick look around the shop. It was small, but had a large variety of firearms. He finally spotted the other customers, two men, standing in the back corner admiring a handgun. Both had tattoos down their arms and wore patriotic shirts.

A door banged shut, and Vincent turned around. Edward thrust a sheet of paper toward him. "There you go. Everybody who bought one since we started selling them about a year ago. You'll need a warrant if you want anything else."

Vincent snatched the paper out of his hand. "Don't worry. I won't be back."

"Good," Edward called after him. "We don't need any more of your kind around here."

Vincent ignored the comment and stepped outside. He had never been targeted like that before. In a different situation, he might have thrown some punches at Edward. It bothered him that racism like that existed here. He had spent all of his life in New Mexico and Colorado and was as American as anyone else in this country.

He drove back across town on Highway 82, trying to control his anger. There was going to be a lot of melting done today, but the Weather Channel was already forecasting some more snow tomorrow night.

He parked in back next to a Toyota Sequoia that belonged to Stuart Rockford. The officer hadn't been here when Vincent left. Brown had wanted everyone here by 9:00. Rockford was over three hours late.

134

The sheriff was in his office with the door closed, so Vincent figured he'd give the list to Alex. His door was open slightly, but Vincent knocked anyway.

"Yeah?" Alex looked up from his computer.

"I just came from Precision Small Arms. I've got a list of everyone who purchased a Springfield XD-S in the past two years." He set the piece of paper on Alex's desk.

"Thanks." Alex pushed the list aside. "Can you just go through these two quick and see if any names match up?"

Vincent scanned the names of the gun owners and then moved on to those who owned Chevys. His memory was good; not photographic, but he knew that he'd remember if he saw a name twice.

There was no overlap between the two lists.

24

"You understand, sheriff, the position that you're in. You need help."

Sheriff Brown shifted in his chair and pulled the phone away from his ear. He was on the phone with an agent from the FBI office in Denver. Mary McCarthy. She was getting on his nerves.

"I understand," he said, speaking into the phone. "But we're making real progress this morning. I have officers out following several leads, and I'm sure we'll have a big break soon."

"I know how you feel," McCarthy replied. "I used to be a cop in a small town. We are not doing this to show your incompetence. Any law enforcement agency would have trouble with what you're dealing with. The murder of one cop is serious, let alone two. I have a team of four agents getting assembled as we speak. Like it or not, they're flying out as soon as possible and will be in your town within the next couple of hours. They will work alongside your officers, but if you refuse to cooperate, they may take control of this investigation and leave you on the sidelines."

"All I'm asking is for a few more hours. Like I said, there are several major developments we're following."

"Sheriff, I get it. But you are stretched thin right now. Your department is small to begin with, and it doesn't help that many of your officers are likely gone for Christmas. My agents will take your directions and behave as if they are your officers. If the pattern continues, you'll be dealing with another dead cop within the next few hours. I want to make sure we do everything in our power to prevent more deaths. I'm sure you want the best for your town. And that means taking a suspect into custody as quickly as possible. You'll be seeing my agents in a few hours, sheriff. Thank you for your time."

He slammed the phone down. "Damn FBI," he muttered. What could they possibly find that he and Alex hadn't?

Mentally, he reviewed the officers he had today and what they were working on. Alex was practically free to do as he pleased. Vincent was still at Precision Small Arms, as far as he knew. Dylan Kessel was looking once again through traffic cameras. Stuart Rockford had come in twenty minutes ago. Brown hadn't been happy with him coming in two hours late. Rockford had claimed that he had an important meeting that morning, but hadn't offered any details. That's when Mary McCarthy had called, so Brown wasn't able to push him any further. Something odd was going on with Rockford. The officer was being secretive about something, and Brown wanted to know what it was.

The rest of his officers were out on the streets, as Alex had suggested. It was nearing 12:45, the time that the other two murders had occurred. If another murder did occur, maybe they could stop this guy before he disappeared again. McCarthy was right; they were stretched thin. The force was small to begin with, but the holidays had caused it to shrink even further. He was going to have to look into hiring a few new officers once the new year arrived.

There was a knock on the door and Amanda Thomas stepped in. She was a tall woman with short brown hair and hard gray eyes who had raised two daughters as a single mother in Chicago. Amanda had only been out in Aspen for three years now, and both her children were in college in Denver. When Alex had said that Amanda wasn't friendly, he silently agreed. She definitely wasn't the motherly type, either. He could imagine that things hadn't gone too well with the kids just based on her facial expression.

"Well?" he asked expectantly.

Amanda shrugged and sat down across from him. She didn't like taking orders, which had made for a couple conflicts between the two of them. "Nothing. They barely even said a word to me."

He sighed, but had figured that would be the case. "Okay. Thanks for trying."

"Yeah." She leaned forward and spoke quietly. "This is a really bad age for anything like this to happen. I think they are old enough so they understand what happened, too young to deal with it effectively. They're gonna need a psychologist or something." She paused. "Just my opinion, you know."

"I'll keep that in mind." He stood up and scratched his brow. He really didn't want to deal with her attitude today. "Look, I don't really have any reason to keep you here the rest of the day. I'll call if I need you. Head on home and if I don't see you, enjoy your Christmas."

She headed for the door and spoke more cordially than he had heard her in a long time. "Thanks, sheriff. Merry Christmas to you."

How had Christmas come so quickly? He and his wife had planned to go out to Lakewood to stay with their daughter, but that didn't look like it was going to happen now. Just his luck, that something like this would happen over the holidays.

He followed Amanda out of his office and nearly bumped into a young blonde woman waiting outside. He recognized her as Alex's wife, but couldn't remember her name.

"Morning." He stuck out his hand. "Remind me of your name again?"

"Jen." She smiled and shook his hand. "Alex said you might be able to use a little help?"

"Yeah. He convinced me to let you come in."

"So what is it exactly that I'm doing?"

Of course. Alex hadn't told her that she was going to be talking to four children who had just lost their father, and possibly their mother as well. "There are four children waiting in a room who just lost their parents. He thought you might be able to talk with them."

He saw the surprise on her face. "I'm not sure if I'll be able to help."

"It's worth a try. I'll be in there with you."

Jen hesitated for a second, then nodded. "I guess I'll give it a shot."

"Okay. Right this way."

****

Jen followed the sheriff down a hallway and through an open door. Another closed door waited at the end of the hall. Brown pulled it open, and she saw four children sitting at a long table.

Jen didn't know what she could say to these kids. She had never lost anyone really close to her, so she didn't know what they were going through. And she had no children, no real experience with them. But she did have a nephew who she babysat occasionally.

Alex didn't know it, but Jen was pregnant. She had just found out for herself a few days ago. Her body still looked the same, and it would be several weeks before anyone would notice. She wanted to surprise him on Christmas with the news. Jen hoped that he would be as excited as she was.

The sheriff handed her a sheet of paper. "Here are some questions to ask, if you get through to them. I'll be waiting in here, and I can hear everything you say." He pointed to a door on their right that she hadn't noticed before. "Don't feel pressured to get any answers. I think I'm going to have to bring in a therapist to talk to them."

The door closed behind her, and Jen stepped up to the table. The children looked up at her, their expressions revealing nothing. The boys sat at the left end of the table, the girls further right. She thought the boys looked to be about twelve and fourteen, the girls maybe eight and ten.

She pulled out a chair and sat down at the middle of the table, smiling briefly at each of them. She was much younger than their mother, but maybe they would see her as a sort of surrogate.

Jen briefly looked over the list of questions that Brown had given her. She couldn't just start in on them. There was no way she was getting answers by doing that. Instead, she turned over the sheet of paper and drew a Tic-tac-toe board. She drew

139

an X in the middle and then handed the pencil to the younger boy.

He took the pencil; a bit reluctantly, it seemed, and drew an O in the bottom right corner.

"What's your name?" she asked, when they were halfway through the game. She saw the other children watching her intently.

He drew another O to make three in a row. "Kevin," he answered quietly.

"My name's Jen. How old are you, Kevin?"

He looked down at the table. "Eleven."

"What grade are you in?"

"Fifth." His voice was barely audible.

Kevin, she decided, wasn't going to be of much help. Her best chance was going to be with the other boy. She drew another board and slid the paper in front of him.

"I'm Tyler," he said, before she even had a chance to ask. "I'm in seventh grade." He drew an O in the upper row of the board.

She immediately felt a sort of connection with Tyler. He reminded Jen of her brother. Tyler looked just like Josh had when he was in seventh grade. Josh was twenty now, studying forensics and psychology at the University of Idaho.

"I know you've already been asked some questions today," Jen said, "but I just have to ask a few more."

"Where's my mom?" one of the girls asked suddenly

Jen hesitated before answering. Kevin and Tyler had to know about death, but she didn't know about the girls. She decided to be honest.

"The police are still looking for your mother. If you can answer a few of my questions, it would make finding your mom a little easier."

"Another lady already asked us questions," Kevin piped up. "But she wasn't as nice as you."

Jen was flattered. "Thank you, Kevin. Do you know where your mother might be?"

He didn't answer.

She flipped over the piece of paper so she could see some of the questions. She could feel the sheriff's eyes on her

140

back. The questions all seemed too direct, too harsh. She slid the paper aside and turned to Tyler.

"You and Kevin went to see a movie yesterday, right? What movie did you see?"

"We saw *The Greatest Showman*."

Jen had heard good things about the movie but had yet to see it. "Did you like it?"

He shrugged. "It was all right."

"Did Mandy give you a ride home?"

"Yeah."

"Do you know what your parents were doing yesterday morning?"

"No."

The answers were short, but at least he was talking. "Did you guys go in through the front door when Mandy dropped you off?"

He shook his head. "We always go in through the garage."

"Okay. Were your sisters home when you got home?"

"No. They got home a couple minutes later."

"When you went into the kitchen, what did you see?" She knew it was a difficult question.

Tyler wiped his eyes. "Dad was on the ground. There was a lot of blood." He broke down and began to sob.

She walked around the table, knelt down next to him, and put her arm around him. He let loose the emotion that had been bottled up for twenty four hours.

She let him cry for a good five minutes. She could see the sheriff through the glass, staring at her impatiently. He was going to have to wait, because she had the feeling that when Tyler regained his composure, he would start talking more openly.

And she was right. "I told Kevin to call 9-1-1. I bent down beside dad, but...I knew there was nothing I could do for him."

"Was he still alive?" she asked, feeling a bit of his pain.

Tyler nodded. "He said something to me."

She felt a small surge of excitement. "What did he say?"

141

"It was weird. He said Erik, and then the word 'spent.' At least that's what it sounded like."

Alex had mentioned the name Erik Lawson. Was that who Preston had been referring to before he died?

"Thank you so much for your help." She gave each of the children a long hug before leaving. "I promise we're going to find your mom."

She hoped it wasn't an empty promise.

25

The sheriff strolled into his office without knocking. "Your wife just finished talking to the kids."

"They actually talked to her?" Alex was a little surprised.

He nodded. "You were right. They practically opened right up."

"So?" he asked. "What did they say?"

"One of the boys, Tyler, pretty much confirmed what we know. He walked into the kitchen and found Sam dying on the floor. But he said Sam actually said something to him before passing on. Two words. 'Erik' and 'spent.'"

Alex thought about that for a moment. 'Erik' made sense. That was likely the last person he had spoken to. But 'spent?'

"I'm convinced more than ever that we need to talk to this Erik Lawson. Not the old guy. The guy from California. Have we had any luck contacting him?"

"No. We've got people still trying to reach him, but there's been no luck. Like I said, he's supposedly on vacation in South America. Maybe he doesn't have cell service down there."

Brown slammed his fist down on the desk, startling him. "Dammit, Alex, I know. But he could be the key to everything. This has gotten to the point where I'm almost willing to fly down there myself and find him."

Alex agreed. "I'll find out where he works and give the place a call. Maybe they can connect me to him in some way."

He looked at his phone. "It's past one. Has anybody reported anything?

The sheriff shook his head. "Alex, please just get me something. I've got another press conference coming up, and someone from the FBI just called and said they have a team on their way here."

"We could use the help."

Brown turned on him. "What are they going to find that we haven't? This is going to ruin my reputation, Alex. If we don't catch this guy soon, I'm done. I just can't do it anymore."

Alex understood that Brown was under an extreme amount of pressure. Especially with all the media coverage this case was getting. But he had never seen the man crack like this. Again, he got the feeling that he wasn't getting the whole picture. Brown wasn't just under pressure from this case. There was something else going on, and he wanted to find out what else was wrong.

"Sheriff," Porter entered the office behind him. "I just brought in Teddy Ryan. He's in the interrogation room, waiting for you."

"Interrogation room? I thought he was just giving his statement."

"Something's off about his story. Is it all right if I ask him a few questions?"

"Sure. Alex, go with him."

Ryan looked nervous. His gaze never locked on one place, and his fingers were tapping nervously on the table. It definitely looked like Ryan had something to hide.

"I thought I was just giving my statement," Ryan said as they entered.

"Yeah, well, we've got a few questions for you first," Porter said, taking a seat.

"I already answered them."

"We've got some more."

Ryan sighed. "Fine."

"You said you were skiing the Corundum Creek Trail. How did you end up near Castle Creek and County Road 15?"

"I don't know. I must've taken a side trail or something."

"I know the terrain up there, and it's fairly wooded. I don't think there's any trail that would've taken you near Castle Creek."

"I'm telling the truth, man. I had nothing to do with this."

"And I'm telling you that I don't believe you. I'm going to ask you one more time. What were you doing out by Castle Creek?"

"Look, Ryan," Alex said. "I know you didn't do anything to the woman. But I know you want to tell us something. We can charge you with obstruction of justice if you don't talk."

"I didn't do anything."

"I'm serious, man. You're digging yourself a deeper hole."

Ryan leaned forward and spoke quietly. "Okay. but I don't want to get in any trouble for this."

"Start talking."

"I *was* really going to go skiing at Corundum Creek yesterday. I needed some fresh air. Right before I got to the trailhead, there was a guy standing in the road, so I stopped and got out of my car. I thought his truck might have broken down. Once I got near, he started talking and said there was a missing woman in the woods and I needed to help find her. And it was clear that he was serious. So I parked at the trailhead and skied around the woods, looking for her. I didn't think I'd actually find anything, but when I did, I called you guys."

"Why didn't you call us when he told you there was a missing woman?"

"Like I said, I didn't think I'd find anyone. And then when I found her, I was afraid you guys were going to be angry that I hadn't called and told you right away."

"Okay." Alex believed him. "Can you describe this guy for us?"

Ryan thought for a moment. "Yeah, I think I could give you a pretty good description."

He turned to Porter. "Get Maya in here. She's the closest thing we have to a sketch artist. We'll get the sketch out to the public during the press conference."

145

Alex poured another cup of coffee and headed back to his office while Tanner worked with Ryan. He used his old FBI login to get into a restricted database, then entered the name Erik Lawson. Several names popped up, but he eventually found the Erik he was looking for.

Lawson was employed by a firm called Kruze Consulting, and had been for the past twenty years. He found a number for the firm and gave them a call, not knowing if anybody would be there on a Sunday.

"Kruze Consulting." A woman's voice answered on the third ring. "How can I help you?"

He gave her his name and where he was from. "I'm wondering if Erik Lawson is in today." He already knew the answer to that question.

She put him on a brief hold, coming back about thirty seconds later. "I'm sorry, but Mr. Lawson is not in today. Would you like me to transfer you to his voicemail?"

"No, thanks," Alex replied. "Do you know when he'll be back in the office?"

"It looks like he's on vacation until next Sunday."

Sunday. That was a long time away. They couldn't afford to wait that long.

"Where is he, if you don't mind me asking?"

"He's somewhere in Argentina. Been there for the past week and a half."

"Is there any other way I could get connected with him? This is really important."

"He didn't give me many details of his trip. I could give you his cell phone number, if you like."

He thanked her for her help and hung up, disappointed. Their best lead was five thousand miles away, somewhere cell coverage probably didn't reach. He could only hope that Lawson was only temporarily out of range and entered civilization again soon.

Alex scrolled through the rest of the page, looking for additional information on Lawson. California had been his home ever since high school, and at present, it looked like he was divorced with no children.

He needed to do one more thing before grabbing something to eat. He had a city map, and he unfolded it and spread it out on his desk. There was already a star near Carver's house and another near Preston's home. He grabbed a pen and drew a third star near Castle Creek, where Erin Carver's body had been discovered. Connecting the three points formed a lopsided triangle, its center somewhere south of Aspen. He was trying to create a geographic profile, a strategy he had often used in the FBI. It typically helped investigators locate where the criminal was living, but this triangle was too big to tell him anything. When he added a point at Angela Olmsted's old house, things got a little more interesting. Now it was a four sided shape, with three corners located south of town and one north. Most of the area was south of Highway 82, but everything so far told him that their suspect had turned onto North Mill Street after leaving Daniel Carver's house. That didn't make a whole lot of sense.

Alex needed a break. He was about to head out to the parking lot when his cell phone rang. The number was unfamiliar, but the the display told him that the caller was from Aspen, so he answered.

"Is this Alex Snyder?" It was a female voice. He recognized it, but couldn't place the voice with a name.

"Yeah. Who's this?"

"Mayor Janet Danielson. I need you in my office in twenty minutes." She hung up, without even waiting to see if he agreed.

He really disliked people who thought they could get their way just because they were in a position of authority. Aspen's mayor was a perfect example.

He parked in front of City Hall ten minutes later. Lunch would have to wait, which was fine, because he wasn't that hungry anyway. He'd never dealt with the mayor personally, but the phone call had already left a negative first impression.

A clerk at the front of the building let him inside. City Hall was closed on Sundays, but he figured Danielson was trying to figure out a way to keep fear from spreading. He took a left at the second hall and headed all the way to the end of it. The door was slightly ajar, and he could see the mayor sitting at her desk, her head in her hands. He knocked, then waited a few seconds before stepping into the office.

The office was spacious, with a tall set of windows on the back wall, and a large mahogany desk in the center. Several chairs sat against a wall, and pictures hung everywhere he looked. The mayor didn't even rise from her chair, instead ordering him to close the door, and then motioning for him to sit down across from her.

"I'm going to cut right to the chase, Alex. Is it all right if I call you that?"

He nodded.

"Good. I've known your sheriff for a long time. He does sloppy work sometimes, and I'm sure you've noticed it. I know for a fact that he has never dealt with anything this big, and he clearly has no idea how to handle this situation."

"I'm working directly with the sheriff, and I can assure you that we're doing everything in our power to catch this guy."

"Then why is this killer still on the loose?" She threw her hands up, exasperated. "You know what I think? It's Paul. I don't exactly know you guys are handling this investigation, but it's clearly not working."

"With all due respect, mayor, you don't understand what we're dealing with. Any law enforcement agency would have trouble catching this guy."

She slammed her right hand on the desk. "Not anybody. Just Paul. This is exactly why we have members from the FBI on their way here. After Christmas, I am going to speak with the city council, and request that all of Paul's actions during his tenure be reviewed, and if necessary, ask for a suspension or even a resignation."

"He hasn't done anything wrong." While Alex didn't see eye to eye with the sheriff all the time, he knew Brown was doing all he could to find their guy, and there wasn't much, if anything, that he would be doing differently.

"Easy for you to say."

"What?"

She waved her hand as if to brush away the words. "Never mind."

Danielson had a lot of hatred and anger directed toward the sheriff. That much was clear. And Alex didn't think it all stemmed from this case. She had referred to him as Paul several times, instead of the sheriff or Brown. They knew each other, and there was definitely some bad blood. His thoughts flickered back to his encounters with Brown the last few days. How he had the feeling something was wrong. Was it related to the mayor in any way? Or was the sheriff dealing with another issue besides Danielson? And then he thought about Carrie Prescott Walters. She didn't like the sheriff either. Had Brown done something to turn the whole town against him? Was that what had been bothering him?

"I just wanted to speak to somebody with a little more sense," Danielson continued. "Make sure you know what's going to happen."

Alex stood up. "Just so you know, nothing you said here is going to make me investigate this any differently."

Danielson's eyes followed him as he walked toward the door. As he opened it and stepped into the hallway, a petite woman in a white blouse almost ran into him. He apologized and stepped around her and was almost down the hallway when he heard her voice behind him.

"You're a detective, right?" The words drifted down the empty hall.

"Yeah." He stopped walking and turned to face her.

"I've got something you might want to hear. Do you mind coming back to Janet's office to listen?"

He really didn't want to see the mayor again, but something about this lady's comment intrigued him. He agreed, and a minute later, they were all situated around Danielson's massive desk.

"My name's Kathleen Orso," she said, introducing herself to Alex. "Mostly I deal with anything related to property and land ownership in this county, whether it's private or public."

"Get to it, Kathleen," Danielson said, snapping her fingers. "We don't have all day."

149

Alex saw Orso do a slight eye roll. Unnoticeable to most, but in his line of work, you had to be observant.

"I stopped in because I was looking for my jacket. I thought I may have left it here on Friday. I walked into my office and something just seemed off. So I looked around a little, and a couple of my pictures were out of place. I can tell, because I make sure everything's lined up perfectly before I leave for the day. Then I happened to turn on my computer, and a box popped up on the screen. You know what it said? Download complete. I sure as heck didn't download anything."

"So you think someone broke into your office and messed with your pictures?" Danielson sounded incredulous. "I wouldn't make too much out of it."

Orso slowly turned to face the mayor, anger in her eyes. "I know when my things have been messed with. You on the other hand, would barely notice anything missing with all your... possessions here."

"Careful what you say. I could just say a word and you'd be gone, Kathleen. You know I just keep you here because you're one of my hardest workers."

Alex could see Orso holding back her anger. A feud between these two women was coming to light. Did anyone in this town actually like the mayor? If not, how had she managed to get elected three times? "All I'm asking is your permission to take a look at the cameras."

"I don't think that's necessary. You don't have the clearance to do this."

"Which is precisely why I'm sitting in your office right now. I'd like you to access them for me."

"Again, that's a long process. Without any concrete evidence that someone has been in your office, I'm afraid I can't do that."

Alex stepped in. "I agree with Mrs. Orso. I'd like to see the cameras. If she thinks someone was in her office, then I'm inclined to agree with her. Otherwise, I could call the sheriff and he'll be here within ten minutes."

Danielson's gaze shifted between the two of them. "Fine," she relented. "If this turns out to be a wild goose chase, I am not going to be happy."

The three of them walked through the deserted building, the mayor leading, he and Orso behind her side by side. They took several turns, and Danielson used a key to unlock a door marked *Security*. She pushed the door open and they followed her inside.

Several computers sat on a table up against the back wall. The room was small, no bigger than his office. A single black swivel chair sat in front of the table. All the screens but one had cameras recording.

Danielson turned on the computer on the center of the table and waited for it to wake up. Nobody spoke, making the silence a little awkward. He could tell that Orso was still seething, and he couldn't blame her. The mayor seemed to have the gift of making people angry at her.

"So what exactly do you want me to do?" Danielson asked. "Nobody was in here yesterday, at least not that I know of. If somebody actually broke in, like you claim, it could have happened any time."

"I guess we have to start from the start."

The mayor sighed, but didn't argue. The footage began at 7 P.M. Friday night. It was sped up, but each hour still took over a minute. They all crowded the screen, watching the footage from the camera right outside of Orso's office.

He could tell Danielson was ready to call it quits when something suddenly popped up on the screen. "There," he pointed. Orso had seen it too. She moved the video back a few minutes. A black figure appeared on the screen. Two figures, he saw, looking more closely. The time in the upper left corner said 9:43 P.M.

They watched as the two figures moved into view of the camera walking with their heads down. One was short, the other tall. Neither looked at the camera, instead entering what he assumed was Orso's office.

"What the heck?" Orso murmured. "I always lock my office."

"Maybe a janitor came by and cleaned it and forgot to lock it," Danielson suggested.

Kathleen looked doubtful. "Let's focus on the real issue. Who was in my office and why?"

151

The footage kept rolling, and around 9:54, the two figures left the office. All in all, they had only been on the camera for about ten seconds, but the taller intruder had looked at the camera as he was leaving the office. It was only for a moment, and Alex didn't think the two women had noticed.

He pulled out his cell phone. "I need to make a phone call. I'll be right back."

"Dammit, Stephen," he whispered, pulling the door shut behind him. "What the hell were you doing here?"

26

The next few hours dragged by. Angela poured herself another cup of coffee. She was exhausted. She hadn't slept much last night, no more than a few hours. Her meeting with Stuart Rockford at Poppycock's hadn't turned up much. The cops didn't know much more than she and Stephen. Rockford had, however, told her about Erik Lawson. Both of them. Rockford had discouraged her from going to Lawson's. Instead, she gave him a call. He wasn't very helpful, complaining that he had already talked to a cop. He did give her the number for his son, and she tried it several times, but there was no answer.

So she was back to square one. Stephen was gone, meeting his girlfriend Mariah for lunch in Glenwood Springs. She was alone for most of the afternoon. Spread out on the table were several papers, all relating to the case. She had looked through each of them several times. For some reason, she kept coming back to the property map. It just felt like she was missing a piece of the puzzle, like the map was trying to tell her something and she just couldn't figure out what. She put a dot on the map in the general area where Erin Carver's body had been discovered. It was several miles from where she was, but not too far from her old house. Most of the land surrounding that area was National Forest land,. which probably meant there were no structures of any type in that area. *Probably* being the key word, because occasionally the government granted individuals the right to build on publicly owned land. Or if structures were built and then the land was sold to the government, individuals were allowed to retain their property. She wasn't completely sure. The government worked in strange ways. Stephen could probably explain it to her. He had always enjoyed politics. He had wanted to minor in political science and Angela thought that one day he might even run for office. Hell, if Paul Brown and Janet Danielson could get elected, how hard could it be?

Stephen's future was bright, she knew that. He had long since gotten over his father's death. Angela didn't know much about his girlfriend, Mariah, but from what Stephen had told her, she sounded like a good person. He wanted to spend Christmas with her, and she didn't want this to get in the way.

She was getting up to grab some more sugar for her coffee when there was a knock at the door. Her first thought was that it was Carrie, but she would've called or texted before just showing up. She quickly gathered up the papers and stuck them in the drawer in her desk.

She opened the door to find Alex Snyder standing outside. He wore a black North Face jacket, blue jeans, and a smile that she could see right through.

"Alex." She greeted him curtly. "Is there something I can do for you?"

"I'd like to ask you a few more questions. Can I come in?"

She stepped aside and shut the door behind him. What could Alex possibly want from her? She had already told her all he knew. Unless... She pushed the thought away. There was no way he could know about what they did last night.

She poured him a cup of coffee and brought a bowl of sugar to the table. She pushed her laptop aside and sat down, waiting for him to make the first move.

"What are you doing?" he asked casually.

"Just work stuff." She replied a little too quickly.

"Is Stephen around?"

"He's in Glenwood Springs for lunch with his girlfriend."

The remainder of his smile vanished and he folded his hands on the table. "Look, Angela, I'm going to get straight to the point. Does the name Kathleen Orso ring a bell?"

154

She could tell that he was studying her face to see her reaction. "I've never heard that name before." She kept her voice steady. "Who is she?"

"She works for the city. I was speaking with the mayor this morning, and she comes in and says she thinks someone's been in her office. So we take a look at the cameras, and we find that someone's been in there Saturday night, around 9 P.M. Where were you Saturday night?"

"Why would you think that I would break into this lady's office?"

"Could you just answer my question?"

"I was sitting right here at this table."

"Can anyone confirm that?"

"Stephen."

"Anyone besides Stephen?"

She slammed her coffee cup down hard on the table for emphasis. "This is ridiculous. Why am I being questioned like a criminal?"

Alex leaned forward, and spoke softly. "I saw you guys in the cameras, Angela. I recognized Stephen. Nobody but me knows it was you guys."

She opened her mouth to deny it, but Alex held up his hand. "Stephen looked right at the camera, Angela. There's no use lying to me."

A whirlwind of thoughts raced through her head. Was Alex going to arrest her? She was *not* going to go to jail. It would ruin everything she'd worked for. What was the sentence for breaking and entering, anyway? Just a fine? Alex said he was the only one who knew. She had to figure out a way to deal with him.

"Dammit," she cursed. "I told him not to look at the cameras." She paused. "So what are you going to do? Arrest me?"

"No. I'm not going to arrest you. But if the sheriff knew, he might. He's not happy that you're trying to investigate this on your own. I'll stay quiet about this for now, but you have to answer all of my questions. Truthfully. Otherwise, I can make this very difficult for you."

It didn't seem like a bad deal. "Fine. What do you want to know."

"What have you been up to these past two days?"

She told him about their meeting with Emma Carver, the incident in the meadow, and the break in. Alex's face didn't reveal any emotion, and he didn't say anything until she was done speaking.

"So somebody took shots at you and you didn't even report it?"

"We weren't hurt," she said, knowing how weak it sounded. "And there was no service out there anyway. By the time you guys would've arrived, the guy would've been long gone."

"Still."

"Sorry."

"All right. So can you describe this guy for me?"

"I mean, we didn't really see him close up. He was wearing a hat and stuff, so we couldn't really see his face or any physical features. He was probably about as tall as you. And it was definitely a man. He could be 25 or 50, I honestly have no idea."

"Did you see a vehicle?"

"Yeah. It was an old, dirty pickup truck."

"Model? License plate?"

"We were more focused on getting out of there than getting a license plate. I can say with certainty that it's older than 2000."

"So all you've got is a male who drives an old pickup."

"Yeah."

"There's a lot of guys in this county who fit the descripttion you just gave me."

"I know."

Alex sighed. "We have several witnesses who say they've seen a suspicious red sedan near each crime scene. This could mean our guy drives a truck as well."

"Makes sense to me. There's no way you're getting to that place with a sedan. You need an SUV for sure."

"So why'd you break into Orso's office?" Alex asked, changing topics. "I'm assuming that was your idea."

"We needed to access property records, and I figured the only way to do that was to get into her office when she wasn't there. I figured she wouldn't answer many of my questions unless I had a badge, and I wasn't going to wait until Monday to go in and talk to her."

"Okay. This is important. Did you or Stephen touch anything?"

"I did, but I was wearing gloves. I told Stephen not to touch anything. I swear to God, if he did…"

"He wasn't wearing gloves?"

She couldn't remember. "I don't think so."

"We've got some guys over in Orso's office right now. They're going to be dusting for prints. If Stephen did touch anything, he could be incriminated."

"What's that mean?" She prayed to God that Stephen hadn't touched anything.

"It would be up to the sheriff and Orso, if they want to press charges. It's a misdemeanor, but Stephen could probably get by with just a fine. He has no record, and I'd advocate for him."

"It was my fault," she said quietly. "Stephen wouldn't have done any of this if not for me."

Alex didn't reply right away, and when he did, he changed the subject once again. "There's one more thing I want to ask you about."

"What?"

"Stuart Rockford."

She figured there was no point in hiding the truth. "What do you want to know?"

"What's the relationship there? I'm sort of confused. Are you using him or is he using you?"

"A little bit of both, I guess. He's telling me what you guys find and I'm telling him what I find. How'd you know it was him?"

"That's not important. Why are you two working together?"

"I want to find the person who killed my husband, and he said he could help me."

"What's in it for him?"

157

She wasn't quite sure. "I think he wants to be the one to crack this case, get some name recognition. You know he wants to run for sheriff next year."

"I know. Here's what I want you to do. Every time you talk to him, you're going to give me a call directly after. Tell me anything you've figured out, and anything he's told you that seems important. I don't want him to know that I know what he's doing. Once this is all over I'll spring it on him and then he'll be in some serious trouble."

"You won't mention that I told you, right?" She didn't want to get on Stuart's bad side.

He shrugged. "Look, you got yourself into this mess. I can't control what happens. I'll expect a call from you tonight. You might want to let Stephen know what's going on." He finished the last of his coffee and stood up. "I hope you'll make better decisions from now on."

She sat at the table in silence for a good fifteen minutes after Alex left. Alex was right. Stephen needed to know about this. First, though, she needed some fresh air.

****

He was headed back to the department when his cell phone rang. It was Allison, who was working as dispatch over the weekend.

"Alex, we've got a situation. A couple drivers reported seeing a woman walking down the road with... inadequate clothing." She gave him the location. "I couldn't get through to the sheriff so I figured I'd let you know."

It was Julie Preston. He was almost certain of it. Erin Carver had been dressed in only a sweater, and the location Allison had given him was not far from where Carver's body had been uncovered.

"Allison, I think it might be Julie Preston. I need you to get an ambulance sent down there ASAP. Keep trying to reach Brown so he knows what's going on."

"Will do, Alex."

He tossed his phone on the seat and pushed down on the accelerator.

27

December 26

Christmas came and went. It was cold and windy, with temperatures hanging in the mid-twenties. Snow was forecast to begin later that day and last through the night, giving the Maroon Bells and surrounding area an additional six inches.

Alex spent Christmas at home. Jen was with family out in Colorado Springs. She had understood that he couldn't join her, but that didn't mean she was happy about it. They were supposed to fly to Minnesota at the end of the week to celebrate the holidays with his family, but at the moment, it didn't look as if that would be happening. Which was too bad, because he hadn't seen his family since the wedding.

The woman he had found wandering down the road on Sunday was indeed Julie Preston. She had been dressed in nothing more than a sweater, jeans, and tennis shoes. Julie was talking incoherently when Alex found her, and the EMT's later said her body temperature was in the mid-nineties. It was a miracle, they said, that she had managed to survive. The ambulance had taken her to the Aspen Valley Hospital, before a helicopter came and airlifted her to St. Joseph Hospital in Denver. She wasn't completely out of the woods quite yet, but Alex had just been informed that her condition had been upgraded from critical to serious. It was a glimmer of good news, but the doctors hadn't said any more than that.

The sketch of their suspect was out there, but so far, there had been very few tips. If the man hadn't been wearing a hat and sunglasses, they would have certainly gotten a more accurate sketch. All Alex knew for certain was that their guy drove a red Chevy sedan and an old truck and likely lived alone.

Mitch Warren had finished his tests on Sam Preston's body, but he hadn't found anything out of the ordinary.

The last two days had been a bit of a blur, but they hadn't made much progress. He'd spent most of yesterday at home, doing some more work. There had been no more murders, no more missing women. The FBI hadn't proven to be much help, and all but two agents had returned to Denver. Kathleen Orso's office had been dusted for prints, but none had been discovered besides her own, which was extremely lucky for the Olmsted's.

There had been no word from the younger Erik Lawson. Alex assumed that he was still out of range in Argentina. He had made numerous calls to the number, but every time it went straight to voicemail. Right now, Erik Lawson and Julie Preston were their best leads, and Alex was frustrated because he wasn't able to speak to either of them. The hospital was supposed to call him or the sheriff the moment Julie Preston woke up. He hoped it was sooner rather than later, because it was very likely that Julie knew the name of the person who had abducted her.

Alex sat on the sectional in the living room. It was around 7:30, and it was the first time since Friday that he had actually had a chance to relax. He'd spent Christmas Eve working with the sheriff, before attending midnight mass at St. Mary's and going to bed. Yesterday, he'd joined the Olmsted's for dinner at Angela's house. The invitation had come on Sunday night when Angela had called him. He had no other plans, so he'd accepted. They didn't talk about the investigation at all, which was good.

He glanced out at the stand of pine trees in the backyard. It had been a mild weekend, melting some of the snow on the ground and taking care of the rest that hung on the pine trees. He'd watched the news and heard that some more cold air was moving in, and snow was forecast to start around three. That could complicate any work he had to do outside, but at least it wouldn't be as bad as Friday's storm.

The murders were slowly slipping from national headlines. Some national reporters remained in Aspen, but the

161

majority had left. It was still big news throughout the state, though, as people waited for Julie Preston to wake up and tell her story. Alex wondered if the killer had fled Aspen, since no more murders had occurred since Sam Preston's death.

Several scathing editorials had been published in the Tribune, criticizing Paul Brown's inability to find the criminal. Alex thought each of them were unfair. He was partially in charge of the investigation, and he knew that they were doing everything in their power to find the killer. He didn't think any other law enforcement agency would be doing a better job in their position.

He had taken a box of records from the year 2000 and gone through them. Sara had speculated that the murders might be related to an incident that had occurred a while back. Records were going completely electronic, but until that was complete, there were still hundreds of boxes in a storage room that contained records all the way back to 1990. He was going to go through the years 2000-2004 first, and then decide if he would continue on chronologically or go backwards into the 1990's.

He got up an headed for the bedroom, passing the grand piano on the way. Both he and Jen enjoyed playing, and had decided to get a piano when they bought the house. A book of Christmas songs sat open on the piano. He felt the irresistible urge to sit down and play.

Alex sat down and played *Silent Night*. Halfway through, his phone rang, but he ignored it and continued through the song. The notes rang through the empty house, echoing off the walls. He felt like a lot of the stress he had been feeling was gone.

Until he saw that the missed call was from the hospital in Denver.

28

Vincent stood at his front window, waiting for Alex Snyder to arrive before he went outside. The sheriff had called him just a few minutes ago, saying that he was to go to Denver with Alex and talk to Julie Preston. Denver, he thought, was a long way away. More than three hours. They were going to waste at least six hours of the day driving. But he realized that if Julie Preston could tell them who abducted her, it wouldn't be a waste at all.

He saw Alex's black pickup pull into the driveway and he stepped outside. The wind was biting, ushering in more cold air and snow. He hadn't had a chance to watch the news, so he wasn't sure if they would be dealing with a couple inches of snow or another blizzard this afternoon.

"Hey," he said, hopping into the passenger seat.

"Hey." Alex put the truck into reverse and swung it back onto the street. "Brown call you?"

"Yeah. Julie's awake?"

"The doctor said they're getting ready to pull her out of the coma."

"So she isn't actually awake yet?"

"I'm not sure. " They turned left onto Highway 82, heading west toward Glenwood Springs and I-70. "They're going to wait until we get there to ask any questions. Assuming she wakes up. A couple people from the FBI are going to meet us there."

"It's too bad we couldn't take a plane or something," Vincent said as they drove past the Pitkin County Airport.

"Denver's so far away, especially in the winter. I hope this drive isn't for nothing."

"I know," Alex agreed. "Hopefully I can get us there by eleven."

They drove in silence for a long time, listening to music playing quietly from the radio. The roads were mostly empty, which was good. They turned onto I-70 about a half hour later, and from there it was a straight shot east to Denver. Vincent stared out the window and watched the familiar towns fly past; Gypsum, Eagle, Vail. He wished he were out snowboarding right now, instead of in the middle of this three hour car ride.

Alex finally spoke as they approached Frisco. "You have a good Christmas?"

He shrugged. "All right, I guess. I'll be headed down to New Mexico once this is over."

"You're from there, right?"

"Yeah."

"I've never been to New Mexico. What's it like?"

"It's really nice. We've got mountains, obviously, but nothing as beautiful as here. I'm from Questa, which is a little ways north of Taos. Not too far from the Colorado border. It's got about fifteen hundred people, and I like the small town feel."

"Does your family still live down there?"

"Yeah, my parents, sister, and her husband."

Alex nodded. "Kind of like me. I'm from northern Minnesota, all my family still lives there. Not in the town I grew up in, but in the same area."

Vincent had never been to Minnesota. All he knew was that it had a lot of lakes. "Do you like it up there?"

"Yeah." Alex slowed down as the interstate curved past Silverthorne and Dillon. Both seemed like nice towns, with the Dillon Reservoir visible from the highway. "I miss it sometimes. We lived in kind of a boring part of the state, but we had a cabin on a really nice lake. We were there almost every weekend during the summer. That part I definitely miss. There's hardly any lakes out here. I mean, the mountain lakes are incredible, there's no doubt about it. But it would be great if there were some more accessible, forested lakes around here."

"We get nowhere near as much tourism as here," he continued. "But if you're looking for solitude, go to the Boundary Waters. A million acres of forest and lakes. You could easily spend months out there."

"It sounds like you love Minnesota," Vincent said. "How'd you end up out here?" He knew Alex had been in the FBI, but wasn't quite sure how he had made his way to Aspen.

"Jen." Alex hesitated. "My wife. It's kind of complicated. She wanted to live here in Colorado, where she grew up. I know I've only been here six months, but I'm not sure if I really want to live here. The scenery is incredible, but I don't think that alone could make me stay for the rest of my life."

"What happened that made you decide to join the force?" Vincent knew he might be touching on a sensitive subject.

Alex didn't reply right away. When he did, his voice was quiet. "My partner was killed in a shootout. That was right before Jen and I got engaged. She wasn't willing to move out east. When he died, I figured there was no reason to stay in D.C."

Vincent let a little time pass before his next question. "What's it like being an agent?"

"Not nearly as exciting as the crime shows. We do a lot of paperwork. For the most part, I worked in a team, so we were in the field pretty often."

"Do you miss it?"

"Definitely," Alex said longingly. "I think about it every day. I've been thinking a lot about going back. They promised that if I ever wanted to come back they'd have a job waiting for me. I'm not sure if Jen would ever agree to leave here, though."

"Aren't there, I don't know, field offices in some cities across the country?"

"Yeah." Alex slowed down as a car switched lanes in front of them. "There's about sixty scattered throughout the country. There's one in Denver. I've thought about it, but that would be moving again, and I think Jen's already pretty attached to Aspen."

They grew quiet once again, the hospital only a few miles away. On the outside, Alex seemed calm and collected, but it seemed he had his fair share of problems. Regardless, Vincent liked the guy. Alex was only a couple years older, but it seemed like he had so much more life experience than Vincent. Hopefully when this was all over, the two of them could get to know each other better.

Alex turned left onto a side street, and a few minutes later, they parked in front of the hospital. It was only a few minutes after eleven. It was considerably warmer here, but dark clouds loomed to the west. Snow was coming, and Vincent didn't think they'd be back to Aspen before the storm hit.

A tall man in a black suit approached them as they entered the lobby. Vincent placed him in his mid-thirties. He had a crew cut and a scar that ran from his left ear down to his chin.

He extended his hand to Alex. "You must be Alex Snyder." He had a low baritone voice, and spoke with authority.

Alex nodded. "Pleasure to meet you."

The man offered his hand to Vincent. "And you are?"

"Vincent Martinez."

"Nice to meet you, gentlemen." He turned and headed for an elevator at the far end of the lobby. "I'm agent Matthew Sommers. Agent Baxter was unable to make it here this morning, so I was sent in his place. I spoke with your sheriff earlier this morning. Sounds like a pretty tough situation you have down there."

Alex explained what was going on. He left out several parts, but Vincent didn't feel the need to interject or clarify anything. When he was finished, Sommers said, "Well, let's get right to it then. I haven't been up to her room yet, but the doctor told me that she's conscious. Let's hope she can answer your questions."

They rode the elevator to one of the higher floors. Sommers found a nurse and she led them to Julie Preston's room. The door was ajar, but Vincent couldn't quite see inside.

"Julie's been awake for the past hour or so," the nurse explained. Her name tag read 'Carly.' "She hasn't said much of anything, and we're not quite sure if she's aware of what's going on around her. Her children were here just a little bit ago, but some relatives came and took them out for a while. We'll allow you to talk to her, but please don't push her too far. Dr. Friedman

166

is with another patient right now, but he'll be in to talk to you as soon as possible."

Sommers thanked the nurse and pushed the door open. Julie Preston lay on the bed, wires connected to several parts of her body. Her dark blonde hair was matted to her head, and her skin was very pale. Her eyes followed Sommers as he grabbed a chair and pulled it up next to her bed. Vincent and Alex did the same.

"Julie," Sommers began, speaking gently. "How are you feeling?"

She didn't answer the question, but instead pointed to Alex. "I know you."

"My name's Alex Snyder." He leaned forward. "I work with your husband."

"My husband…" she lingered over the words. "Where's Sam?"

Vincent and Alex exchanged a glance. Did Julie remember anything that had happened to her?

"Can you tell me what you did yesterday, Julie?" Alex asked.

She furrowed her brow. "It was so cold." She looked around the room. "How did I end up here?"

"I found you wandering down the road with nothing more than a shirt on. Do you remember that?"

"It was so cold," she repeated. "We went to his cabin. I don't know why he didn't have the heat on."

"Who's cabin were you at?" Alex asked. Vincent felt a surge of excitement. Was Julie about to give them a name?

"I can't remember," she said slowly. "He… he gave me something to drink. It was so sweet. I was so tired."

"Do you remember who was at the cabin with you?" Alex asked again.

She shook her head. "He took me there after… Oh, God, where's Sam?"

The door opened behind them, breaking the tension. Dr. Friedman gave them a cordial smile and pushed the door shut behind him. A long, white coat dropped past his knees and a stethoscope hung around his neck. He was rubbing his hands as if he had just used hand sanitizer.

"Gentlemen," he said, stopping on the other side of the bed. "I'm Dr. Friedman." He looked down at Preston. "How are you feeling, Julie?"

She closed her eyes. "I'm tired."

"I know you are. I'm going to talk to these nice folks here. Try to stay awake, will you?"

They filed out of the hospital room after the doctor and made a circle in the hallway. Dr. Friedman glanced over his shoulder, back toward the elevator, and then spoke quietly.

"I'm going to skip all the formalities, if that's fine with you," he began. "Frankly, I have a lot of work to do today and not a lot of time to do it. Julie's doing better than we thought. When she arrived here, her body temperature was around ninety-six degrees. Your doctors back in Aspen said her temperature was just above ninety-four degrees when she got in. If it had dropped any lower than that, her vital organs would have basically stopped working, and she would have died. It's really a miracle that she's still alive."

"By the time she got here, she was in a medically induced coma. It's hard to say exactly what happened to her, but we know she had severe hypothermia. Her body temperature is back up to normal. She had severe frostbite on her hands and toes, but we've been able to treat that. I think we'll be able to release her by Saturday."

"What about her memory?" Vincent asked. "None of what she's saying really makes sense."

"It could be her way of blocking out whatever she went through. That happens sometimes, especially in traumatic incidents."

"I think it's more than that, doctor," Alex said. "She said she drank something sweet. The toxicology report on our first victim found numerous chemicals in her system, including a lot of alcohol. Is it possible she was drugged as well?"

"Definitely possible," the doctor mused. "By the time she arrived here, all those chemicals were out of her system. But there are chemicals and certain drugs that have the ability to erase short term memory."

Alex nodded slowly. "If she saw a psychologist, they'd be able to bring the memories back, correct?"

"That usually only works if the patient wants to recall the memories. I'm not an expert on this kind of thing, I'm afraid. Julie is alive, and she's going to make a full recovery. I know you have an important investigation going on right now, but my responsibility is to look out for the well-being of my patients. You can have a couple more minutes with her, then she needs to get some rest."

Dr. Friedman headed down the hall, and the three of them entered the room again.

"You need to help him," Julie said, her eyes closed.

"Help who?" Alex asked.

"He has been so lonely ever since she died."

"Who are you talking about?" Alex asked, a little too forcefully.

She opened her eyes and her eyes locked onto his. "His girlfriend." Her eyes closed once more. "I need to talk to Sam. I'm so tired."

Sommers tried to press her further, but it was clear that she was done talking. Sommers thanked Julie and they filed out of the room. Dr. Friedman stopped them at the elevator.

"So? Was she of any help?"

"There's a lot she doesn't remember," Sommers said. "But I think it was helpful to talk to her."

Alex agreed. "If she remembers anything else, can you please give one of us a call?"

"I've got agents here in Denver," Sommers chimed in. "They could be over here to talk to her within ten minutes if needed."

"Yes, I will call," the doctor replied. "Good luck with your investigation."

The sun had disappeared by the time they walked out to the parking lot. As they approached Alex's truck, Sommers spoke.

"I've been thinking," he said. "How long of a drive do you have back home?"

"Three, maybe four hours," Alex said.

"I'd like to work with you for the rest of this investigation. I can have a plane ready in ten minutes and we can

169

be back in Aspen by 1:15. I don't think we can afford to waste three hours at this point.

Alex looked to Vincent, then back at Sommers. "What about my truck?"

"We'll deal with that later. Your department has a vehicle you can use, I'm sure."

Alex thought it over, then agreed. "I'll follow you to the airport."

Twenty minutes later, they took off in a small, two engine plane from Front Range Airport, flying west toward the line of dark clouds.

29

Alex stared out the window, into the thick sea of clouds. The small plane had begun its descent, and they would land at Pitkin County Airport in about ten minutes. He had already called the sheriff to inform them of their situation. Brown had promised that a vehicle would be waiting for them.

Alex hated flying. He preferred driving any day. But in this situation, time was precious, and the flight was only about an hour long. He'd flown often when he was in the FBI, but those planes were generally pretty comfortable. The one he was in right now was old, and the flight had been pretty bumpy so far. He didn't know if that was because of turbulence, but he just wanted to be on the ground. His family had done plenty of road trips when he was younger, and he enjoyed each of them, even if it was a twenty hour drive. He'd flown overseas on numerous occasions, to Norway, Russia, and even New Zealand. He'd always dreaded those flights, which took eight hours or more. Flying just wasn't his thing.

Sommers, who was in the seat in front of him, turned around and spoke loudly to be heard above the roar of the engine. "Pilot says we'll have some turbulence up ahead. We're running into the leading edge of the storm. Make sure you're buckled up."

His belt was already fastened. He saw Vincent, who was in the seat across from him, pull his tight. The jolting came a minute later, worse than before. If not for the belt, Alex was sure he would have been thrown from his seat. He couldn't see anything outside the window, just the thick gray blanket. He gripped the headrest in front of him, and a few minutes later, he saw the glow of lights and they touched down on the runway. The plane taxied up to the terminal and stopped. The airport in Aspen was a fairly small, mostly used by the wealthy who split their time between Aspen and other places. There were also some commercial flights that departed and arrived from Salt Lake City, Denver, and Chicago, to name a few. Despite that, the tarmac was usually active with private planes instead of commercial jets.

Snow was falling heavily, whipped in circles by the wind. All he could see was the dark outline of the main airport terminal and the hazy glow of a few lights. It was amazing how pilots could land in this kind of weather. He'd always respect them for their ability.

They followed Sommers into the main terminal. It was fairly crowded, but then again, it was the day after Christmas, one of the busiest travel days. There was a large screen on the wall, showing that every flight had been delayed. There was one more flight coming in from Salt Lake City, scheduled to land at 1:36.

They found Paul Brown on their way to the parking lot. He wore a big coat and boots, and his hair and mustache were wet from the snow.

He stepped forward and extended his hand to the agent. "You must be Agent Sommers. I'm sheriff Paul Brown."

"Nice to meet you," Sommers said. "I wish it could be under more pleasant circumstances."

"As do I." His gaze flicked to Alex. "I was hoping Julie Preston would be able to give you a name."

"I think she's suffering some short term memory loss," he explained. "That or she's trying to block out whatever happened to her."

Brown nodded, rubbing his chin. "Let's get back to the office before this storm gets worse. They've upgraded us to a blizzard warning. Eight to twelve more inches of snow by tomorrow morning."

Brown was parked in the middle of the parking lot, in a black Ford Explorer. "This'll be yours until you get your truck back. I expect you to keep it in good condition."

172

They turned onto Highway 82, headed east toward the center of Aspen. The sheriff had the wipers on full blast, pushing the snow off the windshield as soon as it landed. Martinez and Sommers sat in the back, Alex in the passenger seat. He briefed the sheriff on what Julie Preston had told them. When he finished, he realized how little they had to go off of.

The only thing Brown said in reply was, "We'll talk when we get there."

The roads were mostly deserted, with only a few vehicles headed each way. It was ominously dark out. The roads were wet, but soon would be covered because of the rapid snowfall rate. It was one of those days where you just wanted to stay inside and watch a good movie.

They all gathered in the large conference room at 2:00; Sommers, Vincent, Brown, Alex. Dylan Kessel was there, along with Charlie Porter, Stuart Rockford, Jesse Rollins, Maya Tanner, and another FBI agent named Danny Waschkin, who had stayed behind to help out.

Alex once again described their meeting with Julie Preston. There was a look of disappointment on everyone's faces when he was done talking.

"So is she ever going to remember who did this?" Rockford asked dejectedly.

"A psychologist might be able to help her," Alex said. "But it's going to be a couple days before she's out of the hospital. By that time, our guy could he halfway around the world."

"So what do we do?" Kessel asked. "This was a dead end, and Lawson still hasn't returned our calls."

"Julie made it clear that she knew the person who did this. She also said her abductor was lonely because he lost someone he loved."

"And she mentioned that she was at a cabin," Sommers added. "Are there any cabins near where you guys found her?"

"I'll look into that," Brown said quickly. "Hal Jenkins is a guide out here during the summer and he knows this area like the back of his hand, better than anyone else I know. I'm going to go talk to him.

"Stuart and Charlie, Mitch Warren called to say that he finished the autopsy on Preston." For some unknown reason, the autopsy had taken almost three days. "Head on over and check it out.

"Sommers, I'd like to have you look through everything we've got so far. You can use the small conference room. Waschkin, Tanner, and Martinez, I'll have you guys join him."

That left him, Kessel, and Rollins. "I'd like to go through some more records," Alex said. "See if we can dig up anything."

Brown nodded. "Sounds good. Alex, I'd like to talk with you in my office for a moment. Everybody else, let's get to work."

Alex followed the sheriff to his office, and took a seat across from him. Brown shut the door, and with a deep breath, sat down.

"First of all, I want to make sure you understand that whatever is said here stays here."

"Of course."

"Good." He sat down and his eyes locked onto Alex's. "I haven't told anybody this but my wife and children. I have lung cancer."

Alex sat back in his chair. So this was what had caused the change in Brown. "Why are you telling me this right now?"

"I just felt the need to share with someone," the sheriff replied. "I figured you had a right to know what's wrong, and I'll tell everyone else once this is over. I got my diagnosis in early September, but I've been feeling a lot worse lately."

"Is it terminal?" Alex asked.

Brown shrugged. "The doctors don't know. I'm on medication and I go in regularly for treatment. I'm doing everything I can to stay healthy and beat this. I used to smoke a lot when I was in my twenties, and I guess it finally caught up to me."

Alex figured it was a good time to bring up another topic. "So you aren't going to be running for sheriff next year?"

He shook his head. "This job's taken much more of a toll on me than I expected." He lowered his voice, even though nobody else could hear him. "Jesse's made it clear that he has no

174

interest in being sheriff. I was thinking of retiring early and handing over the reins to him, but that option's off the table now. I'll stick with it until November, if I can."

"Why doesn't Rollins want to take over?"

"I asked him, but he wouldn't give me a straight answer. Maybe he'll change his mind. Which brought me to thinking. Would you ever consider running next fall?"

"No." Alex answered automatically.

"No?" Brown seemed taken aback.

"I'm not ready, and at this point, I have no desire to run this department. I haven't been here long enough, don't know enough people. I don't want to plant down any more roots until I know for sure that I'm gonna be staying here."

"God knows you have enough experience. You're probably the most qualified person in this county."

"I'm not sure if this is a permanent job for me. I can't commit myself for four years."

"Okay." Brown seemed to accept it. "If you change your mind just let me know."

Alex wanted to get to those records. "Is that all you wanted to see me for?"

"While we're on the subject, I wanted to ask you about Stuart Rockford. He's made it clear that he wants the position."

"That would not be good."

"Glad you feel that way also. I've heard complaints of misconduct, but I haven't got the chance to talk to him about it yet."

Alex debated telling the sheriff about Stuart and Angela, but decided to keep it to himself. For now, at least. "I'll make sure he never becomes sheriff."

Brown looked at him oddly, but didn't ask any questions. "I don't have any hard evidence of misconduct, but I'll confront him if I find any." He stood up. "We both have work to do, Alex. Let's get this guy."

30

Stephen was bored. It was 2:30 in the afternoon and he was sitting on a couch at his mother's house. If anyone saw him here, they would assume that he didn't have much a life. He did. He just didn't know what to do.

Christmas Eve had been spent with Mariah, and he met the majority of her family. They all seemed to like him, which was good. Christmas Day, he came back to Aspen and spent the day with his mom. She had invited Alex over, since he was alone, and luckily, it wasn't awkward. Nobody talked about the murders.

He had been here the whole day, not doing much of anything. His mother had been out most of the morning and had just returned. She hadn't said exactly where she'd been, only that she was headed upstairs to take a shower. The water had been off for a while now, and he wondered what she was doing up there.

He had to return to work on Friday. That was two days away. He'd told Angela that, but she hadn't responded. He knew he wasn't being forced to stay here, but he was afraid of what his mother might do if he wasn't here to reason with her.

Outside, snow fell heavily. Aspen averaged significantly more snow per year than Glenwood Springs. Stephen wasn't a huge fan of winter, which was one of the reasons he had decided to live farther west. There was no way that he would be able to get home today. He didn't want to risk driving in this weather.

He was about to turn on the television when a phone rang. He hurried to the kitchen and saw that it was Angela's cell phone. The display said 'Unknown caller.' She was still upstairs, so he answered.

"Is this Angela Olmsted?" It was a man's voice, low and raspy. It sounded like the caller was outside.

"This is her son, Stephen. Who's this?"

"Erik Lawson. I've been out of range for the last week and I see I've missed a hell of a lot of calls from Aspen. What's going on?"

Stephen felt a jolt run through him. "Give me one second, Mr. Lawson."

He took the stairs two at a time and knocked hard on his mother's door. She opened it a few seconds later, a hairbrush in her hand.

"Yeah?"

He held up the phone. "It's Erik Lawson."

Her eyes grew wide and she dropped the brush. He handed her the phone and they made their way back downstairs to the dining room table.

"Mr. Lawson?" She put the phone on speaker so Stephen could hear what was being said. "This is Angela Olmsted. Thanks for returning my call."

"Yeah. I told your son that I've got... I don't know, hundreds of missed calls from Aspen. Your voicemail was the first one I listened to so I called you first."

Angela grabbed a notepad that was sitting on the chair next to her. "The reason for our calls, Mr. Lawson, is because there have been a couple recent murders in the area."

"I'm sorry to hear that, but how does this affect me? I've been gone from Aspen for over twenty years."

"One of the victims is Samuel Preston. Your father informed us that you two were friends in high school."

"Sam..." Lawson's trailed off. When he spoke again, his voice was hard. "You guys are police right?"

Angela hesitated. "We're working with the family of a victim and privately investigating. I can assure you that this information will go directly to the police."

Lawson didn't answer right away, and Stephen thought he may have hung up. "When did Sam die?"

"Saturday afternoon. It was right after he placed a call to you."

"Yeah. I had service and was surprised to hear from him. You said murders. Who else?"

"Another cop, Daniel Carver, and his wife Erin."

"Look, I don't want to talk about this over the phone. There's an old friend of mine who still lives in Aspen. Name's Jack Burnett." He gave them Burnett's address. "It's a long story, and my connection's breaking up. Jack will tell you all you need to know." He hung up without saying goodbye.

They exchanged a glance. Did Erik Lawson know who the killer was but hang up without telling them? It sure sounded that way.

"Well, I guess we know what we need to do now," Angela said, standing up.

"In this weather?"

She glanced out the window. "I've seen worse. Anyway, my Jeep's got all wheel drive. We'll be fine."

Stephen sighed. "Where are the keys?"

Ten minutes later, Angela backed the Jeep out onto the street. She had found Jack Burnett's number in the phone book and had given him a call, confirming that he was home. She thought it would be best if they spoke in person, instead of over the phone.

Burnett only lived about a mile away. She kept her speed below 20 mph the whole way, careful because of the thin coating of ice that lay beneath the snow. Several inches had already accumulated and the storm was far from over. A few minutes later, they pulled into the driveway of Burnett's place, a small, one story house that was in need of a new coat of paint.

"Follow my lead," Angela said, shielding her face as she hurried up the sidewalk. She rang the doorbell, and a moment later, a middle aged man appeared at the door. Stephen thought Burnett looked vaguely familiar.

"I'm Angela," she said, pulling the door shut behind them. "We spoke on the phone."

He nodded. "Are you guys cops?"

Angela shook her head. "No."

He took a step backward. "Then I'm not sure that I should be talking with you guys."

"My husband was killed by this man, Mr. Burnett. I'm working directly with the sheriff on this investigation."

He looked doubtful, but finally nodded. "Okay. Let's talk in my office."

"So," Burnett said, once they were situated, "what exactly can I help you guys with? You weren't real clear on the phone but I assume that it's important if you're willing to come out in this storm."

"What is your relationship with Erik Lawson?" Angela asked.

Burnett leaned back and scratched his head. "God, I haven't seen Erik in years. We were pretty close in high school, but once he went out to San Francisco for college, we lost touch. I think the last time I saw him was probably at our fifteen year class reunion."

"How about Samuel Preston? Were you friends with him as well?"

"Yeah, Sam was a great guy. There were four of us in high school; me, him, Erik and Spencer Marshall. Sam and I went our separate ways after high school, but we'd still talk occasionally. I hope you find the guy who killed him."

"We're hoping you could help us with that," Angela said. "You mentioned the name Spencer Marshall. Care to tell us about him?"

"It's really sad, what happened with Spencer. He went to a trade school, met some girl. They were deep in love, and then she went missing in a snowstorm. This was probably fifteen years ago. They never found her body. He changed after that. I guess I haven't talked to him since then. Hell, I guess none of us have. He probably feels like we abandoned him. As far as I know, he still lives alone here in Aspen."

Spencer Marshall. Things were starting to fall into place. Marshall's girlfriend had gone missing during a snowstorm. Did Marshall blame the cops for not finding her? That could explain why he was going after them. But why wait fifteen years?

179

Angela looked Burnett in the eye. "I think Spencer has something to do with these murders."

"Spence? No way. He would never kill Sam."

"You said he's changed. Do you know any more details of his girlfriend's disappearance?"

"I helped search for her. She went missing in mid-January. She was out snowmobiling. They found the snowmobile in the woods, but Jessica wasn't there. A storm hit the next day. Way worse than this. We must've got, I don't know, two feet of snow. The search resumed after that, but we pretty much knew all hope was gone. Spence was devastated. He was only twenty, and he had just proposed to her a few days earlier. I really should have been there to support him. I feel really bad about the way things turned out for him. God, do you really think he did this?"

"I don't know the man, Mr. Burnett. Do you think he's capable of this?"

Burnett shook his head cluelessly. "I have no idea. I haven't talked to him in so long. His mom was always there for him, but I heard that she passed away a few days ago." His gaze locked on his. "That could've pushed him over the edge."

Stephen remembered something Angela had told him. "Didn't Stuart Rockford say that one of Sam Preston's last words was 'spent?' What if he actually said 'Spence' instead of 'spent?'"

Angela had a look of determination in her eyes. "It's him, Stephen. I know it is. He lost his girlfriend, and he blames the cops. Carver and Preston and Will must have been a part of the search. Maybe he blames them." She turned back to Burnett. "Do you know where this guy lives?"

He shook his head, opening a file cabinet below the desk. He pulled out a phone book and tossed it across the table. "Here. Look in there."

Angela flipped through the pages until she found his name. Marshall lived to the west, near Snowmass Village, in an apartment. She thanked Burnett and they hurried back outside to the Jeep.

"Let's go," Angela said, brushing the snow out of her hair.

"Don't you think we should tell Alex or somebody?" Stephen asked

She shook her head. "No cops. We do this my way."

31

Paul Brown drove through Aspen in a dark blue Ford Explorer. It was still before sunset, but almost as dark as night. Days were getting longer now, but winter was far from over.

Hal Jenkins was an interesting man. During the summer months, he was a hiking guide across western Colorado. Brown didn't know what he did during the winter. He did know that Jenkins had hiked *thousands* of miles of trails and was in extremely good shape. He lived in a small house several miles south of Snowmass Village with his girlfriend, Mary. In addition to that, Jenkins had the best aim of any man he had ever seen. People said that Jenkins had served in Iraq, but he wasn't sure if that was true. The snow was coming down harder, but Hal knew the Maroon Bells and White River National Forest better than anyone, so he was willing to get back on the road.

He turned onto the dirt track, which was covered in several inches of snow. His vehicle pushed through it, and he pulled up behind an ancient Dodge Dakota that belonged to Jenkins. There was very little snow on the vehicle, which suggested that Jenkins might have been out recently.

He dashed up the sidewalk, trying to keep his feet dry, and rang the bell. The wooden steps creaked under his feet. Everything about the house was old; the porch swing, the shutters, the paint. He'd never been inside, but figured it would be much the same.

The door opened, and Mary Rice stuck her head out. Her auburn hair was pinned up in a bun on the top of her head. She squinted at him. "What the hell are you doing out in this storm, Sheriff?"

He kicked the snow off his shoes before stepping inside. "Hey, Mary. Is Hal home?"

"Where else would he be?" She turned around and yelled up the stairs. "Hal! The sheriff's here. He wants to talk to you." She turned back to him. "You need anything? Coffee? Water?"

He shook his head. "No thanks. I don't have a lot of time."

"Come sit down, at least." She motioned toward a suede blue couch in the living room.

He accepted, sinking into the sofa. Mary sat down in an armchair across from him. "We heard about the murders. Did you catch the guy who did it?"

He shook his head, and was grateful when Hal appeared. Mary could talk anyone to death.

Jenkins was a tall man built of muscle. He stood about 6'2" and weighed at least two hundred pounds. He had long brown hair that hung to his shoulders and large hands that caught his eye every time he saw Jenkins.

"How've you been, Paul?" he asked, plopping down next to him. "I hear you've got a bit of trouble on your hands."

"Yeah. I was hoping you could help me out, Hal."

"Me? What could I possibly help you with?"

"You know this area better than anyone. Both of the women who went missing were found near County Road 15, pretty close to Castle Creek. I'm not very familiar with the terrain in that area. Are you aware of any private property up there?"

"Well, you've got Grahamster's." Grahamster's was one of the many ski resorts in the Aspen area. While not as popular as Snowmass or Aspen Mountain, he knew it was a favorite among some of the locals.

"Yeah, I know that," he said. "Anything farther south of there that you can think of?"

Hal rubbed his chin. "I've gotta think about that for a second. Trailhead for Corundum Creek's down there. I've hiked that several times, but the trail goes almost directly south.

You've also got that Tibetan Retreat place. Where exactly were these ladies found?"

"One of them was farther south on 15, to the west of the road near Castle Creek. Pretty rugged out there. The other was wandering down 15B. Just north of the Corundum Creek crossing, as I understand it."

"Hmmm," Hal said. "You want any coffee, sheriff?"

"He doesn't want anything, Hal," Mary said.

"How do you know what the man wants?" Hal glared at his girlfriend. They had been together for eight years and still bickered like this.

"I already asked him."

"Guys." Paul held up his hand. He got a headache whenever he spent time near the two of them. "If you can't help me, I'll just be on my way."

"Wait," Hal said slowly. "I recall coming across some cabins up there when I was cross country skiing. Keep in mind that this was many years ago, so they may not still be there. At that time, they were under the ownership of this young guy. Biracial. His name is Clayton King, I believe. That's the only type of private property I know of up there. These cabins are near County Road 15, but I'm not exactly sure where. That's the only thing I can think of."

Clayton King. He thought the name sounded vaguely familiar. "Thanks for your help, Hal."

"No problem, sheriff." Hal walked him to the door. "You planning on running again next fall?"

"I don't really have time to talk right now." He slipped on his shoes. "Maybe we'll catch up some other time."

"We voted for you in the last election, you know," Mary said from behind him.

"Thanks for your help, guys." He left them in their small house and hurried back to the Explorer, which now sat coated with snow. He turned the heat on full blast and cleaned the snow off his windshield. There were three messages on his phone; one from his wife, an old one from Mitch Warren that he had forgotten to delete, and a third message from Charlie Porter. He ignored the first two messages, instead giving the deputy a call right away.

184

"What's up?" Porter said in greeting.

"I'm done here. You guys find anything?"

"Not much." He could hear voices in the background. "We knew he was shot with the same pistol as Daniel. Time of death is what we expected. Near 12:45. Sam had a beer or two before he died. Nothing we didn't already know."

His phone buzzed suddenly. "Okay. Look, I'm getting another call. I'll meet you back at the office."

The call was coming from Vincent Martinez. He sounded worried.

"We finished going through the information and evidence we have, and then I went to see if Dylan and Jesse and Alex had found anything. They're gone, sheriff."

"What do you mean they're gone?"

"We checked the whole building. They're not here."

He was confused. "Are you trying to tell me that they went somewhere?"

"It sure looks that way. Dylan's car is still here, but I don't see Jesse's truck."

"Dammit," he said, suddenly sharing Vincent's concern. "They didn't tell anyone where they were going?"

"No. There's not very many of us here right now. Charlie and Stuart aren't back yet either."

"I know. I just talked to Charlie, and they're on their way right now. Look, I'll be back as soon as I can, and we'll plan our next move from there."

"Sure. One more thing. I'm in the conference room right now, and it looks like they were going through a box of records from 2002. There's a stack of files to my left, which I assume are the ones they've gone through already, and some more in the box. Do you think they found something?"

"I don't know what they found. Did you try calling them?"

"Yeah. There's no answer."

Paul debated what to do. The snow was getting heavier and he was uncomfortable staying out in this weather. On the other hand, he felt that they were on the verge of a major break. He *had* to talk to Clayton King.

"Look, I've got one more person to talk to. Get me an address for a Clayton King of Aspen."

Vincent gave him the address a minute later. "So what do you want us to do?"

"I don't know. You guys work something out among yourselves. Any news at all, you let me know right away. Got it?"

"Yeah. Be careful out there. I heard the plows aren't even going to be out until tomorrow morning, it's coming down so hard."

"I'll be fine, Vincent." He ended the call and plugged King's address into his GPS.

Had Alex found something and not told him? If so, he better have a damn good reason.

32

Jesse Rollins drove as fast as the snow allowed. Alex sat in the passenger seat, Dylan Kessel behind him. They sat in tense silence, each of them thinking about what they had just discovered.

Alex had found the file. It was dated January 21, 2002. He had only been in elementary school at the time. Right away he had the feeling that the file was important. He was right.

The story went something like this. Spencer Marshall was the guy's name. He was twenty years old when it happened. Jessica Fisher was his girlfriend. The file didn't hold a lot of information, but he had used the internet to find more details on the case.

Jessica was out skiing that day and never returned. Sheriff Donny Mitchell, who was in charge of Pitkin County at the time, mounted a search effort to find the girl the day after she disappeared. That quickly came to halt on the morning of the twenty-third. A huge blizzard rolled in, dumping anywhere from two to four feet of snow from Glenwood Springs to Crested Butte, east to Buena Vista and Leadville, and north to Vail, Idaho Springs, and Silverthorne. It even shut down I-80 for more than forty eight hours. It was definitely a storm to remember. Unfortunately, nobody was able to search for Jessica until the weather improved on the twenty-fifth, and by then, almost everybody knew that all hope of finding her alive was gone. Her body was never found.

Needless to say, Spencer Marshall was devastated. Foul play was ruled out, and her death was labeled as a tragic accident. Everyone moved on, except for Marshall. Alex found out that he still lived in Aspen, working as a machinist.

These facts alone may not have been enough to convince him that Marshall was guilty. But there were two additional pieces of information to consider.

Jessica Fisher disappeared on January 21, the same day that William Olmsted was murdered.

Secondly, five officers were listed as major parts of the search. One, Jerome Halst, had moved to Florida. Three of the others were Daniel Carver, Samuel Preston, and William Olmsted. That had made Alex certain. But there was a fifth name on the list, and that was the reason that he was heading east instead of west toward Spencer Marshall's apartment.

Officer Ethan Adams was the fifth name. He had tried several times to reach Adams and his wife, but neither were answering their phones. He hoped that Marshall hadn't already gotten to Ethan.

They hadn't told anyone where they were going. There wasn't time to mount a huge team to go get Marshall. And he didn't completely trust the agents from the FBI. They didn't know this town, and he didn't want them screwing anything up. Rollins and Kessel were two good cops, and Alex knew he could count on them in a tough situation.

"There's one more thing you guys should know," Alex said, breaking the silence. "Rockford's been feeding information to an outside source."

Rollins didn't take his eyes off the road, but Alex saw that he was confused. "What do you mean?"

Alex explained about Angela Olmsted, and how she was investigating on her own and working with Rockford.

"Isn't that illegal?" Rollins asked.

"Yeah. He seems to think that he's above the law."

"That bastard," Rollins said, turning off the highway. "I've dealt with him for seven years and I'm sick of it."

"Why exactly is he doing that?" Kessel asked from the back. "I mean, what's in it for him?"

"He uses Angela's information to solve the case, gets a pat on the back and some recognition, which will boost his chances in the fall."

"Have you told the sheriff yet?" Rollins asked.

"No. I'm deciding what to do."

"Let's take him down," Kessel said excitedly. "I don't think anyone would really miss him."

"I think we wait until after this is finished and then go to Brown," Alex said. "I already talked to Angela. She's got nothing to lose by turning on him. If nothing else, he'll get fired."

"Good," Rollins said, turning onto a side street that was covered with snow. "I want to be there when you take him down."

"Me, too," Kessel chimed from the back.

Alex wasn't looking forward to bringing down Rockford as much. He knew Rockford's ambitions, that sheriff was just a stepping stone to a bigger career. This would ruin it all, and the man might not go down without a fight.

Rollins pulled up in front of Adam's house. It looked dark inside and uninviting. There were tire tracks in the driveway, indicating that someone had been out recently. Rollins told him that Adams had been at his desk for much of the morning, leaving around 1:00, just before Alex and Vincent had returned from Denver.

"This is it?" Kessel asked.

Rollins shut off the engine. "He lives here with his wife. No kids."

All three were armed. It didn't look like Marshall was there, but they couldn't afford to take any chances.

Alex pulled up the hood of his parka and followed Rollins up the sidewalk. Kessel brought up the rear. There were indentations in the snow where footprints may have been, which only added to the tension. The blinds were drawn in the front window, and snow had been blown up and gathered at the bottom of the front door.

Rollins reached forward and rang the doorbell. "Ethan? Are you home?"

The only answer was the howl of the wind. Rollins turned the knob and pushed the door open.

Alex stepped inside, his senses alert. "Check the basement," he told Rollins. "We'll check the main floor."

A minute later, they met back in the kitchen. There was nobody here. Alex had never been inside Adams' home before, and was impressed by it. Dark, hardwood floors, high wood ceilings, a large chandelier over the dining room table. With no kids and two incomes, he guessed they were financially well off.

"What exactly are we looking for?" Kessel asked.

"Anything unusual," Alex said. "Look for signs of a struggle. Let's split up. Call if you find anything."

He headed left out of the foyer and down a hallway to the laundry room. There was a door on the other end, which he presumed led out into the garage. He opened it, and a cold blast hit him. There was one car in the garage, a newer model Buick Regal. Ethan drove a Ford Escape, so that must be his wife's car. The Escape hadn't been in the driveway, so that meant Ethan was gone. But where would he have gone?

He shut the door and was headed for the basement when he heard a shout from Kessel. "Alex, you might wanna come see this."

He and Rollins stood in the kitchen, staring down at the floor. When he got closer, he saw dark drops of blood, forming a trail toward the front door. He must have missed it when they first came in.

He looked around the rest of the kitchen. There was a pan on the stove, a gallon of milk on the counter. It looked as if Mrs. Adams had been making an early dinner. Had Marshall knocked on the door and then forced her back into the kitchen, or had he somehow broken in and surprised her there? And where was Ethan?

"What do you think?" Kessel finally asked.

"He has Megan, that's what I think," Rollins declared. "Where the hell is Ethan?"

"He drives a silver Ford Escape, right?" Alex asked, confirming what he thought he knew.

"Yeah."

"It's not in the garage. There's a Buick in there, which must belong to Megan, but no Escape."

"What the hell?" he said. "He told me he was headed home to spend the evening with Megan."

190

"Here's what I think happened," Alex said. "Megan's in here cooking dinner. Marshall either breaks in or gets Megan to let him in. I don't know whether he shoots her or stabs her, but he leaves with her. Maybe Ethan went after them."

Rollins turned his back and dug his ringing cellphone out of his pocket. "Yeah?"

He listened for a minute, and then said, "Where are you, Ethan? We're at your house right now."

He nodded. Then, "Okay, we'll be right there."

"Ethan went off the road." Rollins headed for the door. "Come on. Let's go find him."

33

Jen left her sister's house in Colorado Springs, but she wasn't quite ready to head west back to Aspen. Her roommate from college, Angelica Varis, was a resident of Colorado Springs, and Jen hadn't seen her in two years. She figured now was as good a time as ever to catch up.

Jen only had two siblings, but Christmas hadn't been a small affair. Her mother had nine siblings, and all of them were still alive. The whole family had gathered at her sister's house, and it had been a fun time. She received a lot of questions about what was going on back home with the murders, but she felt she had deflected them pretty well.

It was warm in eastern Colorado. Temperatures were in the fifties, melting some of the snow that blanketed the ground. She had heard that central Colorado was getting another snowstorm. Since Highway 82 was always closed in winter over Independence Pass, the drive took significantly longer. She would head north on I-25 to Denver, then I-70 east to Glenwood Springs, and Highway 82 south to Aspen. All in all, about a five hour drive. Longer if she ran into bad weather, which was very possible between Idaho Springs and Eagle.

She turned onto the ramp and headed north on I-25. It was rush hour, but traffic wasn't bad, most people probably still off from the holidays. Angelica lived alone in a middle class neighborhood on the northeast side of town. She had been Jen's best friend in college and had double majored in accounting and finance. They had tried to stay in touch but it was a little difficult since they lived so far apart.

Ten minutes later, Jen pulled up in front of the house. Snow lay in patches around the small yard. The houses were packed close together, with a view of the rising foothills and Pikes Peak beyond.

She grabbed the keys and her cellphone and headed toward the house. The front door opened even before she knocked, and Angelica gave her a long hug. Her blond hair hung down past her shoulders, and a lot of people mistook the two of them for sisters. They were the same height, build, had the same hair color, and both played volleyball throughout high school and college.

"Jen," Angelica said, finally releasing her grip. "It's so good to see you."

"It's good to see you too, Angelica." Jen sized her up. She looked the same as she had the last time they had seen each other. "You look great."

"So do you."

Jen glanced down at her stomach. "Yeah, well, not for long. I'm pregnant."

Angelica gasped. "Are you serious?"

"Yeah."

"Congratulations! Come on, let's go inside and talk."

The inside of the house was warm and cozy. Angelica had always been interested in design, and Jen thought she would have been great as an architect or interior designer. They sat down at the small table in the dining room, which was really just an extension of the kitchen.

"So," Angelica said. "How many months?"

"Almost three."

Angelica did the math in her head. "So you'll be due in what, June?"

"Yeah, somewhere around there."

Angelica rubbed her hands together. "I'm so happy for you, Jen. Does Alex know yet?"

"No. I haven't told him yet."

"When are you going to tell him? I mean, he's going to be able to tell pretty soon."

"I was going to tell him on Christmas Eve, but he's been so busy with this case that I haven't been able to."

"Yeah, I heard about that. Any new leads?"

"I'm not sure. There were none when I left."

"So when am I going to see Alex again?" she asked. "He's a great guy."

"It'll be soon," Jen promised. "You should really come out to Aspen. We have a guest room that you could stay in."

"I'm sure you have a lovely home," Angelica agreed. "It's just that, well, you live in *Aspen*."

Jen knew the story. When she was fifteen, Angelica and her parents took a weekend trip to Aspen. Some secrets came to light, and her parents ended up having a bitter divorce. To this day, there was still a hatred that existed between them. Jen knew her father and mother, and they were both nice people, but things just hadn't worked out. Angelica had never been back to Aspen, and Jen suspected she didn't want to bring back the memories.

"I mean, of all the mountain towns, you choose Aspen," Angelica continued. "There's Vail, Breckenridge, Telluride, Frisco, Silverthorne, Winter Park-"

"Angelica." Jen cut her off. "I know. But we can't not hang out just because of the town I live in."

She sighed. "Tell you what. Once you get back, we'll talk, and maybe I'll take you up on that offer."

Angelica's gaze had wandered from Jen and locked on something above her head. She turned and saw a canvas of an endless prairie, the tall grass bending in the wind.

"Do you like it?" Angelica asked.

"It's beautiful," Jen replied. "Where'd you get it?"

"There's a shop here in town. I've gotten several pieces from there." She looked directly at Jen. "You know, sometimes I feel like a blade of that prairie grass. The wind comes and blows me over, knocks me down. But I also get back up, and nothing can keep me down."

Jen didn't know where this was going, but she sat and listened.

"What's wrong, Jen?" Angelica spread her hands. "I love my life. I've got a good job. A beautiful home here. I have an amazing boyfriend." This was news to Jen, but Angelica was on a roll. "I have a nice car, good friends. What more can I really ask for? I look at you, and I think you have it all as well. So what's bothering you? You've even got a baby on the way; you should be thrilled!"

For the next thirty minutes, Jen poured out her feelings, and the two women talked. When they were finished, she felt so much better. She had been holding these feelings in for a long time.

"I know I was saying how great my life was, but there's one thing I should tell you," Angelica said, her voice turning serious. "You can still keep a secret, right?"

"Of course."

"Good. Don't tell anyone. Please. This needs to stay between you and me."

When Angelica finished, there were tears running down her cheeks. Jen held her friend, and then finally broke the uncomfortable silence.

"The cops should know, Angelica," she said.

She shook her head vehemently. "No. It's not going to be a problem, at least not in the near future. I just wanted someone else to know what's going on, and I trust you the most."

"Angelica," Jen said forcefully, "this is serious."

"What are they going to do, Jen? I'll figure out a way to handle this, okay? Promise me you won't tell anyone. Not even Alex."

"Fine. I promise. But you have to promise me that you will call me if anything happens."

Angelica nodded. "Look," she said, wiping her eyes. "It's getting kind of late, and I heard there's another snowstorm out there right now. Why don't you stay here tonight and you can drive home tomorrow? We have some more catching up to do."

Jen didn't have to be asked twice.

34

"Here's the plan," Alex said. Rollins was in the driver's seat, Kessel in the back. He wasn't sure exactly where they were headed, only that Ethan Adams had gone off the road and they needed to find him. "Once we find Ethan we're going back to the station. Ethan's going to stay there, and one of you guys needs to stay with him and brief the sheriff and FBI. Who's it going to be?"

Neither answered. They both wanted to be a part of the action. Finally, Rollins said, "I'll stay."

"Good. Make sure we're all on the same page. Dylan, I need you to go in the back door and find an address for Spencer Marshall. You can use my office. Just make it quick."

"So it's only going to be you two going to Marshall's?" Rollins, again, was confused. "Why don't we do this as a group? That way there's more firepower."

"You guys will come in after us. We just need a fifteen minute head start. Those two agents are going to try to take control, and the process is just going to take too long. We need to wrap this up quickly. And with just me and Dylan going ahead, we can hopefully do that."

The headlights cut a thin beam through the night, but it was still difficult to see. Rollins drove slowly, not wanting to go off the road like Ethan had.

"Should be right up here," Rollins murmured, more to himself than anyone in the vehicle. He slowed down, and saw a set of tire tracks that veered off the road. He pushed down on the brakes and turned the car slightly so that the glow of the headlights was cast onto the area to the right of the road. There was the Escape, the front dented badly, pushed up against a stand of trees. Alex didn't see Ethan and wondered if he was still in the car or had wandered off to find help.

Alex got out of the car and hurried over to the wreckage, aware of the other two officers behind him. Most of the damage had been sustained at the front of the car. Adams had definitely been going fast, and lucky that some of the thick snow had slowed him down as he flew off the road. Alex had seen plenty of damaged vehicles in his life, and he was almost positive that this one would never be driven again.

"Right here." The voice came from his left. Ethan Adams was standing on the road, his dark silhouette barely visible.

"Ethan." Alex's feet grew cold as he pushed a trail toward Ethan with his shoes. "You okay?"

"Fine." Though Alex could tell he wasn't. There was a little bit of blood on his face, and he held his right arm stiffly, as if it were in pain.

"What happened?" Rollins brushed past Alex and reached his friend first.

"I was in the basement, watching some TV before dinner. I was about to head upstairs when I heard Megan scream. When I got upstairs, I saw him taking off in that red Chevy. I knew he must have Megan with him." Ethan pounded his fist into his hand, his anger building. "I followed him. And this is where I end up." He cursed under his breath. "When I find the bastard who did this I *am* going to kill him." He glared at Alex. "And nobody better stand in my way."

"Let's get in the truck," Rollins suggested. "We'll talk on the way back to Aspen."

Alex gave the front seat to Adams and sat in the back next to Kessel. Adams was shivering, even with the heat at full blast. He wondered how long the man had waited there before they had picked him up. Not more than ten minutes, he thought, but even that could chill a person.

"Did you see the guy?" Rollins asked, turning in the direction of town.

197

Adams shook his head. "He was in the car by the time I got outside."

"We think we know who it is," Rollins said quietly, glancing back toward Alex. "Spencer Marshall."

"Who the hell is he?"

Alex gave a nod of permission, and Rollins related the story of Spencer Marshall. When he finished, they were in the parking lot of the police department. They sat there quietly, Adams taking it all in.

"Sure, I remember that search. I had just got hired here. Marshall, if that's the guy's name, was annoying as hell. I felt bad for the family, but by the end of the search, I had no sympathy for him." Ethan turned in his seat. He had calmed a little but Alex could still feel his anger. "So this guy took my wife because we couldn't find his girlfriend? Is that it?"

"Something like that."

Adams grimaced and shook his head. "So what are we doing just sitting here? Let's go after him."

"We need to go inside and talk with the sheriff." Alex tried to phrase the words so that it didn't seem like they were leaving him behind. "You might need to get some medical attention."

"Bullshit. I'm fine." He squinted toward the building, which was barely visible through the snow. Adams unbuckled his seatbelt. "I'll go talk to the sheriff, but there is no way you guys are leaving me here."

Rollins turned off the truck. "Go ahead, Ethan. We'll be right behind you."

Adams started to say something, but stopped, instead stepping out of the truck and slamming the door behind him.

"Can we use your truck?" Alex asked. "It would make things a lot simpler."

"Sure." Rollins left the keys in the ignition. "The plan's still on, right?"

Alex nodded. "Dylan, go get me that address. Make it quick."

Kessel followed Ethan toward the building, leaving Alex and Jesse. "Please, Jesse. Fifteen minutes."

"Don't worry. I'll buy you some time."

198

"Thanks." He stared out into the snow, watching Rollins disappear inside. The flakes were often beautiful, but tonight, they were a curse.

Kessel was back in four minutes. He jumped into the passenger seat and Alex started up the truck. "Got it?"

"Yeah." He read Alex the address and plugged it into the GPS. "Everyone was in the conference room. Nobody even noticed me." He handed Alex a two-way radio. "I figured we might need these."

"Good work. Do you have any idea what's going on in there?"

Kessel shrugged. "The door was closed. I bet Jesse's gonna get in some trouble."

"I'll explain later. He'll understand why we did it this way."

"So do you think he's going to be at his apartment?"

"Do you?" Alex asked.

Kessel thought for a moment. "No, I guess not. He wouldn't take Megan there."

"Exactly. This is just a starting point. Maybe we'll find something there that will point us in the right direction."

A few minutes later, as they turned onto the road that led to Marshall's apartment, he was blinded by a pair of headlights. The first he had seen since they left the department. As he watched them recede, he thought for a moment that he had seen Angela Olmsted in the front seat.

He shook his head. Lack of sleep was messing with his brain.

35

Twenty Minutes Earlier

Stephen was growing uneasy. They were headed toward Spencer Marshall's apartment, which was on the west side of town. There were very few vehicles out tonight, which told him that they probably shouldn't be out either. A couple of times he had picked up his phone and debated calling Alex, but he knew he couldn't when Angela was around. If he called and she found out, Stephen had no doubt that she would leave him stranded somewhere.

Angela turned left onto a side street that was buried under several inches of snow. Lights shone from the apartment building, a safe haven from the harsh weather.

Angela parked the Jeep in an empty spot and turned to Stephen. "Again, follow my lead. For some reason, I don't think he's going to be here, but you never know." She had shoved her small pistol into her pants at the small of her back. "Do you want to take yours?"

He concealed his pistol, and they got out of the car. It was hard to tell, but Stephen thought the snow had lightened up just a little bit. Even so, it was still coming down pretty heavily.

"How are we going to get in?" he asked as they approached the door. "I mean, Marshall's not just going to buzz us in."

"Don't worry." Angela pushed the button for a 'C. Merrick.' "I've got some friends here."

Friends? His mother had hardly had any friends when he was growing up. Where had all of these friends come from?

200

The door clicked, and Angela pulled it open. Spencer Marshall's apartment was #212, so they headed for the stairs. Stephen had the same feeling Angela had. Marshall wasn't going to be here. He was probably out in the woods. Not holed up in his apartment.

"Here goes," Angela said. They had reached #212. She knocked hard at the door three times. They waited ten seconds, but there was no noise from inside. Angela reached into her pocket and pulled out a paperclip. "Cover me," she said, inserting it into the keyhole.

"When did you learn to pick a lock?"

"It doesn't matter, Stephen. Please."

Stephen looked down the hallway. Seeing nobody, he pulled the gun out from his pants. He held it in front of him, eased off the safety. His heart was pounding. The door swung open, and he raised the handgun, ready to fire if provoked. The living room was empty. A doorway led to the right, and one at the back of the living room.

"Check over there." Angela pointed toward the corner. "I'll check the kitchen."

Ten seconds later they met back in the living room. The place was empty. It was small, with a living room, a decent sized kitchen, and a bedroom and bathroom. Plenty of space for a man who lived alone, Stephen figured.

Angela shoved her pistol back in her pants. "Look." She pointed to the wall above the TV. Stephen followed her finger. He didn't notice anything extraordinary at first, but as they moved closer, he realized that all the framed photos were of the same person. Some of them were when the woman was younger, but it was easy to tell that it was the same person in each picture. There were at least forty photographs, maybe more.

"Who do you suppose it is?" Angela asked, taking one of the pictures off of its hook and examining it.

"I bet it's his mother." He pointed to a young boy who was sitting on the woman's lap in one photo. The boy appeared in several other pictures, but most of them were of the woman alone.

"Why do you think he has all of these up?" Stephen wondered aloud. "No offense, to you, but what guy has forty pictures of his mom up on the wall?"

Angela smiled briefly, but then turned serious again. "I don't know. Nothing about this guy is normal. I'm not even going to try to figure him out."

"So do we have any idea where he might have gone?" Stephen asked, turning away from the photos.

"He clearly loves his mother." Angela said it with a hint of resentment. "At least that's one good thing about him."

"Hold on." Stephen held up his hand. He wasn't going to let that comment slide. "You were hard to love. Especially these past couple years. So don't blame the state of our relationship on me."

"I did my best." She turned to face him. "Where were you when Will died?"

"I *tried* to be there for you, but you just shoved me away." Stephen's anger was building. He had pictured them having the discussion eventually, but not like this.

"I was grieving. You came for the funeral and then you just disappeared."

"I was with you for over a week and we barely spoke." He took a deep breath. "I have a life, mom. I decided to move on. You didn't."

She reached forward and he instinctively stepped back, thinking she was going to strike him. "I needed someone to help me, and you weren't there."

He started a rebuttal, but she held up her hand and stopped him. "We can talk about this later. There's more important things to do right now." She disappeared into the kitchen.

Stephen stood there for a moment, baffled. He didn't understand his mother. You could live with someone for eighteen years and not really know them. And he was slowly coming to the realization that he didn't know his mother, and hadn't known his father.

He followed Angela into the kitchen, staying a few feet away from her. The kitchen was about the size of the living room, and was almost spotless. Unusual for a man living alone.

Or maybe it was just that way because Marshall hadn't been home in a while. He was leaning toward the latter.

"Take a look at this," Angela said. She was standing near the table, which was tucked in near the window.

The post-it-note was stuck to the middle of the table. An address was written on it. '1451 Highland Ranch Road.' It was written in black ink, the handwriting neat and large.

Angela rubbed her thumb across the ink. It didn't smudge. "This is out by Castle Creek," she said, grabbing the post-it. "Near where Erin Carver was discovered."

Stephen glanced out the window down to the parking lot. To get to Highland Ranch Road they had to take County Road 15 south out of Aspen. That road gained in elevation, had narrow shoulders and a couple switchbacks. With snow, it became one of the most dangerous roads in Pitkin County. The fact that it was dark out just made it worse.

He took another deep breath. There was no way this was going to end well. "I'm going to call Alex. We should *not* go out there by ourselves."

Angela was at the door already. "I'm going, with or without you. There's nothing you can do to stop me. If you want to stay here, be my guest."

"I'll call the sheriff. He'll set up a roadblock. There's only one way down there."

"You wouldn't."

"I'm trying to keep you safe. Us safe. Because I know the only way you'll stop is if you're dead. Or in jail. And I have to make sure neither of those happen. Well, the first, at least."

"I'm leaving." She opened the door. "If you haven't caught up to me by the parking lot, I'm assuming you've turned on me. I guess I'll see you when this is all over."

No way was he staying here. He had to protect his mother. Or at least try. He shut the door as he left and hurried down the hallway. He quickly dialed Alex's number, but it went to voicemail. Stephen explained their situation in as few words as he could and stepped outside. His mother had just reached the Jeep. Stephen hurried across the parking lot and got inside just before she put the Jeep in reverse.

203

As they pulled out onto the road, a pair of oncoming headlights appeared, and as they passed, Stephen could make out two men in the vehicle. The driver looked a little bit like Alex, but it wasn't Alex's truck. He just hoped that Alex, wherever he was, got Stephen's message sooner rather than later and was able to catch up with them.

"We don't know what we're walking into here," Angela cautioned, slowing down as they passed through the first stoplight on Highway 82. "It's odd that that piece of paper was just sitting on the table, waiting to be found. Be extremely alert and do not hesitate to shoot."

"I'll tell you what we're walking into," he responded. "A trap. The address was sitting right there in plain sight. Marshall's going to be waiting for us."

"Stop worrying," she ordered, turning off the highway. "I know how to handle a firearm, and I know you do too."

Stephen did, but he answered with another question. "So what's going to happen if we do find this guy? Are you just going to shoot him?"

"You nailed it."

"I know what he did, but you can't just kill him. You'll go to prison." Stephen was getting even more worried, wondering when his mother had gotten this crazy. "Doesn't that make you just as bad as him?"

"Maybe. But I'm killing him for a good reason. He killed my husband. And once I do, this burden's going to be off me, and I'm going to get out of this town. I think I'll move to Alaska. Just be in the wilderness by myself for a few years. I've always wanted to do that."

He prayed that Alex would get the message. He would do whatever he could to stop Angela from killing this man, but he couldn't guarantee that he would be successful. The justice system had its flaws, but Stephen figured the police had more than enough to lock Marshall up for the rest of his life.

They were now south of town on a particularly narrow stretch of the road. Mountains rose up on either side, their slopes not visible in the dark. County Road 15 was the primary route to Ashcroft, an old mining town that was now all but deserted. Occasionally tourists would head down there but most were focused on the Maroon Bells or other, more popular attractions, such as Crystal Mill.

He slid against the window as Angela took a curve much too fast. It was a surprise that they hadn't been in an accident in the past few days, the way she had been driving.

"Slow down," he warned. "Unless you want to get us killed before we even get there."

Surprisingly, she listened to his advice. The headlights were on full beam, the wipers brushing the snow away, but visibility was still greatly reduced. Up ahead he saw the turnoff for Highland Ranch Road. Angela hit the brakes and slid into the turn.

The driveway cut into a thick stand of pines, a narrow track barely wide enough for the jeep. There were no other houses nearby. Snow was piled high across what would have been the driveway, but Stephen could make out a pair of tire tracks that hadn't been completely covered by the snow. Which meant that someone had been here recently. Or was still here.

Angela turned off the car once they were a couple hundred feet down the driveway. She turned to him, the overhead light illuminating her face, and he looked away, unable to meet her eyes.

"I've been looking forward to this."

36

He made yet another stop. Paul hoped it would be his last. It was getting late, now approaching seven o'clock. He parked on the street in front of Clayton King's house, which was only a stone's throw from downtown Aspen. And it looked like luck was finally on his side, because Clayton King was out snow-blowing his driveway. Which was a little odd, considering it was dark out and the storm was far from over, but he didn't care. King was home, and that was all that mattered.

King turned off the blower as Paul started up the driveway. He was a tall man, with thick, dark hair that fell to his shoulders. If not for the different skin color, he might resemble Hal Jenkins. His mother was white and his father, who was of African descent, had left the family when King was young. Despite his tough upbringing, he had attended a local community college and graduated with a business degree and was now married with two young children. Both he and King attended Christ Episcopal Church, which was how they had gotten to know each other.

A sudden bright line shone in his face, and he brought up his hand to block it. "Paul? Is that you?"

"Yeah. Turn off that light."

King pointed the flashlight toward the ground, but didn't switch it off. "I thought I recognized your vehicle, but I wanted to be sure, with everything that's going on right now." King shone the light at him again. "You look cold. I don't imagine you came out here just for a friendly chat. You wanna head inside?"

He didn't want to spend too much time here, but he also realized that he could barely feel his toes. "Yeah, if you don't mind."

King turned and led him around to the back of the house, leaving the blower sitting in the middle of the half-cleared driveway.

King offered him coffee, but he didn't want any. Paul was just glad to get out of the cold. King's wife and two daughters were in the living room watching *The Lion King* and after greeting them, the two men had sat down at the dining room table.

"So what exactly can I help you with?" King repeated. "Again, I don't expect you came here just to visit." He glanced out the window behind Paul. "We've had so much snow, and the winter's only just begun. I wonder what the next few months are going to be like."

Paul enjoyed the weather, but now was not the time to talk about it. "You own some cabins out by Castle Creek, right?"

"Yeah. The Castle Creek Cabins. They're a few miles south on County Road 15. Why do you ask?"

He quickly explained why the cabins were of interest to him. King kept interrupting him with questions, and his impatience grew even more.

"Yeah, there's ten cabins out there. I rent them out in June, July, August, and September. They're full almost all the time, and there's a small building I use for check in and all that good stuff. This year was one of the best years for me."

"How many years have you owned them?"

"Geez." King scratched his head. "They were built a long time ago, but I think I've owned 'em for six, maybe seven years. Bought them from an older guy who'd had enough of the cold and was moving to Texas."

"Is there any other private property up there that you know of?"

King thought for a moment. "No, I think most of it is national forest land. It's pretty isolated up there. Don't mark my words, though."

"Okay." He tried to figure out what he needed to know. "Do you lock them up for the winter?"

"Of course. I winterize them, make sure everything is working properly. I don't get up there during the winter at all, because it's a dirt road that leads up the mountain and obviously it doesn't get plowed. The only people that might even get near them are the snowmobilers or cross country skiers. They're kind of hard to find unless you know exactly where to look."

Paul had lived here his whole life, and he never even knew about the cabins, so that proved that they were off the beaten path. He thought for a moment. If someone was using the cabins, they'd either have to pick the locks, or have a key.

"Do you have records of everyone who stayed there this past summer?"

"Sure," King said. "They're in my office. I'll go grab them."

He came back with a thick stack of papers, held together by a rubber band. "Here you go. So you think someone's been using my cabins?"

"It's definitely a possibility." Paul stood up to go, hoping that King got the point.

"You'll let me know if someone's been up there, right?"

"Yes, Clayton. Now I've really got to get going."

"Sure." He followed Paul outside. "I guess there's no point in doing any more blowing tonight. It can wait 'til tomorrow."

"Thanks for your help." He opened the door to his truck, fighting the wind.

King said something, but the wind took his words. Paul reached in his pocket and dug out his cell phone, dialing Charlie Porter's number.

"Hey." Charlie answered right away. "You've got to get back here."

"What's going on?"

"It's too complicated to explain over the phone. Where are you?"

"I'll be back in five minutes."

"Good. I called in some guys who were supposed to be on vacation. We're going to need every available man we can get."

"Charlie, what the hell is going on?"

"We've got a suspect, sheriff. Spencer Marshall. I think he's responsible for all of this."

"Before you explain all this to me, I need to talk to Vincent. Is he there with you?"

"Yeah. Why him?"

"I'm sending him out to check some cabins. I would send you, but sounds like you're in charge of whatever's going on there."

"Yeah, sheriff?" It was Vincent's voice.

He started the truck and headed back toward the center of town. "Vincent, I need you to go check out some cabins for me." He looked at the stack King had given him and read Vincent the address. "I don't have time to explain, I just need you to get up there and tell me what you find."

"Sure," Vincent said. "Do you need to talk to Charlie again?"

"No," he said, and hung up. He'd find out what was happening soon enough.

He parked his vehicle in back of the station a few minutes later. Inside, there was more activity than there had been all week. Porter wasn't kidding when he said he'd called in every available officer, and most of the activity was centered around the conference room. He ordered a few of the officers out, leaving the two FBI agents, Porter, Rollins, and Rockford. These were the people he trusted the most to have his back in a difficult situation like this.

"Jesse," he said, sitting down next to Porter, "where have you been?"

Rollins explained how they had gone to the home of Ethan Adams, and then related Adam's story.

"Why didn't you inform anybody that you were doing this?"

"Alex said it would take too long, and that it was better just for the three of us to go instead of taking time to form a plan."

He would talk with Alex later. Looking around the room, he realized that the detective wasn't present. "Where is he?"

All eyes turned back to Rollins, who sat uncomfortably in his chair.

"Well?"

"He and Kessel went to Spencer Marshall's apartment."

Before he pressed Rollins further, he needed to know who this Spencer Marshall was and why they suspected him for the murders. "Can someone please tell me who the hell Spencer Marshall is?"

Porter tossed a file in front of him, and he flipped through it, reading about the disappearance of Jessica Fisher. When he was finished, it all made perfect sense.

"What else do we know about this guy?"

"Not a lot," Porter answered. "He's worked at Aspen Machining for over ten years. Lives alone. Not much more to tell."

"Sheriff, were you working here when this woman disappeared?" Sommers asked.

He shook his head. "I moved here a few years after this occurred. Nobody ever mentioned it to me."

"Maybe a lid was put on it because of the investigation," Waschkin offered.

"What do you mean?"

"It doesn't appear as if your department put forth a massive effort to find the girl. More probably could have been done, and I'm guessing that's how Marshall felt."

"This is all in the past," Rockford pointed out. "Let's find Marshall and take him down."

Paul turned to Rollins. "So we know for sure that Marshall took Megan Adams?"

Rollins nodded. "She's gone."

"Do we really think Marshall would take her back to his apartment?" The question wasn't directed at anyone in particular.

"We have no better place to start, sheriff." Sommers spoke. "Here's what I suggest. Choose two of your men to accompany you to Marshall's apartment. Waschkin and I will come with you. I agree with you; it's unlikely that he'll be there, but we need to rule it out. We'll decide where to go from there."

He had no better ideas, and the way Sommers spoke, it sounded more like an order than a suggestion. "Fine."

"Choose two of your men. We'll be waiting out back."

He looked around the room. Rollins would be dealt with for his lack of responsibility. "Charlie and Stuart. Let's go."

He tried calling Alex again on the way out, but there was still no answer.

37

They were in and out of the apartment in about three minutes. He was in the kitchen when he checked his phone and saw the message from Stephen. That's when he started to get worried. Alex did some calculating. The vehicle he saw coming into the parking lot must have actually been Angela's. How had he not realized that? She and Stephen were probably about ten minutes ahead of Alex and Dylan. But those ten minutes could make all the difference. Things could change in a matter of seconds.

"Where are we going?" Kessel asked as they roared out of the parking lot.

"You remember the vehicle we saw when we pulled into the parking lot? That was Angela Olmsted. She was here before us, and she knows where Marshall is."

"So…" Kessel searched for the right words. "Where's she going?"

"Same place we are." He pointed to the address that he had plugged into the truck's GPS. "Highland Ranch Road."

"How do you know that's where she's going?"

"Because her son Stephen called me. We're friends, and that's how I know what Angela is up to. I'm guessing that Stephen had tried to stop her, but figured his best hope is to have me step in."

"So what are we going to find here?"

Alex shrugged, but knew Kessel couldn't see it in the dark. "Stephen said to get there as fast as we can. This could be where Marshall's holed up."

Kessel fell silent for the time being, probably trying to process everything that was happening. This was probably his first big case. Alex didn't know him well, but thought that they could be good friends. He'd never seen Kessel shoot and hoped the officer would have his back in case things went south.

They were on County Road 15 now, heading south. The road had not been plowed, which allowed him to see the fresh set of tire tracks that were in the southbound lane. He didn't know what he was going to do if he caught up to Angela and Stephen, but one of the thoughts on the top of his list was handcuff Angela to his vehicle. She was going to cause trouble unless she was locked up.

His phone rang suddenly, breaking the uncomfortable silence. It was Jesse Rollins. He put the phone on speaker and set it on the console next to him.

"They're gone," Rollins stated bluntly.

"Who?"

"The sheriff, FBI agents, and Rockford and Porter. They left me here."

"They're headed to the apartment, right?"

"Yeah. Porter called in every available officer, so this place is swarming."

Alex thought for a moment. "Are you alone?"

"Yeah. I'm sitting here in the conference room."

"Who's in charge right now?" Alex imagined Rollins opening the door and looking out.

"Wyatt, I would assume."

Good, Alex thought. At least it was somebody with a bit of sense. "Can you come meet us out here? I think we're going to need backup."

"You guys have my truck," he pointed out.

"You can use my car," Kessel suggested. "The keys are in the drawer of my desk."

"Okay. I'm going to slip out," Rollins said. "Where am I headed?" He paused. "I could get in some more trouble for this."

Alex gave him the address. "I'll handle Brown. Just be careful. I'll call you if there's anything else I know."

"I'll do the same," Rollins replied. "See you there."

213

"Here's the turnoff," Kessel said. Alex slowed down and swung the big vehicle onto the narrow road, the set of tire tracks still visible. The snow was slowing down a bit, but still accumulating.

A minute later, he saw the driveway. It was hidden well by trees, but again, the tire tracks showed him the way. Angela's vehicle, a Jeep Grand Cherokee, was parked about a hundred yards down the driveway. He pulled up behind it and turned off the engine.

****

On the other side of town, Paul Brown stood in Spencer Marshall's apartment. Agent Sommers was downstairs talking to the landlord. Waschkin and his officers were out in the hall, talking to neighbors. He was waiting for a call back from Deputy Wyatt, who was in charge back at the station. Like he'd expected, Marshall hadn't been home. And Alex still wasn't answering his cell phone.

Porter shoved the door open behind him. Despite the long hours his deputy had been working, he showed no signs of fatigue.

"Neighbors didn't see anything," he reported. "Marshall mainly kept to himself, seemed like a nice enough guy. Nobody's seen him around here since last Thursday."

That was the day before Daniel was killed. "He's gotta be holed up somewhere."

"Where?" Porter asked the question that everyone wanted to know.

"I don't know, dammit," he said.

His cell phone finally rang. He stepped away from Porter and brought it up to his ear.

"I did what you asked." There was a hint of excitement in Wyatt's voice. "The only relative he's got here is his mother. She lives off of County Road 15, south of town. And get this; she drives a red Chevy Cruze. Or used to, anyway. She died last Thursday."

214

Alex had talked about triggers, and he figured that this must be Marshall's. Once his mother died, he snapped. And the fact that her house was south of town just solidified the case.

"Give me the address," he ordered.

"1451 Highland Ranch Road. It's about fifteen minutes from your location, maybe a little longer with the snow."

"Okay." He tried to quickly formulate a plan in his mind. "Grab some guys and meet me there. Make sure you're heavily armed. And make sure Rollins comes with you."

"About that…" Wyatt's voice trailed away. "I don't know where he is."

"What do you mean? The building's not that big."

"What I'm saying is that he's not here. He was in the conference room when you left, and I was going to go in and talk to him but he wasn't there. Amanda said she thought she saw him head out the back door, but she wasn't positive."

Was he losing control of his officers? "Forget about him. He's going to be in a lot of trouble after this. Just get some guys together and meet me out there You got that?"

"Yes sir."

Paul shoved the phone back into his pocket and headed for the door. Porter followed him. "Do you have a lead?"

"Yeah. Go find Stuart and get out to the car. I'll get the agents and meet you there."

He almost collided with them as they were coming up the stairs. Sommers must have seen the urgency in his face, because he asked, "Something wrong?"

"No. We actually got a break for once. We think Marshall is out at his mother's place. She died about a week ago, and she owned a red Chevy Cruze that he might be using."

"Where's this place?"

"About fifteen minutes south of here. There's some rugged terrain out that way."

Sommers looked around him. "Where are your guys?"

"They're waiting at the car."

"Good. You call for backup?"

"Yeah."

He had a bad feeling as they drove out of the parking lot.

215

38

Vincent drove slowly up toward the cabins. He couldn't see where the road was, because it was buried under at least a foot of snow. There was a set of fairly fresh tire tracks, otherwise he would have turned around. Now he wished he had, because the Explorer was struggling up the steep mountain. But turning out of the tracks would almost definitely result in him getting stuck, so the only way he could get back down to the road was to back up, staying in the tracks. He couldn't do that in the dark, so he continued up.

About ten minutes later, the ground leveled out and a small structure came into view. He parked alongside it and hopped out of the car, leaving the engine running.

This was the check-in building, he surmised. There was a sign out front that likely said the name of the place, but the front of it was covered with snow. The tire tracks he had been following led to the left of the building. He couldn't tell in the dark, but it looked like a path might lead to the right as well.

The sheriff had told him to check out the cabins, and he didn't really know what that meant. Should he go inside? He pulled on the door, but it was locked. Vincent decided to continue following the tracks. Someone had been up here recently, and that in itself was suspicious.

He got back in the Explorer and drove to the left of the building. Almost immediately a cabin appeared to his left. The tire tracks kept on going, and he followed them. He formed a plan; he would see where these tracks led, and if necessary, come back and check all these cabins.

He drove past a second cabin; then a third, and a fourth. As the fifth cabin came into view, the tracks swung left and stopped in front of the small cabin. Vincent stopped about thirty feet in front of the cabin, debating what to do. The tracks were fairly new, probably made within the last couple hours, but it didn't look as if anyone was here. Then he saw it. His headlights illuminated the back right tail light of a vehicle. He turned off the engine, got out of the car, and drew his pistol. The truck was hidden on the left side of the cabin, and he could have easily missed it in the dark. He found a flashlight in the glove box and shone it on the truck. It was old, made sometime in the 1990's. It was covered under several inches of snow, but underneath that was a layer of dirt and dust. He walked around to the driver's side and tried the door. It was locked. He peered inside, shining the light around. The interior looked surprisingly clean, besides something long and black on the backseat. He quickly realized that it was a rifle case. And he was suddenly one hundred percent sure that this was Marshall's truck. Was Marshall around here somewhere, watching him?

He instinctively pulled out his cell phone to call for backup, but realized that he had no service. To go back into town, get backup, and drive back up here would take at least an hour. That was too much time. He had to do this on his own.

He turned the flashlight off and moved around to the back of the structure. There was a large area of open, windswept land behind the cabin, and beyond that was the forest. The mountains rose high in the distance, their dark silhouettes barely visible. The snow was still coming down, but it had lost some of its intensity.

He stepped into a rut and shone his flashlight at the ground. It was a snowmobile track, heavily used by the looks of it. He raised his light and cast it out toward the forest. The track was clearly visible, making a straight path toward the trees.

His gut told him that Marshall was gone, but Vincent used extreme caution checking the small cabin. Marshall wasn't there, nor was Megan Adams.

He was alone.

39

Alex hurried up the driveway, followed closely by Dylan Kessel. His feet sank into the deep snow with every step and his shoes were filled with snow by the time they were a hundred yards from the truck.

He was desperately searching the dark for Stephen and Angela. Alex figured he and Kessel weren't more than five minutes behind them. His driving had gotten them here fast; but he figured Angela had done some reckless driving as well. If he didn't stop her, she was going to get herself killed; or worse yet, get Stephen killed.

The driveway was long, and about two minutes later, he saw a light in the dark. At first he thought that they were approaching the house, but then he saw that the light was moving. Away from them. The only explanation he could think of was that it was a flashlight, and the person holding it had to be either Angela or Stephen. He turned to Kessel to point it out, but noticed that the other officer had seen it as well.

They started to run, the going difficult because of the snow. As they got closer, Alex saw a several more lights through the trees. Maybe that was the house.

Three hundred yards further, the driveway straightened out, and Alex could now tell that the house was up ahead and to the left. He could also see that the bobbing light was less than a hundred feet ahead of them. And he could tell from the thin glow that it was two figures; Stephen and Angela. Alex breathed a sigh of relief. Now he had to figure out the best way to confront Angela.

"Hey," he said, loud enough for them to hear. He could see that Stephen stopped moving, but Angela and the light didn't.

"Alex," she said, her voice calm and steady. "I was hoping it wouldn't come to this."

"So was I." He picked up the pace again to a fast walk. "I'm going to have to ask you to stop walking."

"And I'm going to have to ask you to stay away from me." She stopped and turned around. They were now only fifty yards apart.

He ignored her and kept walking. "You're a civilian, Angela. I don't want you to get hurt."

"I said stop." She articulated every word. When he didn't, she reached behind her back and pulled something out. A gun, Alex realized quickly, and stopped in his tracks. Behind him, he heard Kessel draw his gun and click the safety off.

Alex held his hand up behind him, motioning for Kessel to stay put. They both wore Kevlar vests, so he wasn't too worried about his own safety. Would Angela actually shoot him? He doubted it, but all of her actions to this point had been unpredictable. She was capable of anything. He knew that under no circumstances could he let Kessel shoot her. That would create a huge mess of its own.

"Let's talk," he said, keeping his voice even. "We both want the same thing."

"I don't think so," she said, continuing to move toward the house. Stephen walked in that direction as well, as if he were unsure what to do. Alex took a few tentative steps forward, and heard Kessel do the same behind him.

"We both want Marshall. I can promise you that he'll be locked up for the rest of his life."

"I'm done trusting the justice system." She continued her backwards walk toward the house, now emerging from the trees. The house was a few hundred yards away, the driveway not visible underneath all the snow. It sat in a large clearing, with an open backyard. The forest made a sort of ring around the house, with hills rising up beyond. They were now out in the open, and if Marshall was watching, he would have an easy shot.

"Angela," he said, urgency in his voice. "You're out in the open. If Marshall's watching, you're an easy target."

She hesitated, considering his statement for a moment.

"Mom," Stephen said, stepping toward her. "Come on. You've gone far enough."

"Stephen," Alex said, starting to get angry. "Come here. You're a target also. If she wants to get herself killed, so be it."

Stephen walked toward him without hesitating. "You're on your own. I've stuck with you this far, but I'm done."

Alex admired him for finally standing up to his mother. But Stephen hadn't taken more than three steps toward him when a loud crack rang out. It was as if he could see the bullet, its trajectory from the forest opposite them. And a jolt ran through Alex as he realized that he might lose another friend.

****

For the first few seconds, the only thing he felt was a tingling sensation in his fingers. The force of the bullet knocked him to the ground, and he lay in the cold snow, struggling to breathe. Then the pain erupted in his chest, and it was unlike anything he'd ever experienced. It felt like he was on fire, unable to move or breathe. His eyes were open, but all he could see was black. Stephen was briefly aware of the others surrounding him before he started to drift into sleep.

Then he felt something cold on his face. It felt good and bad at the same time. He realized that it was snow, and he tried to reach up and brush it off, but his arm wouldn't move.

"Keep him awake," he heard a voice say, but it sounded distant, and he couldn't tell who it was. He didn't want to stay awake. He felt exhausted, and his breath was coming shallow and fast. His eyes closed once more, and all feeling disappeared.

****

Alex knelt over Stephen. There had only been a single shot, and about thirty seconds had passed since then. He wasn't worried for his own safety. He was entirely focused on Stephen and making sure he didn't lose another one of his friends. Alex

220

tried to remember his medical training, but his mind couldn't focus.

He unzipped Stephen's jacket and discovered what he feared most; the bullet had entered Stephen's chest. Stephen had already lost a lot of blood, his shirt now a dark red. Alex tore the thick fabric and located the wound. It was a bloody mess, and in the dark, he wasn't sure where exactly the bullet had entered.

In the background, he could hear Kessel talking on his radio, calling an ambulance. He didn't know where Angela had gone, nor did he care. All of his senses were focused on the one job in front of him.

Alex had no obvious item to stop the bleeding, so he quickly pulled off his jacket and folded it into a small square, pressing it over the wound. With his left hand, he felt for Stephen's pulse. It was faint, but at least it was there. Stephen's eyes were closed, and he was no longer responding to Alex.

Kessel knelt down beside him. "Ambulance is ten minutes out. What do you need me to do?"

"Hold this for a second." He let Kessel apply the force to the wound. Alex turned around, taking a deep breath. Angela stood behind him, her expression unreadable in the dark.

"Is he going to die?" she asked, her voice trembling.

"I don't know." He tried to keep his emotions under control. "Do you have any medical training?"

"No. I'd just get in the way." She trailed off. She turned around and Alex heard her start to cry behind him.

Alex wanted to yell at her, tell her that this was her fault. That none of this would have happened if it weren't for her. But he didn't have time for that. Another sound split the night, the unmistakable sound of a snowmobile. And he realized that Spencer Marshall was once again getting away.

"Go," Angela said from behind him.

"What?"

She pointed toward the house, and Alex saw a decent sized shed behind it. "There's bound to be another snowmobile or four-wheeler in there. Stephen's fate is out of our hands now. I'm trusting you to go get this guy."

Alex started to protest, but Kessel interrupted him. "There's nothing to be done here, Alex. This may be our only chance to get Marshall. Go."

He was torn. If Stephen ended up dying, he wanted to be here. But he also realized that this could be his one and only chance to catch Marshall.

He hesitated for a second more, then turned and ran for the shed.

40

Vincent stood in the small cabin, unsure what to do. Now that he had confirmed that Marshall wasn't here, it seemed that the logical thing would be to go back into town, or at least down the mountain far enough so that he got some sort of signal to make a call. He cursed himself for not bringing a radio along.

The cabin was cozy and modern. There was a main living area and a kitchen with a stove and oven, and a single bedroom off the side. It was evident that someone had been here recently; a few dishes on the table and some other little things out of place. The cabin wasn't boarded up like it should've been in the winter. And it was warm inside; not seventy degrees, but more like fifty. A lot warmer than it was outside, and definitely warmer than it should be in here, considering how cold the past few days had been. That meant that the heat had been on recently. Marshall had probably been here earlier in the day. But was he still around?

Vincent headed back outside and walked around to the back of the cabin again. His eyes followed the snowmobile trail, and he wondered where it went. It headed directly west from the cabin, but he knew that once it got into the trees it could twist and turn and end up anywhere.

He shone the flashlight back toward his left when something caught his eye. Behind and to the right of the truck, at the very edge of the trees, his light had caught something. He walked toward the truck, his light centering in on the object. It was a four-wheeler, hidden partially by the snow weighing down on the pines. It was plain luck that he had noticed it. And another stroke of luck; the key was in the ignition.

Vincent glanced back at the cabin. The only way Marshall could get back here was if he came by snowmobile. And if Vincent cut off that route, maybe he could trap him somewhere.

He turned the key, and the engine roared to life. The gas gauge read empty, but he prayed that it was wrong and that he would have enough gas to get wherever he was going. He navigated the four wheeler onto the snowmobile track and sped toward the woods.

****

Stephen slept. He dreamt about his father and his past. He couldn't distinguish one dream from another, couldn't remember exactly what they were about. All he knew was that if felt good to sleep, and the pain went away when he closed his eyes.

Then he felt a sharp pain in his chest, and suddenly he was back in Aspen, lying in the cold snow. The pain was more intense now, and he squeezed his eyes shut once more, trying to block it out.

"Can't… breathe," he managed to say.

"The ambulance is almost here," he heard a voice say. It didn't sound like Alex, but he didn't open his eyes to see who it was.

He tried to stay calm, but the pain overwhelmed him. He thought of Mariah. He didn't want to leave her, didn't want his life to be over so early. But as he tried to inhale for another breath, he couldn't find any air, and he felt everything start to fade away. He heard sirens in the distance and a voice say, "Hold on, Stephen," but everything turned black once more.

****

The sheriff was approaching the turnoff for Highland Ranch Road when he saw a pair of flashing lights behind him.

224

As he slowed and pulled to the side of the road, an ambulance flew past him, turning ahead of him onto Highland Ranch Road.

"What the hell?" Sommers said from the backseat, breaking the silence.

He sped up and took the right turn, staying a few hundred yards behind the ambulance. His fears were confirmed when it turned at 1451, the home of Spencer Marshall's late mother. Either Alex or Dylan had been shot, and he knew that's what everyone else in the vehicle was thinking.

He turned onto the driveway, which was covered by a thick layer of snow. The storm, for the most part, had moved east, leaving only light snow showers in its wake. Three vehicles were parked a few hundred yards down the driveway. He recognized Jesse Rollins' truck and Dylan Kessel's SUV, but the third, a jeep, looked unfamiliar. Until he remembered the meeting he'd had with Angela Olmsted last Monday. She had driven a jeep, and it looked remarkably similar to this one. The flame of anger in his chest was replaced by worry and confusion. If she was here...

They pulled up behind the ambulance about a minute later. The large house sat in the middle of the forest, with a big, open yard and ringed by trees on all sides. All the activity was centered twenty feet to his left. He turned off the car and jumped out, his heart pounding.

He came closer, but was unable to see what was going on because of the ring of paramedics. Kessel was kneeling on the ground and Angela stood to the left of him. He didn't see Alex, or Jesse Rollins, for that matter. He caught Kessel's eye and motioned him to step aside for a conversation.

"Who is it?" he asked, as soon as they were out of earshot.

"Her son. He got shot." Even in the dark, Paul could see that Kessel had blood all over his hands. "I don't know if he's going to make it."

"What happened?" He spoke as calmly as he could. "Start from the time you and Alex got here."

"They were here ahead of us. Alex and I caught up to them right before we broke from the trees. Alex confronted Angela, and she pulled a gun out. He tried to convince her to let

225

him handle it, but she kept moving closer to the house, into the open. Stephen had stepped away from her to come join us when he was hit. It was just a single shot. It was probably, I don't know, ten or fifteen minutes ago."

"Where's Alex?"

"Marshall escaped on a snowmobile. Alex went after him."

"Go tell this to Porter. I'll join you guys in a second." First, he had to confront Angela, and he didn't want Kessel to be nearby."

"Angela," he said, returning to the circle of paramedics. They were now loading Stephen's body onto a stretcher, and Paul caught a glimpse of him. His eyes were closed, and he wasn't moving at all. The medics rushed him to the hospital, one of them beginning CPR. The sirens were still blaring, cutting through the calm night.

She turned around slowly. They were only a few feet away from each other. He could see tears on her cheeks, but felt no sympathy for her.

"I hope you're happy with what just happened. You've been asking for this."

"I found him before you guys, and I don't have many men or resources at my disposal. What does that tell you?" Even in the midst of tragedy she was still defiant.

"I have no idea what you've done this past week, but I'll find out soon enough. Right now, you're going back into town and then I'll decide what I'm going to do."

"My son was just shot. Don't you think that's punishment enough?"

"Rockford," he called to the officer. "Come here."

The officer broke away from the FBI agents. "What?"

"Take Angela back to town. Make sure she stays away from this place. Then get back up here."

"Yes, sir." He directed Angela back toward the vehicles. "Come on, Angela."

Angela? He could call her Angela, because they knew each other fairly well. But Stuart? He had a sudden uneasy feeling, and it wasn't only because Marshall was still out there.

226

A vehicle pulled up next to him, and he saw that it was his backup. Five more officers hopped out of the vehicle, each armed. He quickly briefed them on the situation.

"Fan out and search these woods," he ordered. "Use extreme caution. It sounds like he left on a snowmobile, but he definitely could have doubled back."

"Sheriff," Sommers said, "we should search the house. This Adams woman could be in there."

He had completely forgot about Megan Adams. "Let's go," he said.

Before they reached the front door, he dropped back to speak with Kessel. "Has Jesse shown up here?"

"Yeah. He arrived right before you guys. He had some cross country skis and was going after Alex and Marshall."

Though he was still angry at Rollins, he knew the deputy was a good shot and a quick thinker. If anyone could help Alex, it was Jesse.

There was a loud crash from inside, distracting him from the conversation. Sommers put a finger to his lips, and on the count of three, turned and threw the door open.

41

There had been two snowmobiles in the shed, along with a mess of other things. It had taken him a couple minutes to find a key, but once he did, Alex started the machine and drove out into the woods. He had used his jacket to stop Stephen's bleeding, and he had no hat or gloves either. The snow had all but stopped, but the wind was still strong, blowing the fluffy powder right into his face. He ignored the stinging pain, intent on catching up to Marshall. Alex figured he wasn't more than three or four minutes behind him.

He tried to focus on the task at hand, but his thoughts kept drifting back to Stephen. The shot had come from the other side of the woods, which was a pretty long and difficult shot, especially in the dark. It had sounded like a rifle, but Alex wasn't completely sure. Had Marshall been aiming for Stephen, or had he just taken a shot in the dark, attempting to hit anybody? Alex wasn't sure. He knew that if Stephen didn't make it, he was going to blame himself, just like he blamed himself for Jarred's death. One thing was certain; Marshall had been expecting them, and they had walked straight into his ambush. Where he was headed now, Alex had no idea. There was a lot of open land up here, and Marshall could easily lose him. Alex was following the lone snowmobile track right now, but if the trail branched out, he would be guessing at where Marshall had gone.

One question kept surfacing in his mind; How had Angela known? The one option he could think of was that Stuart Rockford had called and told her. But that seemed very unlikely, because it didn't benefit him. And how would he have known that they would end up at Marshall's mother's place? She hadn't reported anything to him; he hadn't really expected that she would keep up her end of the agreement. But the question kept nagging him, and he wanted an answer.

The trail gradually ascended, twisting through the dense forest. Trees flew by him, the speedometer pushing fifty. He was flying blindly around these curves, but his only chance at catching Marshall was to go fast. His heart dropped as he saw what was up ahead. A split. He stopped the snowmobile, leaving the machine idling. Both tracks looked fresh. He knew if he chose wrong, they could lose Marshall forever.

****

Vincent was a less than a mile east of Alex, driving the four wheeler at a little slower speed, using caution on the narrow trail. The lights were on, but they were weak, only casting a glow a few feet in front of him. He'd only been on the trail for a few minutes, but it felt like forever. Elevation had remained level since leaving the cabin, but up ahead, he could tell that it started to descend. He knew that if he kept going west, he would come across a county road. Either the trail ended before there, or it curved back to the south or north.

Vincent had never actually driven a four wheeler, which was odd for having grown up in the west. He'd feel a lot more comfortable if he were on a snowmobile. But he'd had no choice.

These thoughts disappeared from his head when he collided with something and heard the crash of metal. Suddenly he was airborne, his body somersaulting in the dark. He lay on the ground, the wind knocked out of him, trying to recover his breath.

****

"Sheriff, you check the basement," Agent Sommers ordered, taking control of the situation. "I'll check upstairs, you three spread out and check this floor."

Paul hurried toward the stairway, not happy at being ordered around in his own county. Six descending stairs were visible, the other six to the left of the landing. He made it to the first landing and stopped, drawing his firearm. Based on what Kessel had told him, it seemed unlikely that Marshall was here, but maybe he had doubled back.

He was about to take the next stairs when he heard something. It was barely audible, and sounded like something scuffling around. He inched down the stairs, listening intently. He stopped on the last stair to listen again. This time he heard breathing, short and shallow. It sounded like the other person was just on the other side of the wall. He held his pistol out in front of him, ready to fire if need be. He took a deep breath and swung around to confront the person.

He stood face to face with a terrified Megan Adams. She held a small lamp over her head, but she let if fall to the ground when she saw him. He loosened his grip on the trigger, realizing how close he had come to pulling it.

"Sheriff," she cried, dropping to her knees. "Oh my God, I thought it was him." Besides being frightened out of her wits, she looked all right.

Megan," he said, kneeling down beside her, "are you okay?"

"I'm fine." Her fingers drifted to her forehead. "Besides this. It hurts a little but nothing serious."

"Are you sure?" he asked.

She nodded. "Yeah." She looked up the stairs. "Is Ethan here?"

"No."

She turned around, surprised. "Why not?"

"He went off the road when he was chasing after you. I wouldn't let him come up here. He's in the hospital right now, getting treated and having some tests done."

"How serious is it?"

"Nothing too bad. I'm sure he'll be relieved to know that you're okay."

The two agents and Porter had finished their search and were gathered in the foyer, discussing something quietly. All three looked up when he and Megan entered.

"He broke in when I was cooking dinner," she said. "He must have knocked me unconscious, because when I woke up, I was in the kitchen here, tied to a chair. He seemed troubled. He never said anything to me and kept pacing around."

"How long has it been since he went outside?"

"I don't know. Maybe fifteen minutes."

He saw Sommers and Waschkin exchanged a glance. "Do you have someone who can take her into town?"

Paul looked to Kessel. "Sure," he said. "Do you want me to come back here when I'm done?"

"Yeah. Make it quick." The two of them left, and he watched out the window as they headed down the invisible driveway.

Inside, there was an uncomfortable silence until Agent Sommers finally spoke. "How well do you know Megan Adams?"

"Me?" Paul asked? He wasn't sure if the question was directed at him or Porter.

"Either of you. Just tell me about her."

He thought it was an odd question, but answered as best as he could. "I've known her husband for over ten years. I haven't gotten to know her too well, but she seems nice enough. She's a psychologist, no kids. I don't know what else I can tell you."

"This all seems just a little suspicious to me. She wasn't nervous at all. And her demeanor just now was so calm, as if nothing out of the ordinary had happened. This is just a theory, but what if the two of them were working together?"

"That's the biggest load of bullshit I've ever heard," Porter scoffed. "Ethan and I have been friends for a decade, and our wives are good friends as well. There is no way in hell that she's a part of this. She's a psychologist, for God's sake. Maybe she knows how to deal with her fear."

"Working together?" Paul didn't believe it for a second either. "This whole time, we've been maintaining the belief that Marshall's worked alone. Why would he need a partner?"

"Like I said, it's just a thought." Sommers held up his hands. "I'm sorry if I offended you."

Porter turned away, disgusted. "I can't believe you might actually think that. You don't know the people around here."

"Megan wasn't a part of this, okay?" Paul said, before Porter got too worked up. "But there is one thing that has been bothering me."

"What?" Sommers tone indicated that he didn't really care what Paul was about to say. He was starting to dislike these agents more and more. He wondered if Alex dealt with guys like this.

"Why wasn't Ethan shot? In the case of Carver and Preston, they were both killed before their wives were abducted. Why was this different?"

"She said her husband was downstairs, right?" Waschkin said. "Maybe he would have heard Marshall coming."

"I thought that same thing," Porter said, "but I've been thinking about the disappearance of his girlfriend. She went missing, and he had to deal with the pain. Maybe Marshall wanted Ethan to feel the pain of losing his wife, just like he felt."

It was a valid conclusion. Then something came to him. "Ethan was the last officer involved in that investigation." He turned to Porter. "What if he's going back into town to take care of him and then getting out of here?"

Porter was already dialing Ethan's number.

42

Stuart Rockford slid into the driver's seat of her jeep. They were short on vehicles up here, which was why they had to use hers. She could tell that he was angry at her, especially when he shoved her roughly once they were out of sight of the sheriff.

He didn't say anything to her until they were onto County Road 15. Now that the snow had stopped, the plows were out, clearing away the heavy snow that covered the pavement. The wind was still strong, blowing some snow back onto areas of the road that had been plowed. Angela looked at her phone. It was only nine, but it felt much later. This had to be the longest night ever. And it had barely just begun.

"I hope you know that this is all your fault," he said, slowing down noticeably. That meant he wanted to talk, and she didn't really want to, nor did she feel comfortable alone with him. Stuart was not somebody she wanted to cross. She prided herself on not being afraid of much, but he was one person that she was truly scared of.

"You think I don't know that?" There was an emptiness in her chest, much like what she had felt when Will died. Stephen was probably the only person left on earth that she actually loved. A lot of people considered her hard and distant. Which, in a way, was true. If Stephen ended up dying, she didn't know what she would do. She had been raised to be strong and steady despite the challenges she was facing, but she didn't know if she could do it anymore.

"I'm making sure you know it, and I'm going to keep reminding you of it." He turned to her, which was a little unsettling because the road conditions weren't good. She wanted to yell at him to pay attention, but knew he wouldn't listen to her.

"You ruined this for both of us. If you had only called me, things would have turned out so much differently. Marshall would be dead. You'd have this burden off your shoulders. I'd be a local hero. Your son would still be alive."

It jarred her to hear him say that. "He's not dead."

"Not yet, at least. I've seen people shot before. From what I gathered, Stephen was shot right in the chest. Not many people survive that. The odds aren't very good, maybe one in ten. It's a pity, because it's all your fault." He articulated the last three words, as if he was making sure to get his point across.

She wanted to cry, but not in front of this man. "Stop *saying* that."

They had reached the city limits of Aspen, and lights from town sparkled in the distance. Nobody in town knew what had just happened, but word would spread quickly. It always did in small towns.

"Take me to the hospital," she ordered. It was coming up on their left, and was where the ambulance had rushed Stephen.

"Not yet," he said, driving past without even slowing down. "Our conversation isn't over."

"What else do we have to talk about?" She turned to him in the dark. "Why do you even *care*? Did your son just get shot? Did you lose your husband to this bastard? Is your whole world falling apart? I don't think so. Why can't you just leave me alone?"

He took a left at the roundabout, now headed west toward Snowmass on Highway 82. "I'm working under an incompetent sheriff," he complained. "If I had gotten this guy, it would have proved that I'm more than capable to do the job. It would practically be a walk in the park until election day."

"That's not for eleven more months. Do you really think people are going to remember this in eleven months?"

"Yeah. They are. This is the biggest thing that's happened in this town since I've been here. People aren't going to forget about it anytime soon. And my name would be associated with it, if you hadn't screwed up."

234

Rockford made a U-turn at the next stoplight, and Angela realized that they were headed back toward town, toward the hospital. She wondered what was happening to Stephen right now. Was he in surgery? Was he even alive?

"I figure this will have bigger consequences for you than for me," Rockford continued. "People will shake their heads when they hear how you tried to do this yourself, how you dragged your son into this. Me, I won't get any recognition, but that doesn't matter. I'll figure out a way to draw some attention to myself."

A hatred for Stuart Rockford had been ignited inside of her. It only continued to grow as he spoke. If she ever got a chance to crush his hopes and dreams, she would do it in a heartbeat. The fact that he had revealed sensitive information to a regular citizen, was that a crime of any sort? She didn't think so. But she'd get him eventually. And then he'd be sorry how he had treated her.

He turned right at the roundabout and pulled into the parking lot of Aspen Valley Hospital a minute later. He pulled into the drop off lane and turned off the engine.

"I'm driving this back up there," he informed her. "I don't want to leave you with it in case you decide to try and get yourself into more trouble."

"How am I supposed to get home?"

"You'll find a way." He unlocked the doors. "You have a long night ahead of you, with your son and all. I'm sure you'll be hearing from the sheriff in the next few days. And I hope you think about all the trouble you've caused."

If he hadn't taken her pistol, she would've been tempted to shoot him. "Screw you, Stuart. You're going to regret this."

She slammed the door of her Jeep and hurried into the visitor's entrance of the hospital, desperately hoping that Stephen was still alive.

****

Angela waited in the lobby, her thoughts wandering. Nurses and doctors came and went, but nobody acknowledged her. All they had told her was that Stephen was in surgery, and

235

no, she couldn't see him. The last time she had seen him, when he was lying in the snow, he had looked so still. Did that mean he had already passed away? Was that why the void in her heart seemed to have grown? She remembered when she had found Will dead in the living room. He, on the other hand, hadn't looked peaceful. It would be a sad and ironic story if her son died the same way her husband had, and by the same man.

She wasn't looking forward to dealing with the sheriff. Would he charge her with anything? She had seen how angry he was. Maybe if they got Marshall, his anger would fade, and he would give her a break. Alex had agreed not to bring up the breaking and entering charges, but she had broken the deal. Would he change his mind? She didn't know.

The wait was agonizing. But it finally came to an end when a doctor pushed through a set of double doors and came straight toward her.

She closed her eyes and braced herself to receive the news.

43

What Alex encountered surprised him for two reasons. First, a snowmobile and four wheeler had apparently collided, both vehicles basically totaled. Secondly, he hadn't expected to find Vincent Martinez up here.

Alex had spotted Vincent in his headlights from a distance, and he had stopped just shy of the wreck. Vincent looked like he hurt.

"What the hell happened?" he asked, jumping off the snowmobile.

"We crashed." He said it as if it were obvious.

Alex scanned the adjacent woods for any signs of Marshall. He couldn't get far on foot, especially in the deep snow. And maybe, hopefully, he had been injured in the collision.

"You okay?" he asked.

"Yeah. Just a little winded."

"Did you see Marshall at all?" he asked.

Vincent shook his head.

Alex took off a glove and touched the snowmobile. The metal was still hot. "How long have you been here?"

"I don't know. A couple minutes."

Alex's eyes searched the woods again. Where was Marshall? The four wheeler was larger than the snowmobile, so it was likely that Marshall had sustained some injuries. Especially if he was going fifty miles per hour, like Alex had been. A head on collision like that could severely injure a person, even kill them.

Alex walked around the four wheeler and found the spot where Marshall had landed. It was in the middle of the trail, several feet from any trees. Which was unfortunate, because if Marshall had been thrown into a tree, he would have almost certainly sustained some major injuries. Even being thrown into the snow could result in injury, especially if Marshall wasn't wearing a helmet. Footsteps led into the trees on the right side of the trail. They were easy to follow, but Alex wasn't sure if he wanted to go after Marshall alone. There could be an ambush waiting for him, just like there had been at the house. Was Marshall watching him right now? He backed away from the trees and returned to where Vincent was waiting.

"Where'd you come from?" he asked, curiosity getting the better of him.

"Sheriff sent me to some cabins up there." He pointed to the east. "I found a truck there, and then saw the four wheeler. There was a fresh snowmobile track leading this way. I followed it."

The trail obviously connected the cabin to the house. Was that where Marshall had been heading? To get his truck and get out of town? Or was he going to stay in the woods and risk being caught? He didn't try to understand, because the man he was chasing was an enigma.

"Are you armed?" he asked quietly, in case Marshall could hear him.

Vincent looked around, then shook his head. "I must have lost it in the crash."

It didn't matter. In this state, Vincent probably couldn't hit anything anyway. It was him against Marshall, and he had the advantage because he had a Kevlar vest on and Marshall was likely injured. But *he* was searching for Marshall, not the other way around. That neutralized his advantage.

"Stay here," he told Vincent. He realized he still had the radio in his pocket and handed it to Vincent. "Call the sheriff. Tell him to get up here as quick as he can. I'm going to find Marshall."

He didn't look back to see if Vincent obeyed. Alex needed to catch up to Marshall before he got too far away. There was enough wilderness up here to stay hidden for days.

238

The trail of footsteps led straight into the trees. His senses were alert, and he noticed everything in the forest. The sound of snow falling from the branches, the faint smell of pine. And then he heard something to his right. He'd been following the trail for about two minutes, but now he stopped to listen, his handgun loaded, finger on the trigger. It sounded like something gliding over the snow, but he couldn't imagine what it would be.

Then a figure appeared out of the mist, coming toward him faster than someone could walk. He thought for a second that it was Marshall, and then he saw the familiar face. It was Jesse Rollins. And he was on cross country skis.

"Jesse," he said, as Rollins dug his poles into the ground next to Alex. "I almost shot you."

"Glad you didn't," he said, speaking quietly. "What's going on?"

Jesse had come straight through the forest, instead of taking the trail he had. Which meant he hadn't seen Vincent or the crash. Alex figured it must have been slow going with all the trees, but maybe Rollins had found a different, more direct route. With all the twists and turns of the trail, he figured they weren't more than a couple miles from the house.

Alex pointed to the footsteps. "He's injured. Can't have gotten far."

Rollins didn't ask any questions, which Alex appreciated. Time was precious. The officer took off his skis and tossed them into the snow a few feet away. They were basically useless now in the closely packed trees.

"I'll parallel you over here." He pointed a little ways off into the trees, where he likely wouldn't be visible to Alex. "Are we supposed to shoot first and ask questions later?"

"No. I'm going to try to talk to him, if possible. Use your best discretion, I guess. Do you have a vest on?"

Rollins nodded.

"Good. Let me do the talking. If that doesn't work, all bets are off. Got it?"

Rollins nodded again, his face tight.

They parted without saying anything more, and he returned to the trail of footsteps. Occasionally, he cast glances over to his right, trying to catch a glimpse of Rollins. He knew the officer was there, he just couldn't see him.

Up ahead, the terrain descended down to frozen Castle Creek. Somehow, the trail had looped back here and now they weren't far from the road. On the other side of the creek was a thin stretch of forest before another descent to the highway. If Marshall went left, he would follow the creek north back to the highway, but if he went south, he would parallel the highway to Sawyer Creek and easily get lost in the woods once more. Alex shined the flashlight down to see where the footsteps went, but he didn't see any. And then he heard the click of a gun being loaded from behind him. He started to turn but felt cold metal on the back of his neck.

"Drop your weapon," he heard Marshall say from behind him.

"Marshall-"

"Drop it."

Alex's mind was racing, trying to figure out a way to get out of this. Could he turn around turn and shoot him before the man got a shot off? He tossed the pistol on the ground, not willing to take that chance.

"You could have let me be," Marshall said, his voice steady and calm. "I only killed those who needed to die."

"Listen to me, Spencer."

"No. Walk straight ahead until you're standing on the creek."

Alex obeyed. The creek was completely frozen, but he felt the ice shift as he walked out onto it. He stopped and turned to face Marshall, but all he could see was the outline of the man in the dark. He stood just a few feet in front of Alex, on the bank of the frozen creek.

"Turn around." He heard a hint of remorse in Marshall's voice.

"No." Alex took a step forward, and he heard the ice groan beneath him. "Look me in the eye and shoot me."

"I said turn around."

A light suddenly flashed to his left, and Marshall turned to look. Alex saw his chance and took it. He lunged forward and grabbed Marshall's jacket, pulling the man toward him. There was a loud crack as the ice shattered, and suddenly he found himself lying in the frigid water. It stunned him for a moment and then he saw Marshall scrambling toward the bank. Alex grabbed him once more and Marshall fell into the water next to him. He got to his feet and pushed Marshall's head under the water. Marshall's right hand stayed above the surface, and Alex saw that somehow he had managed to retain his grip on the handgun. He reached out to wrench it from Marshall's hand when it suddenly went off.

The bullet hit his vest, the impact knocking him back into the water. Before he knew it, Marshall was on top of him, shoving him beneath the surface. He tried to fight back but his body was temporarily paralyzed from the impact. The icy water had turned his hands and feet numb and he couldn't feel anything except a desperate need for air.

Marshall's weight suddenly disappeared from on top of him, and he broke the surface, gasping for air. It took him a moment to realize what had happened.

Jesse Rollins had just saved his life, and Spencer Marshall was dead.

Alex closed his eyes, took a few deep breaths, and tried to stop shaking.

44

Alex sat on the hood of the snowmobile, drinking coffee from a styrofoam cup. It was a few minutes after midnight. Marshall's body had been taken from the creek by Porter and Wyatt, who had arrived just moments after Jesse Rollins had shot Marshall. Alex was angry at himself for not being more careful, and he realized how lucky he was to be sitting here with no major injuries. He'd already been treated by paramedics at the house. They'd wanted him to go with them to the hospital, but he'd insisted that he was fine. Activity had decreased dramatically, most officers realizing everything was over and being sent home or back to the station. Alex had to repeat his story several times, as did Rollins and Martinez. Vincent had been taken to the hospital for a few tests, the sheriff fearing he might have a severe concussion. Alex did a little mental math. All in all, five people dead, including William Olmsted. Nobody seemed to know the condition of Stephen, which is why he was headed to the hospital in about two minutes. He'd called Jen to let her know what had happened, only to find that she wasn't even home yet. She had left him a message saying that she decided to spend the night in Colorado Springs with her college roommate, Angelica.

There were still a lot of things that had to be cleared up, and a ton of paperwork awaited him. He also had to figure out what to do about Angela Olmsted and Stuart Rockford. But that could all wait until tomorrow. Right now, the most important thing was to find out if Stephen was okay. He borrowed Rollins' truck once more and drove toward the hospital, worried about what he might find.

242

****

She knew it was bad when the doctor looked her in the eye. He was tall and bald and had dark circles underneath his eyes. She composed herself and waited for him to speak.

"Are you Ms. Olmsted?"

"Yes."

"We did everything we could. Your son sustained too much internal damage." He took a deep breath. "I'm so sorry."

She didn't cry, but knew she would later. "I'd like to see him"

"I don't think that's a good idea."

"Let me see him."

He left her alone in the operating room with Stephen. His eyes were closed, as if he were sleeping. A blue sheet covered most of his body. He was only twenty four, and his life was already over. She thought of Mariah, and the call she was going to have to make. And the thought broke her heart.

"I'm so sorry, Stephen." She bent down to whisper in his ear. "I should never have dragged you into this."

She couldn't hold back the tears now, and they came freely. She cried for Stephen, for Will, for Mariah, for herself. There was a hollow feeling inside of her, as if her soul hadn't been ripped out of her body.

"I'm so sorry," she whispered, over and over again. She didn't know how long she stood there. She was vaguely aware of Alex coming in and putting his hand on her shoulder. He didn't say anything, just stood there with her in the dim light.

"Why did this happen to me?" she whispered. If there was a God, why had he taken everyone away from her? Why had the world been so cruel to her? Was this some sort of punishment? She wiped her eyes but the tears kept coming.

Eventually, he led her outside and drove her home. He tried to comfort her, but the words went in one ear and out the other. She sat in the dining room at 1:30 A.M. and she knew it was time to make the call. Mariah answered after a few rings, and Angela fumbled for the right words. Before she started sobbing again, she told Mariah what had happened. And when

243

she hung up, she felt so terrible that she didn't even want to live anymore. She realized just how alone she was in the world.

****

Alex headed back to his office after dropping Angela off. Jen wasn't home, and he knew he wouldn't be able to sleep. His mind was still spinning and his chest was sore from the impact of the bullet.

He sat at his desk for a long time, letting everything sink in and wondering if he could have done anything to save Stephen. The answer, he thought, was yes. If they had arrived a minute earlier, he could have stopped Angela before they got out into the open. He could have driven a little faster, been a little more forceful with Angela. If he had checked his phone right away when he felt the vibration he could have gotten to the house ahead of Angela and stopped them. If he had stayed with Stephen instead of going after Marshall, would he still be alive? Should he have let the sheriff know what was going on, and let him make the decisions? At the time, he thought he was doing what was best, but maybe he was wrong. Alex knew Angela would be blamed for Stephen's death, but he would always feel responsible for it.

There was a knock on the door and Sheriff Brown stepped into his office. His eyes were weary, his expression blank. Alex thought the sheriff would've gone home after the long day. He sat down, and the two of them sat like that for a few minutes, not speaking, each of them in their own thoughts.

"Did he make it?" the sheriff finally asked.

Alex shook his head. He wasn't as close to Stephen as some of his other friends, but he felt that they would have formed a tight friendship eventually. This death hit home, not just because Stephen was his friend, but because Alex felt like he could've and should've saved Stephen. "I don't really want to talk right now."

"You're never going to want to talk about it, Alex. But we need to talk. Why didn't you tell me the second you knew that Spencer Marshall was our guy?"

Alex tried to think back, but if felt like forever ago. "I don't know. I just figured we didn't have time to wait around. I thought I was doing the right thing at the time." He paused. "When Jarred and I went after the gang in Baltimore on our own, I thought we were doing the right thing. He's dead because of it. I thought I did the right thing tonight, but look what happened. What if my instincts are completely wrong?"

"You couldn't have done anything to save him, Alex. He made the choice to go there with Angela. You did what you thought was best, and nothing is going to change that. Angela was a step ahead of us the whole way. If anything, this is my fault. I should've paid more attention to what she was doing."

Brown hesitated. "Alex, if you need to take some time off, I completely understand."

"I'm fine."

"Are you? What if Rollins hadn't been there? You're lucky to be sitting here right now."

"My job is to protect people, sheriff. I've been in dangerous situations before. That's part of the job. I'm aware of the fact that I may get injured or even die doing my job. I accept that. So when I say that I'm fine, I'm being honest with you."

The sheriff dipped his head respectfully. "You did good work this week, Alex. I hope you decide to stay here in Aspen."

When he finally arrived home a couple hours later, he realized how empty his house felt, and wondered if Angela felt the same way he did.

****

The next few days were a blur. Alex attended funerals for Erin and Daniel Carver and Samuel Preston. There were so many reporters in Aspen that he could barely go anywhere without being swarmed. The FBI left the day after it all went down, which Alex was thankful for. He hadn't liked either of those agents, and hoped he never had to see them again. After numerous press conferences and interviews, he just wanted things to return to normal.

Alex confronted Stuart Rockford in the parking lot a couple days after the murders. The past few days had been bright and sunny, and some of the snow had begun to melt. From the two storms combined, some areas had received over five feet of snow.

"Alex," Rockford said, sensing something was up.

"I know that you did some questionable things during this investigation. I think that if somebody told the sheriff, your hopes of a political career would go down the drain."

Rockford glared at him but didn't say anything.

"Do things right from now on. Don't try to be the hero. If anything else comes to my attention, the sheriff and city council are going to hear about this, and you're going to be without a job."

He started walking toward his truck, aware of Rockford's eyes following him.

"I'd watch my back if I were you, Snyder," he called.

Alex knew it wasn't a hollow threat.

Epilogue

The funeral for Stephen Olmsted was held at St. Mary's Catholic Church on New Year's Day. The church was packed, every pew filled. Angela and her sister sat alone in the front row.

Alex and Jen sat in the fourth row, next to Dylan Kessel. Sheriff Brown and his wife sat behind them, and Alex recognized several people from Aspen throughout the church. As the service went on, he found Jen continuously reaching for tissues. He hadn't realized how close she and Stephen were.

Mariah Winwood sat in the front row next to her parents and two brothers. She didn't speak, but had a box of tissues in her hands the whole time. Alex couldn't imagine what she was going through.

A friend of Stephen's from high school spoke, portraying Stephen as a great guy with a bright future that was tragically cut short. But Alex knew that everyone was waiting to hear what Angela had to say.

She finally stepped up to the lectern a few minutes later. Angela wore a short black dress and black heels. She looked physically exhausted, and Alex was wondering how she was dealing with this.

"I was at Stephen's apartment a few days ago, going through some of his things. I... found a ring in his bedroom. He was about to propose to you, Mariah. I just want you to know that.

"I know all of you are angry at me right now. It's my fault that we're all here today. But I don't want Stephen's legacy to be associated with me. He was a perfect son, even though I was a terrible mother. I just wish I would have been able to spend some more time with him these past few years.

"I've lost the two most important people in my life, and I've been doing a lot of thinking. Why has this happened to me? What did I do to deserve this? And I can't find any answers. I.." She struggled to find the right words. "I'm just so sorry to everyone here today. Hold close those you love. Stephen and I drifted apart, and just when I thought we were mending fences, this happens. I.... I'm lost right now, and I'm not sure if I'll be able to get back on the right track." She paused, composing herself. "I've ruined a lot of lives, and for that I am truly sorry."

Angela left town the day after the funeral. Her large house sat quiet and empty, a constant reminder of what had happened. Rumor had it that she went to Alaska.

It was a long time before she returned to Aspen.

Made in the USA
Columbia, SC
31 January 2019